Sheila NEWBERRY

The Meadow Girls

ZAFFRE

First published in 2009 as *The Watercress Girls*

This edition published in 2020 by
ZAFFRE
80–81 Wimpole St, London W1G 9RE

A CIP catalogue record for this book is
available from the British Library.

ISBN: 978-1-78576-190-4

Also available as an ebook

3 5 7 9 10 8 6 4 2

Typeset by IDSUK (Data Connection) Ltd
Printed and bound in Great Britain by Clays Ltd, Elcograf S.p.A.

MIX
Paper from
responsible sources
FSC® C018072

Zaffre is an imprint of Bonnier Books UK
www.bonnierbooks.co.uk

PROLOGUE

AUGUST, 2005

The old farm gate, stuck fast in a tangle of brambles, refused to budge. Tilly climbed over first, after dropping her canvas bag on to the ground on the other side. She liked to have drawing materials with her, in case she was suddenly inspired to capture a moment in time.

'Pass Aunt Evie's basket to me,' she told her companion as he made to vault over.

The grass was long and damp; trainers and trouser hems were soon caked with mud. They skirted the patches of thistles, strolling hand-in-hand across the meadow in the late-afternoon sunlight. The midges were beginning to bite, the birds to circle in the vast skies overhead. Tilly had been told that her great-great-grandfather once kept a small flock of sheep in what now appeared a long-forsaken place.

Earlier, Evie said: 'I hear watercress still grows in the stream; Mattie and I used to gather great bundles of it when we were girls – why don't you get some for tea?'

Tea, the girl thought, with a wry smile. Here, that still meant bone-china cups and saucers, thin slices of bread and butter cut into triangles on matching poppy-patterned plates; small, warm tomatoes picked from the lean-to greenhouse, cottage cheese with chives; home-made raspberry conserve to spread with little knives with mother of pearl handles. The tea itself would be freshly brewed in a round-bellied pot, with a crocheted cosy to keep it hot, milk would be sweet and creamy in the jug with its beaded cap, and sugar lumps lifted with silver tongs. When they left the old house, there had been the tantalizing smell of rich fruit-cake baking in the oven and, on the kitchen table, she'd glimpsed a tray of plump scones, gently steaming. Her great-grandmother's sister Evie was a marvel, doing all this, at ninety-seven. She'd managed on her own, since Mattie died.

This was very different from the meal Tilly and Tom threw together in the shared student house on their return from art college each evening. Pasta, often mixed from ends of packets; sauce from a jar, sniffed to make sure it hadn't gone off; grated hard cheese melted on top of the dish – eaten on plates balanced on knees as they sat together on a settee with twanging springs, staring at the portable TV she'd brought from her bedroom at home. The table was used not for meals but for homework, strewn with great sheets of paper, jars of brushes in turps, tubes of paint, rags, charcoal, pencils and half-drunk cups of coffee.

'It's so quiet here,' Tilly observed. She hoped he didn't mind, being a city boy.

'No roar of London traffic,' he said ruefully. She'd had to persuade him that a weekend in the country, with an elderly relative, would be fun. They'd travelled by coach, which had taken hours, but they'd slept most of the way.

They reached the stream. The water rushed clear, clean and cold over small shining pebbles shifting on a fine, sandy bed.

Tilly sank to her knees, cupping her hands in the water. Droplets ran down her chin as she drank. 'It's delicious!' The tips of her long hair, coppery in that golden light, were wet, too. She fingered the locks back behind her ears.

'Are you sure the water's safe to drink?' he asked anxiously.

'Evie and Mattie always slaked their thirst here – they never came to any harm. And watercress only grows in fresh water . . .'

'Come on then,' Tom said. 'We should follow the stream to find it.'

Tilly slipped off her shoes, tied the laces together, slung them over her shoulder. She pocketed her socks.

'Well, I'm going to paddle my way there, how about you?'

'We'll have to roll our jeans up.' Tom was the more practical of the two.

'The water's not deep, look.' She stepped in with a splash. 'But it makes you gasp!'

They gasped again when they came upon the profusion of glossy green watercress. Tilly nipped a tender sprig to taste it before getting down to serious picking.

'It's not bitter like the cress you buy in the London markets,' she reported. 'This is tender and sweet.'

Like you, Tom thought. This was not something he could say to her. Instead, he observed awkwardly, 'You've bits of green in your teeth.'

'Try a piece – go on. It's good for you! Full of iron for growing girls – and boys, I shouldn't wonder,' she teased him.

At nineteen Tom was a lanky six-footer. Tilly, too, was tall and skinny. Evie had exclaimed that she obviously didn't eat enough, hence the rich fruity cake to come.

Back at the house Evie didn't comment on their wet footprints on the worn carpeting. Her bent old fingers ruffled the brimming watercress in the basket.

'You've done well! You know, this was Mattie's basket; they called us the watercress girls ... When Plough Cottage was still the village inn, and we had visitors staying in the summer, we picked some nearly every day for them.'

'Can I make a quick sketch of it before you serve it up for tea?' Tilly asked.

'Of course you can. Put the basket in the centre of the table, it'll go well on that yellow cloth. Mattie always loved that colour ... she wore a yellow dress when she had her picture painted. You look a lot like her, so it's right you're named for her, Matilda.'

'No one's ever called me that . . . What picture? I've never heard of one.' Tilly positioned her sketch pad, selected stubby pastels from a tin. Finger and thumb were soon powdery with colour as she deliberately but delicately smudged her drawing.

'I'll tell you the story after tea. Your young man looks hungry, don't keep him waiting too long, will you? We'll eat watercress like a second Nebuchadnezzar, eh?'

'Where does that expression come from?' Tilly smiled. One to store up and bring out nonchalantly, on occasion, she decided.

'Dickens, my dear – *Sketches by Boz*. You should read them. Old Neb was a king mentioned in the Old Testament. Daniel tells us he went mad and ate copious amounts of grass. Watercress is far superior!'

PART ONE

ONE

Mattie was dancing about in the stream, spraying her sister with silvery showers of water. It was a blazing hot day in late August, 1914. The girls had come down to the meadow to cool off. Later they would fill the basket with watercress, but there was only one guest to enjoy it for Saturday tea, at present. The rest of the visitors had departed abruptly at the beginning of the month when War was declared.

Six-year-old Evie retreated from the bombardment, stumbled and sat down inadvertently in the water. 'Look what you've made me do!' she cried reproachfully.

'You've got your bloomers wet!' sang out her sister, but she waded over to help Evie up. She was twelve, twice as old as Evie, but her mother often reminded her that she didn't act her age. Lately, she'd added that it was time for Mattie to grow up 'now the whole world's gone mad'.

'We'll have to go home.' Evie sniffed.

'Not yet. Your clothes will soon dry out in this heat. Come on, we promised to take back some watercress!' She felt in her pocket. 'Here's a piece of toffee. It might have a bit of fluff on it, but you can rub that off, can't you?'

Mollified, Evie tagged along behind Mattie to the watercress bed.

Some of the young men of the village had already volunteered to join the army. Last week there had been a march of new recruits through the main street and everyone had emerged with flags to cheer them on their way. The lads of the Boys' Brigade had played their polished brass instruments and banged their drums. The girls had watched from the doorway of the Plough Inn with their parents to wave a last, public goodbye to their two elder brothers. Afterwards they'd observed tears in their father's eyes despite his proud beam. Their mother, Sophia, whispered apprehensively, 'They won't take you too, will they, Will?' He patted her arm. 'Not at forty, old girl,' he said gruffly.

They both knew that difficult times lay ahead. They'd miss the support of their strong sons, although the bar was now half-empty each evening with the regulars gone.

Still, there was their paying guest, Mr B. They called him that because his name was difficult to pronounce. He had come to this country some forty years ago as a young man. He was an artist, quite a famous one, it was rumoured, whose pictures had been hung in the Royal Academy. He was a regular summer visitor, paying extra for the use of a wooden chalet in the garden as a studio where he could, he said, 'breathe in good, clean air, look out on pastoral scenes, paint in peace and quiet . . .'

Mr B had a hawklike profile, dark, oiled-back hair and deep-set eyes under beetle brows. Despite his stern appearance he was kindly, and tolerated the giggles of the girls when they counted under their breath the number of times he stirred the three sugar lumps in his tea. Fourteen twirls of the spoon, to be exact. He was very fond of watercress too.

'Thank you girls – thank you, Mrs Rowley,' he declared, in his slightly accented voice, when he joined Sophia and her daughters for tea. 'I tell my mother how very nice this is, the way you serve the watercress, with a touch of vinegar and a pinch of sugar.'

The girls were full of mirth again, thinking of one so old still living with an even more ancient parent.

Sophia's look quelled them. She said: 'Mattie, Mr B has asked my permission first, and now he has a question for you.'

Mr B dabbed at his mouth with a linen napkin. 'Yes, this is so. I have been commissioned to paint a portrait of a young girl, ah, about your age; my client has supplied me with a photograph and details of her colouring, but I am used to painting, ah, from life. It seems to me that you would be a suitable model, and, yes, in particular for the hair, which is described as golden, long and luxuriant. The eyes are blue—'

'But mine are green!' Mattie interrupted.

'I should explain – I shall not paint *your* face. Your figure only. The only requirement would be, you must wear a yellow dress. If you have not one suitable, it shall be provided. Would you like to sit for me?'

Mattie always made her mind up quickly. 'Oh, yes please!'

'What about me?' Evie asked in an aggrieved voice. She nibbled her watercress like a rabbit, which she had been told was impolite in company.

'You, my dear child, can act as chaperon,' Mr B suggested.

'What's that?' she demanded.

Mattie had the answer. 'You can watch and tell Mother if I fidget too much!'

Mattie could just about manage to keep her pose for one hour. She sat in a straight-backed chair with an uncomfortable rush seat, looking pensively into space. Her bright hair was carefully brushed, allowed to fall loose over her shoulders; the simple yellow dress, made by her capable mother, was smoothed over her knees. She wore dancing-pumps on her feet. Crossing her ankles was not permitted. Mr B looked pained when once she sneezed.

The chalet door was left open, at Sophia's request, which enabled Evie to go in and out – to sit on the lawn and make a long daisy-chain. Being a chaperon was somewhat tedious, she'd soon discovered. She envied her sister her role.

Mattie wasn't allowed to look at the picture until Mr B said it was finished, when there was a formal viewing by the girls and their parents.

There was a definite autumnal twinge in the air by then. After careful laundering, the yellow dress was folded in tissue and placed in the trunk with their summer clothes. Last of all, lavender-bags were tucked inside, ones that she and Evie had painstakingly sewn.

Today, like her sister, Mattie wore a warm, cinnamon-brown dress with a velvet collar, and a lace-trimmed pinafore over it, wool stockings and neat little boots. Her hair was restrained in a single plait which hung down her back, secured with a large satin bow. Mattie envied Evie's hair. Evie didn't have freckles – Mattie hoped hers were not evident on her portrait!

It was Evie who first realised that the girl in the picture had no discernible features. Her face was a perfect oval, with a hint of flesh-pink, but that was all. She opened her mouth to say something, and Mattie clapped her hand over it. 'Shush,' she hissed.

Mr B seemed preoccupied, not quite himself, but he essayed an explanation.

'I hoped to stay a few more days, to complete the painting from the photograph, but the telegram I received this morning . . . I must return to London almost immediately.' He spread out his hands. 'I am required to register as an enemy alien.'

The family were silent, trying to take this in.

The artist added: 'I have a favour to ask of you, Mr Rowley. When I have packed the picture, with a letter of explanation to my client to say that when this matter is cleared up I will finish the assignment at his home – please would you arrange for the package to be collected by carrier, and taken to the address I shall give you? I will provide money to pay for this, and to settle our account.'

Will shook hands with Mr B. 'Of course I'll do it,' he promised. 'Good luck.'

They never saw or heard from the artist again. Had he been interned – or even deported? Surely, if he had been allowed to stay in his adopted country, he would have eventually got in touch . . .

*

Mattie didn't wear the yellow dress again. By the following summer she was thirteen and maturing rapidly. It wouldn't have suited Evie with her more sallow complexion. Also, it was a time for more sober clothes. Her elder brother, Robbie, had been lost in the battle of Ypres. In fact, almost a whole generation of village boys, for most were scarcely more than that, would not return home.

Within two years of the end of the Great War the Plough was forced to close because the brewery did not sanction credit. They were able to stay on in the house, where Will had been born, lived all his married life and which, later, he inherited from his own father. The lambs brought in a tiny income. Ronnie, who had come through the recent terrible conflict almost unscathed physically, joined an uncle employed by the railway as a crossing-keeper. Ronnie's wages as a trainee porter were a godsend to the family.

Mattie worked part-time in the village post office, as assistant to elderly, arthritic Miss Hobbs, selling stamps, weighing parcels and wiring telegrams. She doubled up as shop assistant, serving boiled sweets from glass jars, selling farm eggs and fresh local vegetables, which included, in season, bunches of their watercress. The rest of the day she helped her mother in the house. She yearned for more excitement in her life.

Sophia suffered from bouts of depression after losing her eldest child. Every afternoon she sat on the window-seat watching out for Evie returning from school, taking the short cut home across the field. It was Mattie who cooked their supper, who talked to her young sister about the day's events, for Sophia was also prone to long silences.

After her eighteenth birthday, when she had been at the post office for three years with no prospect of promotion, Mattie determined to venture away from home. If she had a better job, she reasoned, she could send money to help her family. She felt guilty that she would be leaving her sister behind but Evie, at twelve, was still at school. Mattie whispered that she might help out and perhaps gain a little pocket money by picking, then selling water-cress at the gate.

Maybe, subconsciously, Mattie resented the arrival of Ronnie's young wife in the family home in the summer of 1920. She had been at school with Ena but they had never been close friends.

Ena ingratiated herself with Sophia and was pandered to, particularly since she announced that she was expecting a baby the next May. Ena took over the housekeeping purse and held out her hand each Friday for Mattie's contribution. It was understood that in due course Ena would be the lady of the house.

'I have expectations, you don't,' Mattie was told spitefully by her sister-in-law when they had a falling-out one day. Ena made sure Sophia was not in earshot, naturally.

This was true, Mattie acknowledged to herself. It was time to go.

As for the picture, it went down in family lore as the painting of an unknown girl – the only clue to her identity being the name and address to which the picture had been sent. This piece of paper Sophia locked safely away in her writing-box.

TWO

1921

In April, Mattie went from her village in Suffolk to the west country. This momentous event was recorded simply in her diary on the appropriate page: *Today I travelled by the GWR to Plymouth.*

In fact, she made the journey over two days. When it came to it, Mattie was not permitted the excitement of setting out into the unknown and finding a job for herself. Her mother was suddenly galvanised into action. She and her husband both came from large families; they had relatives in what she termed 'far parts'. Although most of the siblings, cousins and in-laws were mere names to her own family, Sophia determined to get in touch with the more likely prospects. The Fulliloves, in Plymouth came up trumps.

Ronnie, recently promoted to railway-ticket clerk, was asked to make the travel arrangements and to accompany his sister on the train to London. 'Aunt Mary from Mitcham will meet you,' Sophia said. 'She has a bundle of baby clothing for Ena. Ronnie, of course, will have to return here by the next train.'

'What about me?' Mattie endeavoured not to sound resentful, but it was difficult.

'You, dear? Why, Aunt Mary will take you home with her, she'll provide you with a meal and a bed for the night. In the morning, your cousin Walter will escort you to Paddington to board the express train to Plymouth.'

'Then?' Mattie prompted.

'The Fulliloves will send someone with a conveyance to pick you up at Plymouth.'

Evie was listening in. 'I hope they *are* full of love, not the opposite!'

'Evie!' Sophia scolded. 'They have been kind enough to offer Mattie a position in their emporium, with free board and lodging.'

'I would have preferred to have made my own arrangements,' Mattie told her. She thought: free board and lodging likely means low wages. 'Goodbye and good luck, Sis,' Ronnie said, after they alighted from the train at Liverpool Street station. He hesitated. He had got out of the way of giving his sisters spontaneous hugs, with Ena looking on disapprovingly. 'Here's Aunt Mary,' he added.

'Thanks, Ronnie,' Mattie said, as a stout lady in black bore down on them.

'For the baby,' Aunt Mary puffed, handing over a large, ill-tied parcel. 'Ena's due next month, I understand. My Effie said a florin will suffice . . .'

Ronnie looked embarrassed. This was women's talk. 'Thanks,' he mumbled, feeling in his pocket for the coin, then slipping it to Aunt Mary. 'You'll excuse me – my train will be in, any minute now.'

'Fortunately I can see a porter with a trolley,' Aunt Mary said pointedly. She added, 'At least *you've* a free travel pass, eh?'

He nodded, suddenly grabbed his sister, held her close and hissed in her ear: 'If it don't work out, Mattie, don't be afraid to say, to come back . . .'

'I won't, don't worry,' she whispered in return.

'Nice lad,' Aunt Mary remarked to Mattie as Ronnie beat his retreat. 'Mind you, he's not as likely to succeed as Robbie would have been, if he'd been spared.'

Although, as a child she'd been closer to happy-go-lucky Robbie than Ronnie, Mattie wasn't having that. She flared, 'Ronnie looks after the family.'

'Now, now.' Aunt Mary looked amused. 'Quick to fly, like your mother. I don't know how your father's put up with it, all these years.' She was Will's eldest sister.

The house in Mitcham was beyond the common, nearer the cemetery than the lavender fields, a thriving commercial enterprise, but a tiring walk after their bus ride.

Mattie carried her cases, while Aunt Mary led the way. There was an ominous throbbing in Mattie's temples. The roar of London's traffic was diminished here, but the rows of identical brick villas, in what had been known as a garden suburb at the turn of the century, seemed endless, to her.

Walter, Aunt Mary's only son, was on his Easter break from college. His books and papers were spread out all over the dining-room table. He was a lanky youth, with a pale face, fluffy moustache and protuberant blue eyes. He gave Mattie a friendly grin. She was wearing a neat grey costume, new lisle stockings, the toes and heels of which she'd rubbed with beeswax to prevent holing, and well-worn black shoes. Her mass of golden hair was hidden under a plain felt hat. It was an outfit more suited to a thirty-year-old.

'Coffee?' Walter offered. 'We seem to be out of tea.' He pulled out a chair for her to sit on. Aunt Mary had left her in the hall and disappeared upstairs.

Mattie paused for a brief moment. She'd never tasted coffee. Perhaps now was the time to try it. 'Please,' she said.

When he passed her a cup, it was full of black, strong liquid. She wondered whether to request milk, but decided not to. There was, however, lumpy brown sugar. Mattie tried not to make a face as she drank. She suddenly remembered she was still wearing the hat. She pulled out the hatpin, laid the hat on the table, and shook her head with relief. She didn't often wear her hair up, and it was her mother's hat, after all.

She suddenly caught Walter's eye. He winked, to show his appreciation of the transformation. Embarrassed, she tucked stray locks back behind her ears.

'The shingle hasn't reached your part of the world, then?' he asked. He idly picked at his frayed shirt-cuffs. What with his yellowing celluloid collar, he was shabby like his mother – like this house, Mattie realised.

'Father won't allow us girls to cut our hair,' she said primly.

'He'd think my sisters hussies, then. Our pa left us years ago.'

'Oh, I didn't know Aunt Mary was a widow – I'm sorry.'

'Left, I said, not died. Ma had to take in lodgers to make ends meet – she still does. My sisters married young, so she says she's investing in me and my education. It'll be my duty to look after her in her old age. That's why we couldn't do more for you. But you might have been better off here than with the Fulliloves. Long way to go, too.'

'You've met them, then?' Mattie felt even more apprehensive now.

'Put it this way – *heard* of them,' Walter said. 'Our rich relations, Ma calls 'em.'

'I wonder why it is that families became so spread out?'

'The younger members, particularly girls, left home to go into service, mostly. I am talking of thirty or forty years ago. They didn't have the chance of further education, instead they travelled miles away. In time, they settled or married where they'd landed, so to speak, but they kept in touch with their old home, even if they never saw it again.'

Aunt Mary reappeared. She gave a big sigh. 'Had to get out of those wretched whalebone corsets, pinch me something cruel, they do. Oh good, the cup that cheers. Drink up, then Walter can carry your baggage upstairs to your room. You might like a wash and brush up, and a lie down before supper.'

'Thank you,' Mattie said. She caught another swift wink from Walter. She was warming to him, despite her first impression that he was a mother's boy.

As he ushered her politely into the small bedroom at the top of the stairs, they heard the front door opening, then closing. There were voices in the hall.

'The lodgers are back,' Walter observed. 'Ma prefers gentlemen, they're not so particular as the ladies. Mr Stubbs will have brought a packet of tea, I hope. He don't drink coffee. Hope you'll be comfortable here. This is my room, so I tidied up.'

'Oh dear.' Mattie exclaimed. 'I'm sorry to put you out, Walter.'

'I'll sleep on the sofa, after the lodgers have vacated the sitting-room tonight.' He went towards the door. 'Must gather up my books from the dining-table now.'

'What are you studying?' she asked.

'He made a face. 'Accountancy. Though I'd rather be a draughtsman. Ma's starting on the supper, I believe. I'll see you later.'

After eating, a stodgy meal and a silent affair, with the two middle-aged lodgers one side of the table, Mattie and Walter on the other, and Aunt Mary presiding over the teapot at the end, the lodgers went to the sitting-room. Mattie helped Walter to wash up, then, at Aunt Mary's suggestion, gratefully retired for the night.

The sheets were patched but clean, she climbed into bed, and was soon asleep.

The Great Western Railway, like its competitors, was justly proud of its service, and the trains. The smart green and red livery, the comfortable carriages, assured the passengers of a relaxing journey.

Walter climbed aboard first, deposited her luggage, then assisted Mattie into the carriage. 'Worth getting here early,' he said, 'you've got a choice of seats.'

Remembering Ronnie's advice, Mattie selected a window seat, back to the engine.

'Would you like a newspaper or a magazine?' Walter asked.

Mattie thought, he probably can't afford it. He paid my bus fare, after all.

'Thank you Walter, but I've a book in my bag. Time at last to read it.'

'Good, Well then, I'll leave you, before the whistle blows. Don't forget to eat your sandwiches at lunch-time. You can buy a cup of tea in the restaurant car. Mattie . . .'

'Yes?' She wondered why he appeared reluctant to go.

'Ma said to tell you that you're welcome to come back if—'

'I know – if things don't work out. It's very kind of her, and you.' She held out a gloved hand. 'Goodbye, Walter.'

'I hope we meet again.' he said sincerely. As he shook her hand he pressed a small packet in her palm. He was gone before she could examine it. A sample bottle of Mitcham lavender scent. Pleased, she tucked it in her handbag.

Mattie settled back in her seat as clouds of steam drifted past her window, then the initial jolting of the train took on a reassuring rhythm as it gathered speed.

She opened a rather tattered small book, purchased for a penny at a recent jumble sale in the village. It was a guide to Plymouth, that great seaport. Saltash, she learned, was the secure harbourage of HM ships. She read of the Great Breakwater, erected stone by stone and completed in 1841 across the middle of the Sound, to protect the ships from the south-westerly gales. Inside The Breakwater was one of the world's strongest forts. Drake's island was also heavily guarded. This was hardly light reading, she thought.

Mattie stifled a yawn, allowed the book to slip from her hands on to her lap. Then, like her fellow passengers, she closed her eyes and dozed intermittently.

She was wide awake when they approached Exeter and enjoyed the coastal view.

Plymouth: pocket watches were checked, tapped; the train pronounced to be on time. Mattie allowed the other travellers to disembark first, before she reached down her suitcases. The carriage door swung open, and a dark-haired man enquired: 'Are you Miss Matilda Rowley?' She nodded shyly. The man smiled. 'I am Griffith Parry. My stepfather, Mr Rufus Fullilove, asked me to meet you. Allow me to take your cases.'

'Thank you,' Mattie said. She followed him along the platform, handed her single ticket to the collector, while Mr Parry waited on the other side of the barrier, then led her to the promised conveyance. Her eyes widened when she saw the dark-green delivery van with the gold lettering on the side: EMPIRE EMPORIUM, PROPRIETOR, R. FULLILOVE, BARBICAN.

Mr Parry opened the rear doors and made room for her luggage among the packages already stacked in the back of the van. He turned to Mattie. 'There is a step up,' he advised her, as he settled into the driving seat, 'I must make a couple of deliveries on our way back. My stepfather insists I make the best use of my time.'

Oh, does he! Mattie thought. What about me, weary after my journeying? She said aloud, 'He keeps you busy, then, Mr Fullilove?'

Mr Parry grimaced ruefully. 'He does indeed. Well, what is your first impression of Plymouth, Miss Rowley?'

'Mattie, please! We are cousins, after all.'

'I should tell you, Mattie, that actually we are not. My late mother married Mr Fullilove when I was a child. She was his housekeeper, a position she took on after she was widowed. I was sent away to boarding school when my mother died. I didn't come home for the holidays. I didn't really mind that, because, as you will soon discover, my stepfather is a hard man. His present wife, my stepmother, is your actual relative, your second cousin, Sybil. She had money at the time; I guess that's why old Rufus married her, to save the emporium. That's an anachronism, since the war changed the world.

'You'll like Syb, I think. When I returned to Plymouth and reluctantly began work in the store she was kind and persuaded me to stay. My own inclination was to study art.'

Mattie bit her lip. 'You asked for my first thoughts on Plymouth. Well, it is so different from any place I have been before, I really can't be sure. It is very historic, of course. Particularly the Hoe. It's nice to know I'll be able to walk there and look out over the sea. I understand you can see miles of coastline from the cliffs. May I call you by your first name? Even if we aren't cousins, I can see I shall need a friend!'

'I was known as Griff at school. My real father was Welsh.'

Hence the dark and brooding looks, Mattie thought. He was a typical Celt.

The van drew to a stop outside an imposing house whose front door was flanked by marble columns. 'My first delivery. I shan't be long.'

Mattie had time to collect her thoughts. She was, she suspected, the latest in the long line of impecunious girls to leave her family. She could well languish, far from home.

THREE

'We're here,' Griff announced. He signalled with his raised open palm to a following motor as they drew to a halt outside another imposing Georgian house in a residential street.

He turned to Mattie. 'This is the Fullilove pile! Rather grand, isn't it? But mortgaged to the hilt, I suspect. Old Rufus is more concerned with importing luxury goods from the Empire and the Continent, despite dwindling sales. Sybil brought her maid with her, shrewd lady. She didn't intend to follow in my poor mother's footsteps.'

'Stop trying to put me off.' Mattie was quick to 'fly' as Aunt Mary put it.

Griff smiled disarmingly. 'I'm only trying to prepare you for what lies ahead.'

The door was opened by a tiny woman, who at first sight appeared to be a young girl. Closer to, Mattie took in a rosy, wrinkled face and twinkling blue eyes. Her slight figure was almost swamped by her black dress and neat white apron. On her silvery hair, the maid had pinned rather rakishly her badge of office, a frilled cap.

When she spoke, it became obvious that Sybil's maid was a Londoner, born and bred. 'Miss Rowley, do come in. Miss Sybil – Mrs Fullilove – is in the drawing-room. I'll take you upstairs first. Have a tidy-up and come down when you're ready.'

'This is Hilda Bunn,' Griff said in Mattie's ear. 'She's a real good sort.'

'I heard that!' Hilda beamed. 'Griff, you can follow us with the luggage.'

A little later she ushered Mattie into the drawing-room, announcing: 'Miss Rowley.'

Sybil was not at all as Mattie had imagined. She was possibly not much more than thirty years old, slim and vivacious, attired in a stylish afternoon frock in rose-pink, with wide sleeves and knee-length skirt. She wore a matching headband on bobbed platinum-blond hair. Her make-up was startling to Mattie, who'd only experi-mented with face powder, then been sternly advised to scrub it off by her mother. Sybil's lips were painted a glossy scarlet, her brown eyes and long lashes emphasised with kohl.

'I've been so looking forward to your arrival, Mattie.' Sybil's voice, too, was a surprise. Breathless, with a capti-vating lilt. She held out her hand, a silver charm bracelet jingling on her wrist. 'Come and sit by me. How was your journey?'

'Rather tedious, but comfortable,' Mattie said. She thought wryly that it had been a waste of time dabbing Walter's Mitcham lavender on her hanky because Sybil's perfume was almost overpowering.

There was a rattle of crockery as Hilda wheeled in the tea trolley. While she poured out, Sybil proffered a plate of brandy-snap biscuits, filled with fresh cream.

'Dinner will be at seven. I should say, we change for that, so don't eat too many.'

'Oh, good. Hilda does sometimes take note of my heavy hints,' Griff exclaimed, as he joined them, spotted the delicious sweetmeats and helped himself to a couple.

Then footsteps were heard going along the hall, followed by an irritable masculine bellow. 'Sybil, where are you? Hilda, run my bath!'

Sybil leapt to her feet. 'Excuse me – my husband is back. Entertain Mattie, Griff!'

As she hurried out, Griff said to Mattie, 'We all jump to his command. Don't look so apprehensive, old Rufus has a penchant for young blonde ladies, hence Sybil, eh? It was the photograph of you your mother sent that made him decide to employ you.'

Mattie hadn't heard 'penchant' before, but she could guess its meaning.

'I wish I hadn't come here,' she said frankly.

'But you don't have a return ticket?' Griff guessed.

'No. I'll have to save up for that out of my wages.'

'I don't blame you. Still, it was worth coming, just to meet me, eh?'

Mattie couldn't help smiling at his audacity. She'd met two attentive young men in a short time, she thought, but she already knew which one she found more attractive.

'I have another dilemma now,' she confided. 'What to wear this evening.'

'I happen to know,' Griff told her, 'that Sybil thought of that. Hilda's hung some suitable clothes in your wardrobe.'

'That's very kind of Sybil! But won't Mr Fullilove realise . . . ?'

'Sybil chose things she bought herself, before her marriage. I should have let her tell you herself, but I didn't want you to worry.'

Mattie didn't meet Mr Fullilove before dinner. When Sybil returned she resumed her cheerful chat, but Mattie noted the flickering of her eyelids, the glances at the door. Eventually, after the trolley had been taken away, Sybil looked at her wristwatch. 'Well, Hilda gave me a nod to let me know she has tidied up the bathroom. You will find everything you need, I hope, in there. Look in the wardrobe, too. We'll assemble downstairs at five to seven. Don't be late.'

Mattie was standing in her petticoat, following a reviving soak in the bath, regarding the clothes in the wardrobe, when there was a rapping on her door. For a moment she hesitated, then called: 'Come in.'

To her relief, it was Hilda. 'Thought you might like me to help, Miss Mattie.'

'Oh, would you? Which dress, d'you think?' There were three to choose from.

'Miss Sybil is wearing blue. How about this sprigged muslin? Not too revealing.'

'I'm glad of that.' Mattie smiled, thinking of Mr Fullilove and his penchant.

'Now,' Hilda said, deftly tying the bow at Mattie's waist, 'I'll dress your hair.'

Mattie sat at the big dressing-table, where she had arranged her few toiletries. The triple mirrors reflected her solemn expression, as Hilda brushed and combed her long hair, twisting it into a simple knot in the nape of her neck. It was certainly more becoming than the tight plaits she'd wound round her head first thing today.

'Well, I'll have to leave you to it, and get back to the kitchen! I left everything throbbing on the stove. Cook flounced off last week,' Hilda said wryly.

'If the brandy snaps are anything to go by, I look forward to my dinner! Thank you Hilda, you've made me look presentable.'

When Mattie entered the dining room, she mentally braced herself for the encounter with the formidable Mr Fullilove. He stood with his back to the fireplace, holding a glass of wine, which he deposited on the mantelpiece, when he saw her.

Like his wife, he was unlike the picture she had conjured up. Mr Fullilove was very tall, broad-shouldered with an aquiline nose and a piercing gaze. He wore a scarlet silk smoking-jacket, embroidered with Chinese dragons. He was perhaps ten years older than Sybil, dark jowled, with thick iron-grey hair. She tried not to flinch as he gripped her hand. She was aware, as she had been with Sybil, of a lavish use of perfume.

'Good evening, Mattie. I gather you prefer to be called that? Be seated next to Griffith. He is adept at light conversation, I am not.' The sarcasm was lightly veiled. 'Would you care for a drink?'

Mattie found her voice. 'No, thank you, Mr Fullilove'

'I should say, you will naturally be treated as one of the family in my home, where you may call me Rufus. However, you will appreciate that at work you will address me formally. Is that understood?'

'It is indeed.' Mattie turned to Griff as he pulled out a chair for her at the oval table. 'Thank you, Griff.' She couldn't help thinking that being treated as one of the family in Mr Fullilove's case was not exactly to be recommended.

Sybil, on her right, leaned forward, whispering as her husband topped up his glass, before taking his seat. 'You look very pretty, Mattie. I'm sure Rufus approves.'

I don't want him *to approve of me*! Mattie wished she could say.

'Didn't have no time to make a first course,' Hilda announced grimly, as she wheeled in the trolley once more.

Mr Fullilove rose to the challenge in her tone. 'Not good enough,' he said curtly.

Hilda slammed his dinner plate on the table before him. The condiments rattled in their silver holder. Mr Fullilove, lips tightly compressed, grabbed his glass.

'Veal cutlet.' Hilda looked defiant. 'Bloomin' palaver – cook's book said to dip 'em in melted butter, egg yolk, then breadcrumbs, grated lemon peel *and* chopped parsley.' She brandished a finger tied around with a strip of bandage. 'Chopped me bleedin' finger, too. Comes of having to rush around doing two jobs, as you're well aware – *Sir*. I nearly forgot to mash the potato, and stick a roll of fried bacon on top of each cutlet. Serve with a good tomato sauce, it said in the recipe – I never had time for that, so I admit it come out of a bottle. Here, Mr Griff, pass the rest of the plates for me, will yer?'

Griff cheerfully obliged. Sybil picked up her cutlery. 'This looks delicious, Hilda. Eat up, all of you! Thank you Hilda, what would we do without you?'

'Starve, I reckon,' Hilda muttered as she went back to the kitchen.

Mattie glanced covertly at Mr Fullilove. He was slicing into his tender cutlet, but his expression was thunderous.

She became aware that Griff was addressing her. 'Sunday tomorrow. Time for you to recover from your journeying, and a day off for me. If it's fine, I like to take a stroll along the Hoe. Perhaps you would like to join me? We could take a packed lunch.'

Before Mattie could answer, Mr Fullilove said dourly, 'I shall require your attention for an hour from ten in the morning, Mattie, to discuss your duties at the emporium. You will then be able to take them up with a minimum of fuss on Monday at 8.30 a.m.'

'Naturally,' Mattie returned smartly. To Griff, she added; 'Yes, I'd enjoy a picnic.'

Over the rhubarb tart and custard Mattie felt her eyelids begin to droop with sheer fatigue. She sat up with a start when Griff gave her a discreet nudge. 'Oh dear, how rude of me. I'm so sorry . . .' she said weakly.

'Please don't apologise,' Sybil exclaimed. 'We've expected too much of you, after your travelling. You are, of course, excused. Griff will escort you to your room. We breakfast late, at nine, on Sunday mornings. Have a good night!'

'Thank you, you're very kind,' Mattie said.

As they left the dining room, they were aware of raised voices from within. Mr Fullilove was obviously haranguing his wife.

'Best for me to retire early too,' Griff said ruefully, at her door. 'Sunday is Hilda's day off too. Breakfast will be made by me, boiled eggs and toast. Then I'll make us some sandwiches from left-overs from the emporium delicatessen. I brought home some tender prime ham which didn't really fit that description . . . we take pot luck at dinner. No roast joint and trimmings! Rufus will be at his club, anyway. 'Night, Mattie.'

'Goodnight, Griff,' Mattie said, as she closed her door.

The strong sea breeze on the Hoe, that great cliff towering around a hundred feet over Plymouth Sound, made Mattie and Griff scurry along the promenade, pausing only to admire the bronze statue of Sir Francis Drake, to find a sheltered spot. Mattie was glad of a long cardigan over her blouse and skirt, but she was ruefully aware that she had not placed the hairpins as skilfully as Hilda and her hair had tumbled loose around her shoulders. It must resemble a bird's nest, she thought.

They plumped down on the rug, which Griff gallantly spread on the grass. 'Here,' he said, after rummaging in his rucksack, 'binoculars. Know how to use 'em?'

'I can find out,' she told him, truthful but determined.

Griff smiled, but left her to it. She adjusted the glasses, then gazed entranced over the grey swell of the sea, at a large grey vessel on the horizon, at waves rushing in and out of the inlets in the rocks, as gulls wheeled overhead. Griff took a sketchpad from his pocket and unwrapped a stick of charcoal. With swift, spare strokes, he captured

Mattie with the wind in her hair as now she concentrated on Drake's Island.

'I'm hungry,' Mattie said at last, with a meaningful glance at the rucksack. 'I didn't get a chance to have another piece of toast for breakfast, when Rufus told me it was time for our talk.'

'Interrogation, don't you mean?' Griff asked. 'Can you hold out ten minutes longer, I wonder? You see, I am waiting for a friend to join us. A lady friend.'

Mattie was candid as usual. 'Is that why you asked me – as a cover-up?'

'Oh, you've found me out! However, I am enjoying your company.'

'Why the secrecy?'

'Christabel is also employed by the emporium. All the female staff are selected by Rufus for youth and good looks, apart from Miss Teazel, in accounts, who's known as a bit of a tartar! When I joined the company my dear stepfather warned me not to become romantically involved with any of the girls.'

'And have you?'

Before he could answer, they heard a cry of 'Yoo-hoo!' Griff scrambled to his feet to greet the new arrival, who was holding on to her daisy-trimmed boater.

'Gosh, I'm hungry.' The girl smiled at Mattie. 'I'm Christabel, by the way.'

'I'm famished, too! I'm Mattie.'

'And I'm the universal provider,' Griff said, as he unwrapped the greaseproof parcels. He handed out the serviettes. 'Tea or coffee? I made two flasks.'

'Our boss's face would turn puce if he could see us, enjoying his prime ham,' Christabel said cheerfully, holding out her hand for a second sandwich.

Mattie warmed to her immediately. Christabel's short, wavy hair was sandy-brown rather than the blond Rufus was said to prefer, and there were freckles all over her pert little nose. She had a shapely figure, wide china-blue eyes and a smile which accentuated deep dimples in her rounded cheeks. Her accent was as rich as the Devonshire cream Mattie had sampled earlier.

'You'll be working with me in the drapery department,' Christabel informed her.

'I'm glad about that!' Mattie replied, meaning it.

'Your predecessor got the sack for inappropriate behaviour.'

'What was that?'

'Put it this way, she had to let out the seams in her uniform, and Sir deduced why.'

'How unkind of him. She probably needed her wages if she was pregnant.'

'Never use that word when Rufus is within hearing,' Griff advised Mattie.

'He was actually affable this morning. He hoped I'd be happy at the emporium.'

'I told you,' Griff winked at her, 'he's got a—'

'Penchant – I know,' Mattie said.

Later, they returned along the promenade, linking arms.

'What a lucky chap I am,' Griff observed, 'escorting two lovely ladies!'

When it was time to part company, Mattie rested on a seat, pretending to look in her bag for a handkerchief, while the other two stood a little apart from her. After a quick glance round Griff embraced Christabel briefly.

'See you tomorrow,' Mattie heard him say.

Christabel gave Mattie a wave in passing, echoing, 'Yes, see you tomorrow.'

Mattie was really glad to have friends to support her at the emporium on Monday.

FOUR

'Leave your shoes outside your door,' Griff said, when he bid Mattie good night. He'd deduced that she'd only the one pair, now scuffed from their excursion.

Mattie retrieved them first thing, polished to a pleasing shine. He was a thoughtful young man: not only had he cleaned her footwear, he'd advised her to use the facilities in the bedroom instead of the bathroom in the morning. 'Rufus takes priority then. Hilda will bring you a jug of hot water at 7. You and I will breakfast in the kitchen at 7.15 – porridge, I expect. By then, Hilda will be overseeing washing-day in the scullery, she has help on Mondays. Sybil, by the way, will stay in bed until we've gone.'

Sybil, Mattie gathered, was truly a lady of leisure. However, it was all too apparent that she didn't have sufficient staff to run this big house. Mattie's mother had been rather vague about her cousin's background, but – *I'll find out!* Mattie determined.

Griff drove Mattie to the Barbican in the delivery van. 'Rufus will already be at the store. A cab collects him every morning and brings him back in the evening.'

'Doesn't he drive?' Mattie asked. She was glad Rufus wasn't travelling with them.

'No. He likes to cogitate on the day ahead while smoking a small cigar. Very different from the way he started his working life.'

Mattie was curious. 'How was that?'

'You don't know?'

'No. Just what you've told me. Rufus marrying for money to save the emporium.'

'He didn't have an auspicious start. He was a foundling, brought up in a local orphanage. They gave him the name Fullilove after the chaplain, who took an interest in his welfare, and also suggested his first name. He was a good scholar, but he had to leave school at fourteen, when he was given help to set up in business. He bought a barrow, piled it with tea he had bagged up himself, salvaged from a warehouse damaged by fire, and made his first profit. Seven years on, he rented a shop, and after another ten he was able to take on the emporium. You have to admire him, eh?'

'Yes, but I don't think I like him . . .'

'Not many do. I'm grateful, though, that he didn't cast me out when my mother died. He knew what it was like to be an orphan. Any worries about today, Mattie?'

'I hope my uniform fits.'

'Oh, it will, Mattie. Your mother was asked to supply your measurements.'

Mattie's face was decidedly flushed. She couldn't help thinking that maybe, along with the photograph, this had made Rufus decide she was suitable for the emporium.

Still fifteen minutes to go before opening time. They went through the staff entrance, then took the lift to the first floor. Mattie glimpsed assistants unveiling their counters, before Griff led her to the drapery department, where Christabel was waiting.

'I must leave you here,' he said. 'I'm on the ground floor, the food hall. Good luck!'

Christabel welcomed her with a smile. 'Your uniform is in the washroom. See you in five minutes.' She indicated a door.

The dark green linen button-through dress, with its skirt of decorous length, was a perfect fit. She folded her own garments and placed them on a shelf labelled MISS MATILDA ROWLEY. A quick tidying of her hair, and she was ready.

She emerged to the ringing of a bell: time to stand by, the emporium was open.

As their first customers did not arrive until after nine o'clock Christabel was able to acquaint Mattie with the location of the most frequently asked-for commodities. There were many deep drawers below the counter and shelves along the walls. The drawers were packed with smaller items, like ribbons, tapes, braids, cottons and silks, hooks and eyes, press fasteners and buttons, scissors, needles, thimbles, darning mushrooms and tape measures. On the shelves were bolts of material, varying in colour and texture from the sober to the exotic. Hanging from rails were translucent silks in all the colours of the rainbow.

'Those are quite dazzling! Beautiful!' Mattie exclaimed, in awe.

'From India. Can't you just picture them made up into saris?' Christabel brushed a stray thread from the counter, indicated the shining brass measure along the edge. 'Have you done much dressmaking yourself?'

'I'm afraid not. My mother makes most of our clothes; she has a treadle machine.'

Opposite the drapery department was the linen hall. The assistants there were almost hidden by pyramids of plump goose-feather pillows and Egyptian-cotton sheets.

Mattie watched the hands on the clock. She felt an urge to tap it, like the men with their pocket watches on the train, to hurry it up. She gave quite a start when the doors swung open and a middle-aged woman in black came bustling up to the counter.

'Watch me, this time,' Christabel whispered to Mattie. 'Good morning, madam.'

'Good morning. I require serviceable blue cotton for our maids' summer frocks.'

'How many maids?' Christabel enquired, reaching down a bolt of saxe-blue cloth.

'Three. I believe you stock ready-made detachable collars and cuffs, in white?'

'Yes, madam.'

Mattie was fascinated by the confidence with which Christabel flipped the bolt of cloth over and over on the counter, estimating the yardage required. Taking up a pair of large scissors with curved grips, she sliced decisively across. She didn't nick the material, then tear off the piece, as Mattie had seen her mother do.

The customer rubbed the end of the cloth between finger and thumb, looking thoughtful. 'This should wear well,' she decided. 'Wrap it up.'

A neat brown-paper parcel was deftly tied with string. The cuffs, collars, cotton and other necessaries were placed in a large bag, neatly folded over at the top.

'Does madam require a pattern?' Christabel asked.

'No, thank you. Mrs Trembath's seamstress knows exactly what is required. Certainly not the latest fashion! Kindly send the bill to Knockwood Hall in due course.'

When the customer had departed, Mattie observed: 'What a grim-looking lady!'

'Oh, you must learn to tell the difference! Mrs Barnes is not exactly a lady, even though she sounds like one. She's the Hon. Mrs Trembath's housekeeper. However, she's entitled to be called "madam".'

'I must admit I'm dreading cutting the cloth . . .'

'Don't worry by the end of the day you'll be expert at it!' Christabel assured her. 'Though Monday is always slow. Most of the drapery customers are of a similar status to Mrs Barnes. The real ladies are to be seen in the millinery or couture departments, later in the day. They try on the new lines, but they don't always buy. The bridal suite was hard-hit by the war, and now, as there are not many eligible young men, they say ours will be a generation of spinsters.'

'Maybe more of us will make a decent living wage in occupations which have always been regarded as men's work,' Mattie said. 'Though I imagine *you* will marry.'

'You are thinking that Griff and I . . . ?'

'Well, yes.'

'It's likely that it's just a flirtation on his part. He talks of emigrating when he's twenty-one. He will come into a little money then, left in trust by his grandfather.'

'How exciting! I wonder where he intends to go. Wouldn't you like to travel too?'

Christabel shook her head. 'I have a sick mother to consider. My father was killed in the war. I'm the breadwinner in my family. By the way, don't mention to Griff what I just told you, will you?'

'Of course not,' Mattie agreed, as a potential customer approached them.

'All yours!' Christabel whispered.

'Stay close by, then. I may need your help!'

On Tuesday mornings, the Fullilove kitchen was always full of steam. Flat-irons smoothed out the creases from the newly laundered clothes. Little Hilda mopped her damp brow and muttered under her breath.

Sybil, of course, wasn't involved. Wearing a pristine white overall, with a turban, she was happily occupied in what had been the butler's pantry in more affluent times. Having unlocked a cupboard, she selected various flagons, pots and waxed cartons and set these out on a work table. Then she took from the drawer a notebook with marble-patterned covers. She turned the pages, a silver propelling pencil in hand.

'Hilda,' she called presently, 'Time for a cup of hot chocolate, I think!'

Next door, in the kitchen, Hilda sniffed, but set the flat-iron in its rest. The pan of full-cream milk was already heating on the stove, as she'd anticipated this request. She grated half a tablet of dark Belgian chocolate into the milk and stirred until it was dissolved, adding a tiny piece of cinnamon to enhance the flavour. The cups were filled, long-handled teaspoons, a bowl of white sugar and paper napkins placed on the tray.

'Thank you, Hilda,' Sybil said graciously.

'Nothing on the boil yet?' Hilda asked, glancing at the empty containers.

'No. I've been studying last week's orders and checking our stock of ingredients.'

Hilda sipped the delicious drink. 'Aren't you worried Mr Fullilove will find out?'

'What if he does? I am investing the allowance he grudgingly gives me – from my own money, I suspect – and what else could I do with my time?'

Hilda bit back a retort. She relished the thought that they were foxing the aloof Mr Fullilove. She said instead, 'Your roots need touching up, before the next meeting. I'll get the peroxide from the bathroom. Griff borrowed it to dab on a mouth ulcer.'

'Comes of eating too many slivers of the emporium's strong cheese! It's good to have two young people in the house. I wonder how Mattie's doing?'

'Oh, you needn't worry about that one, *she*'s got the measure of Mr Fullilove'

'I'm glad the Hon. Mrs Trembath is our hostess on Thursday morning. My husband complains we use too much expensive ground coffee when I entertain the ladies here.'

'Still rationed, are we?' Hilda drained her cup, moved to light the spirit stove. 'What d'you want me to do? I've a pile of ironing waiting . . .'

'Athenian hair-wash. You can manage that, can't you?' Sybil wheedled.

'Remind me of the recipe then.'

'Weigh a quarter of a pound of sassafras wood, add to a gallon of rose-water in a vessel. Bring to the boil, simmer until dissolved. Cool, then add a pint of pure alcohol and an ounce of pearl ash,' Sybil recited. 'Try it on your hair, Hilda. It's a tonic.'

Hilda sniffed again. 'I ain't got time to prink and preen, Miss Sybil.'

'I'll make the black hair-dye – three of the ladies requested that,' Sybil said. 'They don't want their husbands to suspect they're going grey.'

She pulled on a pair of protective gloves. This mixture, which must be stored in a blue bottle, indicating its toxicity, involved dissolving silver nitrate and nickel sulphate in distilled water, with a dash of strong ammonia, which made her eyes smart.

'Enhancing brown hair is easier,' Sybil said with feeling. 'Just a tincture of walnut shells, scented with oil of lavender. Not that our ladies realise that.'

Hilda checked the notebook. 'No saffron?'

Sybil shook her head. 'I daren't ask my husband for that – it's so costly. It gives a glorious tinge to auburn hair. I'll substitute black tea with rum for Mrs Ginger Stevens. I can charge almost as much for it, and it's so easy.'

'Watch out, Mr Fullilove ain't marked the level in the rum bottle, then!'

Later, when the hair lotions were bottled, Sybil began a favourite task: lip pomade. She'd make extra as a gift for

Mattie. This was a startling red and she hoped it would cheer her up. Mattie had looked solemn since starting at the emporium.

*

'Come in!' Mattie was startled by the tapping on her door. She'd not been in long from work, had kicked her shoes off, and was resting on her bed. 'I hadn't realised how tiring it is when you're on your legs most of the day,' she had said to Sybil when she came into the room.

'Never mind, here's a little something to cheer you up,' Sybil said.

Mattie sat up, took the small jar and read the label. '*Lip pomentum* – what's that?'

Sybil smiled. 'See my lips? I mix all my own cosmetics. Rufus doesn't object, believing I am thrifty. Shush! He doesn't know I also sell to exclusive clients.'

Mattie had to smile then. Curious, she unscrewed the top, looked inside. She rubbed the tip of her little finger over the glossy salve. 'Is this how you apply it?'

'Yes, or with a sable brush. Go to the dressing-table, you need the mirror.'

Mattie gazed back at her reflection. She couldn't say, 'I don't look like me!'

'I can tell you're not sure about it,' Sybil said, over her shoulder.

'Oh, Sybil, it's just that—' Mattie wasn't sure how to answer.

'You're right – you're a natural beauty, my dear. I'll wipe the colour off for you before it sets, and I'll exchange this pomade for a pot of my skin cream, eh?'

'I'm curious,' Mattie admitted a little later, 'to know how you started all this.'

Sybil glanced at her gold fob watch. 'Well, I expect we've got time for a chat – dinner will be half an hour later this evening. Rufus rang to say he was held up in his office, going over the accounts with Miss Teazel. She is probably only a halfpenny or two out, but that's too much in his opinion . . .

'Now, I'm surprised at how little you seem to know about me, but your mother was never one for tittle-tattle, eh? Sophia and my mother were first cousins, they grew up in the village where your parents still live. My mother, being older, was married first, by that time she was living and working in the West Country. I was an only child, and my father was a farmer. They could afford to have me educated privately. I even took science lessons at school and dabbled with the idea of making science my career.

'As I grew up, I found country life restricting. I rebelled, left home as soon as I could, and joined a small travelling theatre company. I dreamed of becoming an actress. I assisted the wardrobe mistress, who was also skilled in stage make-up. She shared her secrets, and I discovered I had a flair for it. We made our own preparations, as

I do still, and after a few years I branched out on my own. I was much in demand. I actually made money from something I loved doing. I had a nice little nest egg when I met Rufus. He was introduced to me backstage – he'd been invited to a performance given by the company I was with then. He remarked on the artistry involved with the character make-up.' She paused. 'It may be hard to comprehend, but it was love at first sight.'

'For both of you?' Mattie ventured.

'It seemed so. He was a widower; we married within six weeks of meeting.' She added: 'I suppose he thought an educated wife would be an asset. I realised all too soon I'd made a mistake. There is . . . no passion in our union. I suspect he seeks that elsewhere. Are the visits to his club a cover-up for a liaison?'

'Do you really care?' Mattie wondered.

'Not any more. I have my ally, dear Hilda, and now, you. I feel I can trust you.'

'Thank you. Though I'm afraid I now care even less for Rufus.'

'He hides his kinder side very well. He brought Griff up, after his mother died.'

'He banished him to boarding school!' Mattie reminded Sybil.

'He paid for him to have an excellent education; social grooming. He is fond of Griff in his own way, but doesn't show it. Well, I must dress for dinner, so must you.'

As she opened the door to leave they saw Griff standing there.

'I was wondering where the pair of you had got to,' he said, unembarrassed.

'We'll be down shortly,' Mattie and Sybil said in unison.

Mattie closed the door. How much, if anything, had Griff overheard, she wondered?

Miss Teazel pleaded a headache and asked to be excused. She'd seen her employer's covert glances at her assistant. A pretty young thing, but with little aptitude for book-keeping. The discrepancies had been in Miss Coe's child-ish handwriting.

When her superior had left, Miss Coe smiled nervously at Mr Fullilove.

'I promise to do better, sir.'

They were in his office. The building was deserted, apart from the caretaker in his basement. Rufus pulled down the blinds, switched on the desk lamp.

'I've made you late for your meal. I apologise.'

'Oh,' Miss Coe said disingenuously, 'I have to fend for myself. I only have a gas ring in my bedsit. It will have to be bread and cheese tonight.'

'I feel responsible for your welfare. Allow me to accompany you to a restaurant meal.'

'I . . . don't know what to say . . . it's very good of you, but—'

'I insist. While you fetch your things from the cloak-room, I will telephone my wife.'

'Won't she mind?'

'My dear young lady, I assure you, Mrs Fullilove will not mind at all,' Rufus said.

FIVE

Evie, although she was coming up to thirteen, was blissfully ignorant of the facts of life. She knew Ena was about to have a baby, of course, but matters concerning the birth were conveyed in whispers, between her mother and her sister-in-law.

Evie wisely kept out of Ena's way as much as possible. Ena's temper did not improve as the weather grew warmer and she became heavier and weary. The cradle, which had last been used by Evie as a baby, was brought down from the attic and painted white. The muslin hangings were washed and starched. Sophia removed the faded pink bows and sewed on new blue ribbons at Ena's request. Ena was convinced the baby was a boy. Sophia secretly hoped so: to compensate for, even if he could never replace, her own lost son, Robbie.

It was May, and Mattie had already been gone a whole month. She wrote to her parents once a week. In her latest letter she proudly enclosed a five-shilling postal order, as promised. This was almost a week's wage. Her earlier suspicions had proved right. Her board and lodging were obviously taken into consideration, were not free at all. Mattie also included a note for Evie.

I miss you dear Sis, even our little differences of opinion! I have been quite homesick. I have to say, this place, my job, have not exactly proved to be a dream come true. I hope you will not have to leave school before time, like me. A good education is so important. Read all you can!

However, Sybil is very nice, and I do like Griff (Mr Fullilove's stepson). I also have a good friend at work, called Christabel.

I expect Ena is happier without me around. How much longer before the baby arrives? You will be the big sister then!

How I wish I could go down to the stream with you and pick watercress for tea. But I suppose those carefree days are gone for ever.

With fondest love from Mattie.

Tears pricked Evie's eyes. Ena was able to undermine her in all kinds of devious ways, now that her own big sister was not around to protect her from the barbs.

She thought, as she tucked the letter away where she hoped Ena would not find it, our parents found me amusing when I was a child – I was the spoiled one, I know. Now,

Mother tells me off when Ena moans I've not done my jobs properly. Oh, how I hate washing-up! When I leave school, I shall ask Mattie to send for me! I miss her, too.

Evie's parents were on their fortnightly shopping excursion to the Friday market in town. The bus was packed, and Sophia chatted to the doctor's wife, who was having a rare day off from answering calls to the surgery. Her husband had planned a fishing trip, she said, adding, 'I hope your Ena doesn't decide to have her baby today.'

'Well, the midwife called yesterday and she reckons Ena'll go another ten days or so.' Will *I* last out? Sophia thought. Ena has been a real trial this last month . . .

Sophia was flattered that the doctor's wife had singled her out to talk to, according her the status she'd enjoyed when the Plough was a going concern.

'How is your Mattie faring in Plymouth?' They were communicating across the gangway in the bus. Will tactfully gazed through the window at the local scenes as they rumbled along, but others were listening avidly.

'Mattie is doing well in her new employment, thank you.'

'Such an attractive young lady. She will be much in demand socially, I imagine.'

'Oh, Mattie is quite emancipated. She intends to concentrate on her career.'

Will gave Sophia a discreet nudge. 'Town Hall stop coming up. Make ready.'

As they walked towards the market square, he observed. 'Bit sharp, weren't you?'

'Mattie is not like other girls of her age. *She*'ll make something of herself.'

Will squeezed her arm 'You've expected great things of Mattie ever since she had her portrait painted! Now she's left home we should concentrate on Evie, I think.'

'Evie is different. She'll stay at home unless she marries. You'll see!'

'We mustn't take that for granted,' Will reminded her wisely.

'It's traditional,' Sophia insisted. 'The youngest has certain responsibilities.'

'You've got Ena now . . .'

'Ena! *She* pulled the wool over my eyes. She won't last the course, that one!'

At that moment, with a wry smile, Will thought, but didn't say, how alike Sophia and her elder daughter were, both in looks, for Mattie was fair like her mother, while Evie was dark-haired like himself, and in the way they spoke their mind.

Evie hurried home from school at lunch time to see Ena, as she'd promised an anxious Ronnie, first thing, before he left for work. 'You can make sandwiches for you both, can't you?' As he said that, he was hurriedly cutting bread for his own packing-up.

Evie had assured her brother she would do as he asked. When she entered the house by the back door she went straight to the kitchen. She found things as she had left them, the table wiped clean, the plates on the wall rack. There was no sign of Ena.

She called out anxiously: 'Ena, where are you?' There was a faint thumping on the floor above, in reply. Ena must be in her bedroom.

Evie tore upstairs, turned the corner and burst into the room without knocking.

Ena, still in her nightgown, was writhing on the rumpled bed. Her face was contorted. 'What . . . took you . . . so long.' she managed in a hoarse whisper.

'I ran back from school. Is it . . . the baby?'

'What do you think!' Ena gasped. She groaned as another spasm racked her.

Evie was galvanised into action. She gripped Ena's hand. It seemed to help.

After what seemed an eternity, Ena relaxed, opened her eyes, struggled to sit up.

'The bed's soaking. Get a big towel to put under me. Then run like the blazes for the midwife! Tell her . . . the pains . . . oh leave the towel – just go!'

A shocked Evie realised that Ena was in agony. 'I'll be as quick as I can!'

Five minutes later she was hammering on the nurse's door. Her husband, home from the fields for his lunch, answered. He stood there with his sleeves rolled up, as he'd been at the sink, washing his grubby hands. He wiped them ineffectually on his clothes. 'If you want the missus, she's out on a job. Is it your Ena? I can get a message to her, tell her to leave off lancing Charlie's boils, and to come to yours.'

'Thank you!' Evie was still out of breath. She turned at the gate. 'What can I do?'

'Get plenty of water boiling on the stove. Then sit with the poor gal.'

There was a pump over the Belfast sink. Evie filled kettles and a big pan and set them on the gas stove. She wasted several matches, because her hands were shaking.

She went upstairs, pausing to grab towels from the linen cupboard on the landing.

There was a scream from the bedroom. Evie dropped the linen on a chair, rushed to the bedside. This was all happening so quickly: it was like a bad dream.

Ena was clutching her bent knees, her gown rucked round her waist. 'The baby's being born ...' she panted. 'Help me, oh help me!'

Evie snatched up the biggest towel, eased it under her sister-in-law. As she bent to this task, she was shocked to see what was happening. Instinctively she caught the baby in her hands as it emerged into the world. It gave an indignant wail. This was one cry which Evie was relieved to hear.

Ena subsided limply back on her pillows. 'There's more to come,' she said weakly.

'What . . . do you mean?'

'Lay the baby down, wrap it in the other towel, then leave well alone. The nurse will deal with the rest of it . . .' She closed her eyes dismissively.

Evie suddenly recalled the water which must be boiling furiously on the stove. As she came downstairs, two at a time, she heard the banging on the front door. Thank goodness, the midwife was here!

'The baby's come,' she greeted the nurse.

'What is it?' came the brusque question.

'Oh – I didn't look!' Poor Evie was sobbing now.

'Never mind – got the kettle on the boil? Bring up a jug of hot and a jug of cold water, then make tea for three – you've had a shock, too, my dear.'

First, Evie washed her hands under the pump, then consigned her dress to the clothes basket – what would Mother say when she saw the stains on it? She took down a clean frock from the airer and slipped it over her head. *Now*, she thought I can cope with the nurse's requests.

There was more tea to make and explanations as to why she was not back at school, when her parents arrived home at four o'clock.

The nurse was still with Ena and the baby. Sophia couldn't wait to see her new grandson. Evie and Will sat in the kitchen, drinking their tea and eating Bourbon biscuits, a treat Sophia had brought home.

'You did well, Evie,' Will said presently. He suddenly reached across the table to ruffle her hair. 'I hope it wasn't too much of a shock for you. Messy business, having babies. But they clean up nicely, and then you forget all that.'

'I don't think I'll ever forget,' Evie told him. She wouldn't be unkind and add that the baby was all crumpled-looking and lobster-red; she hoped he would improve with keeping!

Tucked up in her bed, in fresh linen, Ena turned away from her baby. 'You can nurse him for a bit,' she told her mother-in-law, 'then lay him in the cradle.'

Nurse whispered conspiratorially to Sophia, 'I don't like the colour of her. She seems to be rejecting the baby . . . she won't try to feed him. Doctor should be back home shortly. I'll call and give him the news. Ask him to look in tomorrow.'

Sophia gently kissed the little downy head, still damp from bathing. '*Robbie.*' she said very softly. 'Grandma will take care of you, my darling.'

Ronnie apologised for waking his mother soon after midnight. When the baby stirred and was obviously hungry, Ena had hissed, 'Tell your mother to make him a bottle.

You can move the cradle into your parents' room. Let me go back to sleep!'

Sophia had been prepared for this eventuality. There was a tin of formula milk and half a dozen of the new glass feeding-bottles. While she busied herself with mixing, then cooling the milk in the bottle, Ronnie rocked the baby in his arms.

'Pass him to me,' she said presently. 'You go back up and see to the cradle. Put it by my side of the bed. Tell your father, if he's still awake, I'll be up in a while.'

'I know what you're thinking about Ena,' Ronnie said defensively, 'but she'll get over it. She must have been terrified, here on her own, till Evie arrived.'

'We were all in a state, and I just realised: I should have told Evie what a good job she did, eh?'

'I'll tell her tomorrow, Mother. Buy her a little something from the baby. We must send a telegram to Mattie, too.'

At dawn, when Sophia crept downstairs to make the baby another bottle, she discovered Ronnie lying on the old settee which had been put in the kitchen because they were reluctant to throw it out. Visitors often took advantage of it when they called when Sophia was busy baking, but was still glad to have a chat.

'What's this?' she exclaimed. 'The baby didn't keep you awake, did he?'

He shook his head, looking miserable. 'No. Ena refuses to let me share her bed. She says it's all my fault: if I *hadn't*—Well, she says "never again". She's made her mind up to go back to her mother as soon as she's able. She says . . . she says, she doesn't want the baby – we can keep it!'

Sophia hugged him close. 'She'll change her mind. She doesn't mean it.' As she comforted her son, she thought, *but suppose she does . . .?*

There was worse to come. When the doctor arrived, he told them that Ena had a high temperature, that she must be taken immediately to the cottage hospital because he suspected she was developing puerperal fever, an infection following childbirth.

The family could only watch helplessly as Ronnie carried his young wife downstairs, swathed in blankets, and out to the doctor's car. He accompanied Ena to hospital.

Sophia sat on the old sofa, holding little Robbie, securely wrapped in his shawl.

'What can I do, Mother?' Evie asked her.

'You can look after the baby for me, while your father fetches Mrs Moss to help me disinfect Ena and Ronnie's room and strip the bed.'

In the weeks that followed, Evie was often absent from school. She was needed at home to help her mother with the baby. Her thirteenth birthday came and went, without the usual celebration, as Ena remained gravely ill in hospital. Ronnie was the only one allowed to visit her. Ena didn't acknowledge him, she couldn't, as she had become mentally disturbed. Whether it was a permanent state of affairs, the doctors couldn't say, but she'd survived, when many young mothers died in such circumstances.

Evie overheard Ronnie sobbing to Sophia and Will one evening, after his return from the hospital. 'They are going to move her to an institution. What am I to do?'

Sophia looked compassionately at her son. He was pale and thin. He had to keep going because of his responsibilities; at least he had his work during the day and, most important, he had little Robbie, the only good thing to come of all this sadness.

'You are having to bring up a child after your own family are grown,' Ronnie said.

'My dear, we have a new purpose in life, and Evie is a great support, you know.'

'I know. That's a comfort to me, too.'

Evie, who'd been about to say goodnight, turned away from the door. She crept upstairs. She'd write to Mattie, she decided, because who else could she confide in?

SIX

The employees of the emporium looked forward to their annual outing in August, although most suspected this would be a swan song, as staff cuts seemed inevitable.

'Last come, first to go.' Griff felt he should prepare Mattie for this.

'Oh, me and Cissie Coe, I suppose?' Only a few months ago, she thought ruefully, I would have been relieved, but now I'd be sorry to leave Sybil, and, yes, Griff, too . . .

'Rufus can't be seen to favour family. The whole country's in a mess, we're losing the empire trade, our mills closing down. Thank goodness for Lloyd George. Since unemployment soared to a million, he has ensured an increase in dole payments.'

'Men get fifteen shillings, *women* only twelve a week!' Mattie reminded him.

'Well, there's the bank holiday to cheer us up, the charabancs are booked.'

'Where are we going?'

'That's a secret, known only to Rufus and the drivers. Last year we went on the ferry across to Cornwall. On a steep path leading down to a lovely sandy beach Sybil tripped up and sprained her ankle. She had to be carried about the rest of the day by a strapping young assistant from Furnishings. You should have seen Rufus glower. Miss Teazel, in charge of first aid, soaked her hankie in the sea to make a cold compress.' He grinned, adding, 'The chap from Furnishings left the emporium soon afterwards.'

'I'm not surprised! D'you think Sybil will come this year?'

'She will! Have you realised this is the fiftieth anniversary of August Bank Holiday brought in by the act passed in 1871? It was a holiday even before Christmas Day!'

'I read the papers too, you know! I'm also aware that this is the hottest summer ever known and the worst drought since rainfall records began,' Mattie retorted.

*

That evening, after dinner, the two of them sat out in the garden, where it was cooler, as they had done during most of the summer. Sybil preferred to pull the blinds down in the drawing-room. Or so she said. Mattie suspected she was fondly hoping that the two of them would become even closer, but then, she didn't know about Griff and Christabel.

'You must have a new frock for the occasion, all the girls do,' Griff said.

'Oh, I'm not sure I can afford it.' Mattie had just posted off the usual postal order.

'Talk to Christabel. She's bound to have some bright ideas,' he assured her.

Mattie asked Christabel's advice the following morning, during a lull in the drapery department. 'It's Tuesday already – less than a week to go! What do you suggest?'

'Remnants,' Christabel said cheerfully. 'Shilling apiece! I need a new outfit too. How about this cool Indian cotton – feel it, so soft and fine . . .'

Mattie held the swatch of material in front of her, looked into the long mirror. 'Oh, it's just right! White with smudges of green and blue. What about you?'

'Swirls of honey and brown – suits my colouring, as your choice does you.'

'I should remind you I'm not much of a seamstress.'

'Don't worry about that! My mother, bless her, despite being in a wheelchair, takes in sewing. She's determined to do her bit. Have supper with us tomorrow night, and you can tell her which style you fancy – she won't need a pattern.'

'Well, I could borrow one or two of Sybil's fashion magazines for us to look at.'

'That's settled then! Mum's keen to meet you anyway!'

When Mattie told Griff about her invitation he said immediately, 'I'll call for you later on, you mustn't walk home by yourself in the gloaming.'

'Thanks, Griff. You'll be able to see Christabel without Rufus knowing, too!'

He smiled. 'And I shall also seize the opportunity to walk arm in arm with *you*!'

After work the two girls chatted animatedly as they hurried down to the docks area, where Christabel and her mother lived, in a tiny terraced house in a mean street where the front doors opened on to the cobbled pavement.

'My father,' Christabel volunteered, 'worked in the big distillery. He gained a fondness for drink there. Mind you, he was jolly when he'd had one too many, not quarrelsome, so Mum always said we must be thankful for that. He won a medal for bravery in the war, but he was killed in action soon afterwards. So we can remember him with pride.'

'And your mum? How long has she been ill?' Mattie asked.

'For some years now. Her bones are crumbling, the doctors at the hospital say. Her legs are badly affected, she can't walk.'

'However does she manage while you are out all day?'

'We have a kind neighbour who sees to her personal needs and makes her lunch. I boil up a big stock pot once a week with marrow bones and vegetables.'

Christabel's mother was called Dolly, an apt name for one so small and pretty, with straight bobbed black hair like a Dutch doll. While her daughter prepared supper, she considered the illustration in the magazine that the girls had selected.

'The dropped waist is easy to fit, and being sleeveless saves on material.' Dolly propelled her chair over to a long, low table. 'This is where I work. I cut, pin and tack this end, then move on to the sewing machine. Your frock will be ready on Friday. A florin – is that all right, my dear?'

'Thank you, yes. I'm very grateful you can help me out,' Mattie said. Three shillings for a new frock – she was fortunate indeed. Also Friday was pay-day!

'It's my pleasure. Christabel can measure you up later on, eh?'

Christabel laid the dining-table, then brought in the supper plates. 'Pork pie – emporium food hall special. The crust was dented, so Griff got it for me half-price!'

There were plenty of new, minted potatoes too, with a jar of homemade pickle.

When the table was cleared they had a cup of tea, 'Sweepings from the tea-packing factory,' Dolly confided. She was a lively and entertaining companion. Mattie was entranced by her stories. In her youth Dolly, when fit and strong, had been an enthusiastic swimmer. 'One day my friend and I – we worked together at the soap factory, oh, I had such lovely soft skin then, due to all the lanolin! – were enjoying a dip in the sea. We didn't bother with the bathing machines like the young ladies, and we'd made our own costumes from cheap material. The colour ran when it got wet, but luckily it was blue! Then these lads from the blacklead factory, mates of my Joey, swam out to us and started larking around. Joey dived down and grabbed my feet. When he came up for air we had quite a tussle – he stole a kiss, and I tried to box his ears. We were married six months later—'

'And before very long, I came along, eh, Mum?' Christabel said fondly.

'My one and only! My wonderful daughter. What would I do without you?'

'I'll never leave you, Mum. I promise!'

'She was such a bright child, Mattie. If only we could have afforded to let her carry on with her schooling,' Dolly sighed.

'She's the mainstay of the drapery department,' Mattie said loyally.

The front door had been left on the latch. Griff duly arrived just after nine.

Mattie couldn't help noticing how Christabel's face lit up when she saw him.

'Had a good time, I can tell,' he greeted them.

Dolly was visibly tiring now, and Christabel said, 'Well, I'll see you both tomorrow.'

Mattie bent to give Dolly a hug. 'I'll see *you* Friday!'

'I'll make sure you girls stand out from all the rest!' Dolly told them.

Mattie and Griff didn't link arms after all; it seemed quite natural to them to walk hand in hand. When a lamp-post loomed up in the gathering dusk they parted and went one either side; when they came together again he slipped his arm round her waist.

'You should have worn a jacket, but I'll keep you warm,' he joked.

Conscious of the intimacy of this gesture, the pressure of his hand through the thin stuff of her frock, Mattie found herself babbling. When she repeated Dolly's story of her meeting with her Joey, she added: 'I can't imagine Rufus ever being young and full of fun, can you? He's such a *cold* man.'

'Actually, I know I go on about him a bit, but he did have a hard start to life. Not much love to go around. How could there be, with so many other orphans in the same boat? When my mother married him I believe she saw a side to him that Sybil hasn't. I was desolated once when a stray dog I'd adopted was run over. Rufus said nothing to comfort me, just turned away. I raged to my mother how uncaring he was. She said quietly, "He *can't* show his true feelings – a person who appears coldhearted is very often shy." '

Mattie was silent for a few minutes, then she said, 'D'you think Sybil knows that?'

'Maybe. But she doesn't seem able to remedy the situation.'

'Little Dolly took on a lot when she married her Joey, but that seems a real romance to me. You should have seen her smile when she described their first kiss.'

They reached the corner of their road, paused under the leafy boughs of a single tree, some distance from the first house along there. Mattie caught her breath when he drew her close. 'Like this?' he asked softly.

She was pliant in his embrace, thrilled by his ardour, as the kissing began.

Later he whispered, 'I've been wanting to do that ever since we first met.'

Belatedly, she thought of Christabel. Was she betraying her friend? She pulled away from him. 'We ought to hurry – ten o'clock curfew, Rufus said – remember?'

'Wait – have I offended you?' He sounded anxious, hurt.

'No,' Mattie admitted.

'Then why . . . ?'

'Christabel – you and she—'

'Nothing could come of it – we both know that. She'll be happy for us, I know.'

Mattie couldn't help herself, she flung her arms round him and hugged him.

'I'm in love with you, Mattie.' His voice was muffled by their closeness.

'I feel the same about you,' she said.

'We have to keep this to ourselves for now. Things will be different soon. I'll be twenty-one in October, Rufus won't be able to run my life then.'

'I was nineteen in July. I suppose Rufus and Sybil are my guardians while I live with them. Sybil might guess.'

'She might, but she won't say anything. She likes to keep secrets.'

Two open-topped Leyland charabancs drew up outside the emporium to the cheers of the waiting crowd. The drivers, smart in their uniforms with peaked caps, showed folk to their seats. Young girls were wearing flowery short dresses and straw hats, vying for the best trimmings; older female staff were in silks and satins, with hats anchored with chiffon scarves and tied under the chin in case of a sudden gust of wind; young bucks like Griff wore striped blazers, bow ties and boaters; more mature males, following Rufus's lead, were in sober suits, but with a coloured waistcoat.

Mattie was in the front row of seats, between Griff and Sybil; Rufus sat opposite the driver. When Mattie waved to Christabel to join them, she shook her head, mouthed, 'I'm not family!' She indicated she would sit behind Mattie. She was soon joined by Miss Teazel, who clasped a large, black umbrella, 'just in case', and a sulky Cissie Coe, who had hoped to escape her superior's company.

Griff balanced the picnic basket on his lap, while Mattie was in charge of a canvas bag containing towels, plimsolls and a bottle of calamine lotion for sunburn. Sybil, naturally, was unencumbered apart from her handbag.

A few days ago a memo had been circulated to all staff asking them to provide their own packed lunch. This was the first year such a request had been made. However, the blow was softened by the promise of 'a cream tea in a lovely garden, to which you will be transported at 4.30 p.m. before leaving for Plymouth at 6 p.m.'

They motored along winding lanes, where stone walls enclosed pasture land and newly shorn sheep gathered at the gates to watch the charabancs go by.

'Looks like we are staying in Devon this bank holiday,' Griff observed.

After forty minutes they took the estuary road, parking the coaches halfway down in a lay-by. After disembarking the two parties mingled. They crossed over the road to a meadow, golden with buttercups, where a burly man opened a gate marked PRIVATE, and ushered them all through. Then began the trek to the cliff edge and the steps leading to the sands below.

'We are here by permission of the landowner,' Griff reported, having spoken to Rufus, who was leading the band, to keep them in check. 'Rufus paid for the privilege, though.'

There were outcrops of rock on the beach and a scramble ensued, to claim the most desirable to lean against, or to sit on top of a flat boulder, possessions safe from the tide.

Rufus and Sybil sat a distance apart from the younger element, who were already busy setting up stumps for a game of cricket, organised by Griff. Miss Teazel, her expression inscrutable under the unfurled umbrella wedged behind her, sat on a thronelike structure, obviously put together by an enterprising earlier visitor to the shore.

Mattie, Christabel and Cissie giggled as they took off their smart shoes, then wriggled out of their stockings under cover of a big towel. On went the canvas plimsolls, looking as new as, at Griff's suggestion, they had applied whitening powder mixed with milk. 'It won't rub off on your clothes then,' he advised.

Mattie was first in to bat, but was called out shortly after. She trod across a shingly patch to the water, to have a paddle. Shading her eyes, she gazed across at the gentle rise of grassland with a herd of cows on the horizon, over the far side of the estuary. The sun dazzled in a cloudless sky. A sandbank was slowly emerging from the ebbing water. She was tempted to walk across to the meadow, but decided not to risk it on her own. What if it were quicksand?

Sybil took a carton of skin cream from her handbag and began lazily to anoint her bare arms. She wore a new frock too, in kingfisher-blue silk, with a kerchief on her head.

Rufus looked at his watch: another half-hour before he was to call time for lunch. He was conscious of the sensuous stroking of Sybil's fingers as she protected her pale skin from the rays of the sun. She turned her attention to her legs, rolled down her stockings, deliberately pulling her skirt well above her knees. She was aware that he was staring openly now. She bent to her task, wondering what he was thinking.

After a while Rufus said: 'You are making rather an exhibition of yourself.'

'Oh? Don't you dare tell me you are not enjoying the experience!'

'You are entitled to your opinion,' he replied stiffly.

'Rufus . . . you found me desirable once . . . what went wrong?' she appealed.

'In . . . that place where I grew up, we were told that most of us were there because our parents were sinful, lustful, that our conception likely had nothing to do with love.'

'Why couldn't you confide in me before? I could have helped you.'

'My first wife tried. We weren't at all in love, but became friends. You . . . I thought it would be different, but here we are, leading separate lives under the same roof.'

'I'm a proud person, too. You rebuffed me on our wedding night. That was it.'

'We should have talked this out long ago,' he said, 'but it's too late now. You must realise the business is about to go under. We'll have to sell the house to settle our debts. Don't worry, I shall ensure that you are provided for. I don't expect you to stay.'

His hands were clenched in his lap. Impulsively, she reached out and touched his arm. 'I'm not going anywhere, Rufus. I'll help you all I can.'

He cleared his throat. 'Thank you,' he said. 'Time to blow the lunchtime whistle.'

Cissie Coe stubbed her toe, as she scrambled, bare-footed, to where Miss Teazel guarded the lunch bags. Cissie's exclamation of distress was heard. Miss Teazel was prepared this year. She had a phial of witch-hazel lotion and a wad of cotton wool.

'Sit down, and I'll see to it,' she commanded, adding, with a glint in her eye, 'It's a pity Herbert from Furnishings is no longer with us, eh?'

Cissie had joined the emporium after Herbert had departed, but she'd heard the story. 'I wasn't looking where I was going,' she confessed, 'because, oh, you'll never guess! I saw Mr Fullilove kissing *his wife*!'

'That's as it should be,' Miss Teazel said primly. 'I hope you haven't got a guilty conscience.'

Cissie flushed bright pink. 'Sausages and mash, that's all he bought me, not a nice fillet of steak, so I said a smart good-night after that.'

'I'm glad to hear it. Shall we have our sandwiches now?'

That evening, back at the house, Mattie and Griff emptied the sand from their shoes in the garden. Mattie shook her hair loose. 'That's gritty too. I can't wash it tonight.' She scratched at the bites on her arms. 'Maybe I should have had sleeves after all.'

'Darned gnats. Quite spoiled our cream tea by that fish pond.'

'Still, it was a lovely day out, even if we couldn't tell the world we are in love!'

'I expect they guessed,' he said softly.

'Oh, all the gossip was about Rufus and Sybil – can you believe it?'

'Let's take a walk down the garden, no one will see us there.'

Mattie looked back at the house. 'The lights have gone out upstairs . . .'

Ostensibly, Rufus and Sybil shared a bedroom, but after their disastrous honeymoon night he had slept in the single bed in his dressing-room. Hilda knew, of course, but said nothing; it was their business, after all.

After all the fresh air, Sybil was tired. She put her book down, and settled down to sleep. She wasn't aware that Rufus had come into her room, and was hesitating at the end of her bed.

'Sybil – are you awake?' he said, after waiting for a response.

She stirred, sat up. 'Rufus? What is it.'

'I wanted to say, I'm glad we talked . . .'

'So am I. Is there anything else?' she prompted.

'I'm sorry I disturbed you.'

'I'm glad you did. There's something else I should tell you. Best in the dark, with you in bed with me . . .'

They lay side by side, if still apart. 'Well?' he asked eventually.

'I've been deceiving you. I needed more in my life: I had enjoyed quite a successful career before I met you, I missed my work. All those coffee mornings with other bored idle wives like myself – I decided to mix up my potions again, to offer them privately – discreetly – to make a little pin money.'

'Was I really so mean to you?'

'I admit that money was always an issue between us, Rufus. I resented that. Maybe if we'd enjoyed a normal married life, we could have sorted that out.'

'I have a confession of my own to make. The visits to my club . . .'

'You don't have to explain! I think I can guess – another woman?'

'No, much more mundane than that! Every evening I sit in a depressing, dark-panelled room, in a fug of cigar smoke, with a glass of whisky in the company of other lonely men, and discuss the stock market,' he admitted wryly.

'Oh Rufus, how foolish we've been!' Sybil exclaimed. She knew she must make the first move. She moved closer, turned and wrapped her arms around him.

'Are you sure?' his voice was husky, his heart beating as fast as hers.

'I'm sure,' she murmured. 'We've waited six years for this, after all.'

*

There had been a dangerous moment in the garden, when Mattie and Griff had been tempted to carry things further. Mattie had come to her senses first. 'We'd both regret it in the morning,' she whispered.

'I wouldn't!' he protested.

'It could lead to – complications. You know that. When we get married—'

'Oh, you've decided that, have you?' he essayed a joke.

'This very minute!'

'Then I shall make an announcement on my birthday!'

'Come on,' she urged. 'It's very late, and it's work as usual tomorrow.'

SEVEN

There were visitors staying for a few days at the Plough. It was quite like the old days, Sophia thought, except these visitors were not the paying sort, being family. Fortunately Evie was at home for the long summer holiday and could look after little Robbie while Sophia saw to the guests, Will's sister Mary and her son Walter, from Mitcham.

Despite the age difference, Walter and Evie got on very well. He asked after Mattie. 'Is she staying on in Plymouth? I thought she would have been home by now.'

'I believe she would have been, if she hadn't had a good reason to stay,' Evie said. They were strolling across the meadow to the stream. She was glad to escape her responsibilities for an hour or so, was hoping to gather watercress for tea. The scorching heat had caused limp, yellowing grass. The stream had dwindled to a trickle.

'Oh, and what is that?' Walter queried.

'Reading between the lines of her letters, well, it seems she's smitten with Mr Fullilove's stepson, Griff.' She looked at Walter keenly. 'You don't appear pleased.'

'I'm not,' he admitted. 'I took a shine to her, you see.'

'You'll find another girl,' said Evie in her old-fashioned way.

Walter smiled ruefully. Young Evie, he realised with a start, had a pretty, glowing face. In a few years' time . . . He gave himself a mental shake. 'I'm obligated to my mother. Expected to look after her in her old age in return for the sacrifices she made for my education. I rather think it will be the same for you, eh?'

Evie shook her head. 'I'll have to leave school early, as Mattie did, due to our family circumstances. *My* future's mapped out, as nursemaid to Robbie!'

Later, as they paddled in the shallows, Evie, with skirts looped up, her tanned lower limbs innocently displayed, recalled another August day in 1914. She thought, Mattie and I were carefree then, but everything was about to change, and Mattie's childhood was soon over, as mine is now . . .

'Not exactly an abundance of watercress!' she called to Walter, giggling to see his pale feet seemingly elongated in the water as he trod cautiously on the pebbles.

He scrambled on to the verge, set the basket down. 'You get picking then, while I squeeze the water out of my trouser bottoms! I should have rolled them up to the knee.'

'Don't you have any shorts from your scouting days?'

'I was never an outdoors type,' he admitted.

'No bicycling on Wimbledon Common? Mind you, we girls weren't allowed to wander about freely when we were young. I was five before I came down to the stream, when Mattie was considered old enough to keep an eye on me! Mother was always wary of water – *one slip*, she used to say . . . The boys, though, learned to swim in the river.'

'I stuck to my books. I'm a very dull chap, Evie. I don't like admitting it, but maybe I was always destined to be an accountant.'

She placed a small bunch of tender green cress in the basket. '*I'm* too old for my years, some say.'

'You're full of fun today. Good company,' he said appreciatively.

'Well, how about help with the picking? Mother will wonder where we are.'

Sophia was, in fact, wondering whether she should have encouraged her young daughter to keep her cousin company. He was older, though she doubted he was any more experienced. However, she'd have a quiet word with his mother, she thought. Evie was far too young for any romantic notions.

The following day Ronnie came in as usual for his lunch, with half a dozen red rosebuds from the stationmaster's garden, wrapped in a discarded newspaper. Evie placed the stems in a basin of water, saving the paper to read later.

'Mother said you're taking Robbie along to the infirmary this afternoon.' he said. 'The roses are for Ena. Tell her I hope to see her soon, won't you?' He didn't sound very convincing. He was invariably upset and withdrawn after visiting his wife.

Evie bit her lip. How could she tell him that Ena always ignored the baby? Conversation was one-sided. She couldn't pass this on to Ronnie either. Ena ranted on about her early life in London, before her mother returned to her home village with her small girl to escape her violent husband. Ena had never spoken of this time before; now, a shocked Evie learned of the abuse her young sister-in-law had suffered. No wonder, she thought, that Ena had 'snapped'.

Robbie, however, was a delightful baby, smiling and contented – much loved and cuddled by his grandparents, a comfort to his father, and, of course, Evie adored him. If only she didn't have to play the role of 'little mother', she thought, with a sigh.

'I'll walk with you,' Walter offered.

'You won't be able to come inside,' Evie said quickly.

'I hear there's a pleasant garden and a seat or two. I'll take a book to read, eh?'

'I'd come too,' Aunt Mary said, 'but Sophia has decided we'll make strawberry jam, so I can take a couple of jars home. Shame to waste those last small berries.'

Evie wore her Sunday-best frock in pale green organza, with puff sleeves and a sash, made by Sophia from material sent by Mattie. Evie privately thought it rather childish, but Walter complimented her, 'You look very nice!' She wished her hair was as long and straight as Mattie's.

Robbie kicked his legs and waved his arms as he lay in his coachbuilt pram, loaned by the doctor's wife, whose own family were long since grown and flown. He wore a white romper suit, a present from Aunt Alice. Being fair-skinned like Mattie he was shaded from the sun by a fringed canopy, fawn cotton lined with dark green.

Evie was glad of her floppy sunhat. She glanced at Walter. You couldn't call him handsome, she thought, but he'd lost his town pallor after this break in the country, and he was well-mannered, walking on the road side of the pavement.

The infirmary, formerly the old workhouse, was situated on the outskirts of the village. Those suffering from mental problems, whether temporary or long-term, were housed in a separate wing from the cottage hospital. Some of the men tended the garden, growing vegetables; women at the recovery stage helped in the laundry, or in the sewing-room. However, the kitchens were considered out of bounds, because of hazardous equipment.

There were chairs set out on the porch, so Evie suggested Walter wait there with the pram, while she went to find Ena. Carrying the flowers she went through the double doors into a long corridor, with small wards on either side. She met a nurse halfway along, who told her Ena had been moved to a two-bed room at the end.

The nurse lowered her voice. 'She is much quieter. She could well be home soon.'

Ena opened the door. She wore hospital garb, a loose blue dress, as belts were not allowed. She accepted the roses, now wrapped in shiny paper, read Ronnie's message, then laid the bunch on her bedside cabinet. 'Nurse will put them in water later.'

'Robbie is in his pram on the porch,' Evie said tentatively. 'Will you come out?'

Ena nodded, after reflecting for what seemed a long moment. 'All right.' She followed Evie to the entrance.

Walter looked up. He was rocking the pram handle. Robbie was almost asleep.

'Ena, this is our cousin Walter from Mitcham. Walter, this is Ena,' Evie said.

Walter was on his feet, holding out his hand. Ena didn't respond.

'Shall we walk in the gardens?' Evie asked quickly, releasing the pram brake.

'If you like,' Ena mumbled. Her expression was quite blank.

They found a wooden bench fitted round a tree-trunk. The shade was welcome. Evie and Ena sat together, Walter on the far side, with his book.

'Robbie has grown, hasn't he?' Evie willed Ena to look at her baby.

'Yes,' Ena said indifferently. She added: 'They say I can leave here soon.'

'Oh . . . that's good news, isn't it?'

'You needn't worry. I won't come back to the Plough. Or to Ronnie and the baby. It . . . would only happen again, I know that. My mother will have me. She was frightened when I was shouting, but, as you can see, I'm calm now.'

'Does Ronnie know?'

'He will be told, when the time comes.'

'Don't you love him any more?' Evie had to find that out.

'As I said, it would only happen again . . .'

Robbie stirred. Evie reached for his bottle, wrapped in muslin. 'Would you like to nurse him?' she appealed.

Ena jumped up. '*Leave me alone!*' she hissed, and stalked off without a backward glance.

Walter came round the tree-trunk, looking concerned. Evie lifted Robbie up, with tears spilling from her eyes, and offered him the bottle.

Walter's arm went comfortingly round her shoulders. 'You did your best,' he said.

It was October, and Mattie had been gone for six months. Evie had not returned to school in September. She looked forward to letters from Mattie, and now, from Walter. Her mother, she knew, perused them later, but there was nothing she could object to. However, she managed to write to her sister once without her mother being aware of it.

Dearest Mattie,

I need to tell my thoughts to someone, and I hope you don't mind that it is you! You say you have a secret you are longing to tell us, but we have to wait a couple of weeks first! I hope it is about you and Griff. Well, I only have worries to share.

Mother is still hoping that Ena will come back to Ronnie and the baby. Ena's mother is out working all day in the fields, they live in a tied cottage as you know. Mother does not think it is wise for Ena to spend so much time on her own.

You say I should keep up with my studies at home, well, my only chance to read is when I go to bed, and then I am so tired, my eyes close before I turn more than a page or two. The only bright spot this year was when Walter was here!

We will be even busier shortly. We are having paying guests, a mother and daughter. The younger lady is taking up a teaching post at the grammar school in town. Her mother is crippled with arthritis so will need our help. The good thing is they will pay for this too, so we will be much better off.

Well, I must get this in the post. Write as soon as you can, as your letters buck me up no end. Your loving sister, Evie.

Mattie received a letter from Sophia the same day, excited that things were looking up at last, in respect of the paying guests. Mattie decided to write back by return of post.

Dear Mother,

Good news indeed! Just a thought, I don't mean to meddle! Would it be possible now for you to employ a girl to look after little Robbie, and for Evie to return to school for another year or two? I was lucky not to leave until I was fifteen, after all.

Please do consider it!

As promised, I will be home for a few days' holiday shortly. Business is very slow just now, so it is a good time to come. Griff is looking forward to meeting you and Dad and thanks you for the kind invitation. If you have a 'full house' by then, perhaps he could share with Ronnie?

Fondest love from your affectionate daughter, Mattie.

Sophia discussed Mattie's suggestion with Will. 'What d'you think?'

'I think it's a good idea,' he said slowly. 'Maybe we have all expected too much of Evie. Go and see the headmistress this afternoon, ask if she agrees. Don't mention it to Evie until you know if Miss Ashton is agreeable.' He cleared his throat. 'Reckon this young man of Mattie's is coming to impart something important?'

'Reading between the lines, I do!' Sophia said.

The following Monday Evie was welcomed back at school with open arms. Fanny Aldred, like Mattie a former classmate of Ena's, came in daily to look after Robbie, and her cheerful presence was much appreciated by the family, including Ronnie. Of course, he was bound by his marriage vows, so Sophia wondered if she should have a word with him, but William said, rather sharply, not to presume anything of the sort. 'Be glad things are looking better,' he reminded his wife.

After all the stifling weather a storm was brewing. The sky was black with threatening thunderclouds, then came the rain in torrents, filling and then overflowing the stream and the pond at the bottom of Ena's mother's cottage garden, which was their only source of water. In the heat of summer, when the water dwindled, the dirty linen piled up and they had to forgo their weekly baths, in the old tin tub in the outhouse.

It was just after nine in the morning. Her mother had left for work two hours before. A watery sun sent down wavering rays. 'If it clears up,' her mum had said, 'it's high time them sheets came off the bed. Make yourself useful for once. Get the copper lit. You can't say there's not much water in the pond after last night's deluge.'

Ena wore a grey dress, a grubby apron, old slippers on her feet. She wasn't worried about her appearance, the cottage was isolated, no one was likely to call.

She shuffled, clanking bucket in either hand, down the grassy slope. There was a distant rumble of thunder. Startled, she quickened her pace, losing her ill-fitting footwear as she did so. Her bare feet squelched in oozing mud and she dropped the buckets as she skidded inexorably towards the deep water, then tumbled in.

Ena's mother did not arrive home for another eight hours. It was some time before she located her daughter. She spotted the slippers, which had lived up to their name, and the pails which had fallen haphazardly to the ground. Then she shrieked, as she glimpsed a pale foot caught in the reeds. Ena had toppled in head first.

An inquest was held. The verdict was accidental death. The kindly coroner, seeing the distress of her family, said he had come to this conclusion because Ena had stripped the bed as requested, then gone to fetch water to boil the linen in the copper.

The whole village rallied round poor Ena's family. A collection was raised to help with funeral costs, including mourning clothes for her mother. There was a tactful mention in the parish magazine, and prayers were said at the school.

Sophia and William were determined to keep the exact details of Ena's demise from their younger daughter. They said only that they must all make sure that Robbie was well-loved and cared for, as 'Ena would have wished, if she had not been ill.'

Mattie's visit was postponed for a fortnight after the original date, when they were rallying round. It helped that the lodgers must be catered for, regular meals served.

The family decided it was just as well Mattie was coming with Griff, for it would not be right to discuss the recent tragedy in his presence.

EIGHT

Mattie wore a light-weight wool frock in raspberry red, a gift from Sybil. Mindful of the autumnal nip in the air, she'd added a white angora jacket and slouch beret. She said to herself, I want the family to see how stylish I am nowadays! No more dowdy clothes and hats, or thick tan stockings, but the pleasing crackle of silk as I smooth them carefully over my legs, and ensure the seams are straight . . .

She resisted tapping her feet, in court shoes with the fashionable Tbar, to the rhythm of the train wheels; squeezing Griff's hand instead, as they sped through familiar countryside on the last lap home. He lightly touched her inexpensive engagement ring, a twinkling star of tiny diamonds. Griff had spent his savings on it. Mattie had insisted he leave his legacy intact, not say anything at present. He'd slipped the ring on her finger in the train this morning. Mattie wanted her parents to be first to know of their betrothal; until now the ring had been kept in its box.

Anyway, the Fulliloves were preoccupied with problems. Receivers had been called in at the emporium. There had been out-of-season sales in most departments; no new goods were imported. Some staff had left voluntarily, some hung on, hoping they would be employed until the end. Sybil replaced Cissie Coe in Miss Teazel's office. 'I'm good at figure work and you don't have to pay *me*,' she said. The smart delivery van had been sold; Griff now drove the four of them to work in a smaller vehicle.

There had been a muted celebration of Griff's recent coming of age. A cheque for £800 had arrived from a solicitor, in settlement of his inheritance. Rufus shook Griff's hand and congratulated him. He commented: 'At least *you* will have a secure future.'

'If I thought it would help, I'd willingly lend some of it to you,' Griff replied.

'I'm afraid it would be swallowed up, wasted, so we must decline,' Rufus said heavily. 'But we appreciate the offer, eh Sybil?'

She nodded. It still surprised her to hear her husband refer to 'we' rather than 'I'. Their growing closeness, she thought, would sustain them through their troubles.

*

Mattie was prepared to see her mother struggling to cope after recent events, as she had when her elder son was killed during the war. However, Sophia was determinedly cheerful, as busy as she'd been when the Plough was a thriving concern. Will played his part in caring for their lodgers, who had private means and thus were able to pay well for good service. Both sides desired a long-term arrangement: Will pushed the older lady about in her wheelchair and stoked the fire in the bedroom. Mother and daughter were accommodated in the two front rooms off the hall, which had been empty since the brewery removed the bar furnishings which belonged to them.

'Dad painted the rooms,' Sophia said proudly.

Evie gave Mattie lots of hugs, expressing her approval of Griff while she helped her sister unpack in their old bedroom. 'Oh, he's so nice, Mattie! I do like him.'

Fanny, the nursemaid, brought little Robbie to his aunt for inspection. Mattie held the baby in her arms, blushing when Griff winked at her. 'I'm glad they chose *you*,' Mattie told Fanny, who was a real country girl with apple-red cheeks and thick hair braided round her head. Her rounded figure was concealed by a white apron with a pair of spare napkin pins fastened to the bodice. She was very competent, having helped bring up her five younger siblings.

'He's a joy to look after, our baby,' Fanny said proudly. 'I love working here.'

Griff was next door to the girls. That night, when Mattie and Evie were in bed, if not yet asleep, he beat a brief tattoo on the dividing wall, as he'd promised Mattie he would.

Evie giggled. 'I bet you won't divulge what that means, Mattie.'

'You're too young to know,' Mattie said primly, then she burst out laughing. 'He's just saying goodnight, silly!'

'When are we going to learn your secret?' Evie asked.

'When the moment seems right,' Mattie yawned. 'Now, can I get my beauty sleep? It was a long day on the train, you know!'

'You're already beautiful,' Evie said stoutly.

'You, too, dearie! Thanks to all that watercress we picked and ate, eh?'

'D'you *have* to go back to Plymouth, Mattie? Can't you stay here?'

'Oh Evie – as I said, you'll hear our plans for the future, tomorrow.'

'You said "our" so I know that means you *and* Griff!'

It was quite like the old days, Mattie thought, when, joined by the lodgers, they sat round the extended table and ate from plates piled high with succulent roast beef, individual batter puddings, roast and plain potatoes, parsnips, cabbage and diced carrots. There was freshly made horseradish sauce and thick brown gravy. They needed what Sophia called an 'aristocratic pause', before she brought in a large apple pie, a jug of yellow custard and a smaller jug of fresh cream from the local farm. The water carafe was refilled several times. Sophia disapproved of alcohol with meals, despite having been a pub landlady for many years.

'Mother will need a snooze after all that splendid food,' Miss Jackson said.

Will helped Mrs Jackson into her chair. The old lady's head was already nodding. The curtains would be drawn in the bedroom she shared with her daughter. Miss Jackson would retire to the sitting-room opposite. She had school books to mark.

Mattie and Evie collected the plates, and went cheerfully to tackle the washing-up. Ronnie, back from working the morning shift, sat silently at the kitchen table, eating a belated lunch; the baby was asleep in his pram in the corner. Fanny had given him his bottle before going home to join her own family for the rest of the day. Sophia was entertaining Griff in the back parlour. Will joined them there.

They seized the opportunity for a little gentle probing.

'We understand from Sybil that her husband's business is failing,' Sophia began.

'I'm afraid so,' Griff said honestly.

'Does that mean Mattie will shortly be out of a job?' Will asked.

'I imagine we both will.'

'Have you any idea what will happen then?'

'Well,' Griff began, when to his relief, Mattie and Evie joined them. Ronnie remained in the kitchen with the baby. He obviously did not feel up to talking today.

'Tea,' Mattie said, setting down the tray on a small table.

'Sugared and stirred.' Evie grinned, passing the cups.

Mattie waited until they were all seated, sipping the hot liquid.

'Griff has something to ask you, Mother, Dad . . .'

'Mattie and I would like your permission to marry,' Griff said in a rush.

'To get engaged first,' Mattie reminded him. 'We hope to wed next spring.'

Will glanced at Sophia. She smiled and nodded her head.

'I presume you are about to produce a ring?' Will asked. 'Well, go on, you can wear it openly now, Mattie! The answer is "yes". However, in view of the situation in Plymouth, there's not much chance of you saving towards a wedding, eh?'

'As things are with the business, no. But I came into a tidy sum on my twenty-first.'

'Enough to set you up?'

'Yes,' Griff assured her parents. He continued: 'I hope this won't come as a shock, but after we're married, we intend to emigrate to Canada. My father's sister and her husband farm on the prairie, where the nearest town is called Moose Jaw. She's always kept in touch. She says the Canadian government is encouraging immigration and are insisting Cunard keep fares low. We think this is our best chance; life is very hard over here now.'

It was obvious from their expressions that Sophia and Will *were* shocked.

Mattie broke the prolonged silence. 'Aunt Anna's and Uncle Charlie's eldest son and his family moved over the border to a farm in North Dakota in 1915. They built a sod house! We did like the sound of *that*, but . . .' She nudged Griff.

'Immigration is now strictly restricted to the States. I don't think we would stand a chance. Maybe later, eh? Another cousin is with the North Pacific Railway. He lives in Bismark, at the junction with the Missouri river. You've heard of the Missouri?'

Still no response from Sophia and Will, but Evie said loudly in her excitement, 'I have! Shall I fetch my world map book?'

'Good idea,' Mattie approved.

'*Sod* house – is that what it sounds like?' Sophia murmured.

'In the middle of nowhere, I suppose?' Will guessed.

'Five miles from the nearest town, I believe,' Griff said.

Sophia, overcome, was wiping her eyes. Mattie went to her mother, knelt beside her chair, pressing her face against Sophia's shoulder. Her voice was muffled. 'Oh, don't cry – we're not thinking of going to *Australia*, you know! Canada's not *so* far away.'

'Even Plymouth is a foreign place to me!' Sophia said woefully.

'We need to have your blessing to go – that's important to us,' Mattie pleaded.

Griff cleared his throat. 'I promise we'll put aside the wherewithal to come home if things don't work out.'

'You'll have to find employment,' Will reminded him.

'I intend to.'

'What are you trained for?'

'There are big stores over there, too, you know! Thanks to Rufus, I had a good education; I might work in a bank or an office. I'm sure Aunt Anna would let us stay with her, to start with. But I'd really like to buy land, get my hands dirty for a change.'

'And you, Mattie?' Sophia asked.

'I'm looking forward to working alongside Griff, Mother!'

Sophia stroked Mattie's long hair absently, retied the ribbon which kept it back from her face, as she had done so often when her daughter was still a little girl. 'Are you sure you're cut out for that?'

'I'm stronger than you think!'

'Strong-willed is how I'd put it. You've never had to pick up potatoes, feed livestock or milk a cow, like some round here, from an early age. Like Fanny, for instance.'

'I can learn; we both can!' Mattie asserted.

'Do look!' Evie cried, waving the atlas to attract their attention. 'Canada – it'll be very cold there, I reckon!'

'Oh my dears!' Sophia was wiping her eyes again, but she managed a tremulous smile. 'You'll need to wrap up warm in winter – even more than you do here.'

'We will!' Mattie got to her feet. 'We mustn't leave Ronnie out of all this; you look at the map with Evie and Griff, while I go and break the news to him.'

Ronnie had finished his meal, rinsed his plate, and moved to the old couch where he relaxed with his baby son, now wide awake, on his lap. He looked up at Mattie. 'Well, what d'you think of my boy, Mattie?'

'He looks like one of us!' Mattie said proudly, sitting down beside them. Then she realised what she'd said. 'Sorry, Ronnie, I didn't mean—'

'I'm sure you didn't. But he's got a look of poor Ena, too.'

'I didn't like to mention your loss, but I do feel for you.'

'When I came home from the war without Robbie, I thought it was up to me to carry on the family name. Ena and I, well, I jumped the gun, I couldn't wait. We married in haste, because of the baby. I tried to be a good husband. The rest you know.'

'Neither of you was happy, I was aware of that.'

'You and your young man – don't be put off by my experience, will you?'

'You've guessed, then?'

'I have, and I wish you all the happiness in the world.'

Mattie kissed his cheek, then the baby's head. 'Thank you. Griff and I need your approval too! After we're wed, we hope to emigrate to Canada.'

'I thought of doing that, you know – a new country, a new life,' he said slowly.

'Why don't you come with us?'

'How could I manage, with a motherless child to care for?'

'We could help,' Mattie said impulsively.

'No, Mattie. It wouldn't be fair. Maybe, later on, if the opportunity arises, eh?'

'Come and join us in the other room, Ronnie. Don't shut yourself away.' She held out her arms to the baby. 'I intend to spoil *you* this weekend, you know!'

All too soon it was time for Mattie and Griff to return to Plymouth. Mattie had a present to give to her parents: the charcoal sketch of herself that Griff had done the first time they visited Plymouth Hoe. Griff had signed and framed it at Mattie's request.

'It's lovely – but please don't say it's to remember you by!' Sophia said.

'Of course not! Now, please leave all the arrangements for the wedding to us – we'd like it to be in Plymouth, so it'll be a holiday for you, Dad and Evie, who'll be my maid of honour, eh?'

'What about the baby – and the Jacksons?'

'Oh, Mother! Fanny can stay here while you're away, so you needn't worry about little Robbie – she's a good cook too, so she could see to the meals. It shouldn't be a problem for Miss Jackson, either, being the Easter break from school.'

Sophia hugged her tightly. 'I'll treasure your picture, Mattie. I just recalled the portrait Mr B painted of you before the war – I wonder what happened to that?'

'Perhaps we'll find out, one of these days . . .'

NINE

APRIL, 1922

Sybil tiptoed across the bedroom to the window. She didn't pull the curtains but parted them slightly so that she could glimpse the early-morning scene. The street was deserted, blinds still drawn in the houses opposite. It was Saturday, not long after dawn. On Easter Monday Mattie and Griff were to be married. Mattie's family had arrived on Thursday, and would return home next Tuesday. The packing-up here could then begin in earnest. Some of the furniture was included in the sale of the house; the remainder would be put in store while they decided what to do. Just over a week from now, they would say goodbye and good luck to the young couple who were sailing from Southampton on 22 April.

She sighed as she allowed the curtains to fall back into place. She'd believed that Rufus was asleep, but he said: 'It's too early to get up. Come back to bed.' It was unfortunate that he added, 'Anyone would think *you* were the mother of the bride.'

'I'm only ten years older than Mattie!' she said fiercely.

'I'm sorry, I didn't mean— You'll get cold without your wrap.'

Sybil slipped under the covers, but turned her back on him.

Rufus reached out and drew her close. 'You're crying. What's wrong?'

'I'm feeling sorry for myself!' She endeavoured to suppress a sob.

He tentatively caressed her silk-clad shoulders, then, as he felt her slowly relax, he kissed the nape of her neck. 'You've been so good about leaving here, I couldn't have coped without your support, Sybil. I'm so grateful—'

'I don't want you to be grateful – I just need you to love me!'

'I do. It's still difficult for me you know – to express my feelings,' he admitted.

She turned to him. 'You're getting better,' she said softly, through her tears.

Hilda was busy setting out the early-morning tea things on the trays. She muttered aloud: 'One, Miss Sybil and *him* – if he ain't already in the bathroom; two, Master Griff; three, Mr and Mrs Rowley; four, the blushin' bride and her sister—'

'Can I help? I could carry our tray upstairs.' Sybil's voice made Hilda start.

'What are you doing up this early?' she demanded.

'I . . . we couldn't sleep. Too much to think about,' Sybil said. 'This has to be a modest wedding, and fortunately that's what Mattie and Griff prefer, but I want everything to be perfect. It's not fair to expect you to take on all the extra work, so Mattie's mother and I will help wherever we can. Mind you, I'm aware that Mrs Rowley is more capable than me. That wonderful wedding cake she produced from her hat box . . .'

'I don't suppose she'll swan about like you in her night attire! Well, food's one thing we don't have to worry about – all the leavings from the poor old emporium food hall, eh? That pongy cheddar'll be served up as macaroni cheese for lunch today!'

'Scrambled eggs for breakfast?'

'I'll see to those if you like.' Griff now joined them. He picked up one of the trays. 'I'll deliver this to Mattie and Evie.'

Hilda said primly, 'I'm not sure that's proper, Master Griff.'

Griff winked. 'Sybil doesn't disapprove.'

'Take your cup too,' was all Sybil said.

Evie gave a little shriek and disappeared under the bed-clothes when Griff poked his head round the door. Mattie, however, was already sitting on the side of the bed.

'I was just thinking about going downstairs to help Hilda. You beat me to it!'

Evie came up for air. 'You startled me!' she said defensively.

'Weren't you thinking of joining Mother and Dad for morning tea?' Mattie had a glint in her eye. 'It's our chance to talk in private,' she added quickly.

'I'll pour your tea out,' Griff offered, grinning.

'I know when I'm not wanted,' was Evie's parting shot.

'Shall I bolt the door?' Griff suggested.

'Certainly not! I don't know what you're thinking of, Griffith Parry, but—'

'A chaste kiss – or two . . .' he said.

'What's this?' Rufus was amused to see Sybil with a pinafore over her négligé.

'I'm helping Hilda with the chores!'

'You ought to get dressed first, I think.'

'I'm waiting for my turn in the bathroom.'

'Griff was in there earlier. He had the audacity to tell me Mattie was next in line. You might just as well drink your tea in bed like me . . .'

'I wonder where we'll be sleeping a couple of weeks from now?'

He made a face, placed his cup and saucer on the bed-side table. 'I forgot to use the strainer: got a mouthful of tea leaves. Sybil, isn't it time you visited your parents?'

'A reconciliation, you mean? I suspect Sophia gives them news of me. When I left home without their approval my dad said "You'll be back, eating humble pie, before long." My mother said nothing, just turned away. That made me determined that I would do no such thing. It's fifteen years since I saw them.'

'False pride,' Rufus said slowly, 'is something we have in common.'

'The last time I wrote home was when we married. We had a card wishing us well, remember? If I make contact now, they might think I want something from them . . .'

'You do. Not money, we must make that clear, because we won't be exactly penniless, but aren't family the ones you turn to, in times of trouble?'

'*You* had to make your own way in life. I didn't realise how fortunate I was.'

'Think about it. Life's too short for family feuds. Look at all the time *we* wasted.'

'We're making up for that now, aren't we? And despite losing all you worked so hard for, we can build a new life, I know it,' Sybil said. She looked at her watch. 'Not even six o'clock yet!'

Back at the Plough Ronnie was still in bed, as he had the day off from work. No need to rise and shine yet, he thought, the Jacksons having requested breakfast at 8.30. He became aware of movement inside the cot, which he had moved into a corner of his room while his parents were away, followed by a hungry yell. Robbie pulled himself up and rattled the top bar of the cot. He was obviously intent on letting his father know it was time for his early morning sustenance.

Ronnie yawned. 'Be with you in a few minutes. I'm enjoying a lie-in.'

A tap on the door. The handle turned, and in crept Fanny, wearing Mattie's old dressing-gown over her petti-coat. She didn't possess a nightdress. She glanced over at the bed, illuminated by the night light. Ronnie appeared to be asleep.

Fanny went over to the cot, lifted the little boy out and sat down on the low nursing-chair. She loosened the dress-ing-gown cord so that the baby could snuggle against the warm softness of her breasts. She was following the advice of her wise mother. 'He may have lost his mummy, but you can give him that comfort.'

She murmured, 'Ready for your bottle, young man? I'll change you after, and then you must have another nap, your daddy deserves his rest after working hard all week.'

The baby was expert in emptying the bottle in a few minutes nowadays.

'What about you, Fanny?' Ronnie's loud whisper star-tled her. 'You've been working hard all week too, and now through the weekend, too. Shall I brew the tea?'

'That's all right, I'll do it. Just let me see to this nappy. There . . . he's nodding off already,' she said with satis-faction.

'You'll make a lovely mother when you have a baby of your own.'

'I think of Robbie like that. I know it will be hard for me to let him go when you decide to marry again and he has a new mother,' Fanny said in a rush.

'Is that what you think I should do?'

'When you find the right young lady.'

'Fanny, what about you?' There, he'd said what he'd been thinking for months.

'Me?' Fanny was glad he couldn't see her blushes in the half-light.

'Yes. We get on well together, don't we?'

'That's not enough for me,' she said, moving to leave the room.

He was out of bed in an instant, catching her round the waist before she reached the door. 'Will you marry me, Fanny?'

'D'you mean that?'

'I mean it. I know I'm not exactly a catch, but, like Robbie, I need a good woman to take me on. You're so kind and thoughtful – I believe love would follow.'

'I fell for you when you came home from the war, but Ena was the one you saw first. I would never have told you . . .'

'I'm glad you have,' he said simply.

Fanny was facing him now. 'Do you want to kiss me?'

He caught his breath. 'Oh, I do!' With his hands he tentatively brushed back her hair, crimped from the tight daily plaiting, from her flushed face. He kissed her parted mouth then, unable to resist, pressed his lips to her pulsing throat, revealed by the skimpy petticoat.

'Well?' she whispered, hugging him. She thought, he needs this, like the baby.

'I think you're a *wonderful* girl! I'm happier than I've ever been in my life.'

She said reluctantly, 'I must go. We mustn't get carried away. Your parents trust me, you see.'

'Let's get wed just as soon as we can. I know they'll approve! I should say, we'll have to continue living here for a while . . .'

'I shan't mind that!' she said softly. 'I'm a family person, after all.'

Mattie, Griff and Evie were on the Hoe. They'd arranged to meet Christabel, who was to be a bridesmaid with Evie. Dolly had made their matching frocks.

Evie found the sea breezes exhilarating. She felt like turning a cartwheel, but managed to restrain the impulse, reminding herself that now she was fourteen she must be more ladylike. She was due to leave school this summer, but she hoped her parents would eventually agree to Miss Jackson's suggestion that she might, if she passed the test, be allowed to continue her studies at the grammar school. As Walter commented, in his most recent letter, 'You must seize this opportunity! Now I am working and earning a salary at long last, I know all that studying was the key to success. Mother is happy to see me in a white collar and suit!' Evie was unaware that in fact Walter had taken the only job on offer, as a door-to-door insurance salesman.

Mattie and Griff strolled along, with his arm round her waist, oblivious, it seemed, to the brief shower of light rain or to the sights on the Hoe. Christabel steered Evie to a seat. 'You can see a long way from here! No Armada today though.'

'They'll wonder where we are!'

'Nonsense. They've only got eyes for each other,' Christabel said. She giggled: 'Why am I always the brides-maid, never the blushing bride?' she sang.

'Well, I'm blushing now, because people are looking at us!' Evie hesitated, then: 'I'm surprised *you* haven't got a young man, Christabel.'

'What about you?' Christabel countered, jokingly.

'Me? I'm a schoolgirl!'

'And I'm already on the shelf, eh?'

'I didn't mean—'

'I have been in love, you know, though it wasn't returned.'

'Unrequited, isn't that the expression?' Evie asked.

'Yes, and don't you dare ask who the young man was!'

Evie gave her new friend's hand a squeeze. 'I think I can guess . . .'

'You'll keep in touch with me I hope, because those two dear people have a busy time ahead – but they'll have to write home, eh? You can pass on the news!' She added: 'I start my new job on Tuesday. I'm not exactly looking forward to it.'

'What is it?'

'Working in a factory canteen – peeling endless buckets of spuds, I reckon, and endless dirty dishes to wash up. My mum is relieved I won't be stuck at a machine all day doing a repetitive task, and the hours are quite good, if the pay is poor.'

'Oh, Christabel, you deserve better than that!'

'Jobs are like gold dust nowadays. I get a free meal which will help our budget.' She looked at Evie. 'You and me, we've a lot in common, I think. Both ambitious, but both aware of our responsibilities at home. I don't imagine I'll marry. My mum is the most important person in my life.'

'Is she able to come to the church on Monday? I'd like to meet her and to thank her for making my frock. It's quite *à la mode*! My mother makes most of my clothes, but she imagines I still like puff sleeves and sashes!'

'I chose the pattern so I'm glad you think we did well! I'm afraid Mum won't be able to attend the wedding, but we can pose for the photographer. I'm sure you and I will end up in a frame on the mantelpiece! Come on, now we'll catch up with the love birds.'

Mattie almost waltzed down the aisle on her father's arm on Easter Monday morning. She wore a costume in pale pink linen with a circlet of silk rosebuds on her hair, coiffured by Hilda. She carried a posy of expensive hot-house roses and fern. The bridesmaids, in cream silk frocks with layered skirts walked demurely behind, swaying to the music.

Their footsteps echoed as they passed the empty polished pews in the lofty city church. Brass plaques on the whitewashed walls glinted in shafts of sunlight streaming through stained-glass windows. The bridal decorations were confined to the two front pews on either side of the aisle; white ribbons were tied to the lamp standards and there were more of the pink roses in the altar vases. There was no organ music today, but a familiar figure sat at the piano near the lectern. Miss Teazel had offered her services for the special occasion. She had chosen the music. *The Blue Danube* was her favourite.

Rufus, having volunteered to be best man, stood beside his stepson. They both wore smart grey suits with plum-coloured waistcoats. They turned to see Mattie's smiling face as she arrived at the altar steps, while Will and the bridesmaids joined Sophia in the front pew. Sybil sat opposite, with Hilda. It was indeed a modest wedding.

They were unaware of the presence of a little church mouse in the choir stalls, who was concealed in a nest fashioned from shredded hymn sheets. This was just as well, as far as Evie was concerned. She would certainly have reacted to any sighting.

The clergyman was elderly and stooped, with a quavering voice. When they knelt for the prayers, Mattie observed that he was wearing carpet-slippers and she had to tell herself sternly not to giggle.

The solemn vows and rings were exchanged; the clergyman's homily was cut short by a bout of coughing. Miss Teazel fetched him a cup of water before playing the final hymn. It was not the one on the order of service, but the stirring *Rock of Ages*. It was a virtuoso performance by the pianist. The congregation sang with gusto. Pleased, Miss Teazel obliged with an encore. Voices trailed off. Which verse were they to sing?

In the church porch, Griff looked quizzically at Mattie. 'Not quite the wedding we planned, eh?' he whispered.

'I enjoyed every minute of it!' She wiped the tears of laughter from her eyes.

They lined up obediently for the photographer. The pictures would naturally be in black-and-white, but would be tastefully tinted back at the studio. Sophia's floral dress would prove quite a challenge.

The bride's bouquet missed the outstretched hands of the bridesmaids and was caught by a surprised Hilda.

'Well,' Christabel said ruefully to Evie, 'maybe it will work for *her* . . .'

Rufus had laid on a taxi service to take them back to the house. The splendid wedding cake was cut and sampled, and the wine flowed freely.

'Make the most of it,' Rufus told Griff. 'Prohibition in Canada, like the USA!'

Their wedding night was spent at a modest hotel. In the morning they would return to the house because Mattie wanted to spend a precious hour or two with her family before they boarded the train for home. None of them said, but they were all aware that it could be some years before they were together again.

'We'll have a proper honeymoon in Canada,' Griff assured Mattie.

Sensing that she might have reservations about undressing in his presence, he decided to make himself scarce in the bathroom.

Mattie hung her wedding outfit in the wardrobe. She folded her new underwear neatly, rolled down her stockings and hung them over the back of a chair. She looked solemnly at her naked reflection in the cheval mirror, then pulled the silk nightdress over her head. It fell in sensuous folds to just below her knees. She adjusted the straps slightly to a more decorous level. She unpinned her hair, gave it a brisk brushing, pinched her cheeks to give her face some colour, then slipped into bed.

As if on cue, Griff appeared, in his pyjamas. He smelled of Eau de Cologne, and she realised that he had shaved for the second time that day.

'Light on, or off?' he queried.

'Off, I think. I'm tired,' she answered. She realised what she had said. 'Oh, I didn't mean . . .' she floundered.

He put his arms around her. 'It might have helped if we had, you know, before . . .'

'I'm sorry I made such a fuss about it,' she admitted.

'Well, let's just get used to sharing a bed, shall we? We don't want to force things: we've a lifetime ahead of us, after all.'

'A kiss and a cuddle,' she murmured, 'would be good. Thanks for being so patient, Griff.'

'Glad to oblige,' he said gallantly. He thought, that could lead to other things, and I certainly hope it does!

Some time later Mattie whispered: 'Griff?'

'Mmm?'

'If you still want to . . .'

'Shush . . . you don't need to say any more,' he said tenderly.

TEN

SOUTHAMPTON. EMBARKATION DAY

'We're on our way,' Mattie whispered tremulously to Griff. They were among a vast crowd on the lower deck. As the distance lengthened between them and their families on shore, waving goodbye, the gathering fell silent. Most of them realised that this could be a final parting.

The *Empress of Scotland* was an imposing sight, despite her decline in status, but she was once more headline news. Built in 1905 by Vulkan Shipyards of Stettin she had been the largest passenger steamship in the world, until superseded two years later by the ill-fated *Lusitania*. *Europa*, her original appellation, was the pride of the Hamburg-America line. She had been launched by the Empress of Germany and renamed in her honour, *Kaiserin Augusta Victoria*. Her maiden voyage had been to New York, with stop-overs at Dover and Cherbourg. Her passengers were predominantly the affluent and famous, who appreciated the lavish fittings and onboard entertainments, despite the fact that her slightly top-heavy design caused her to roll in rough waters. Her restaurant had been inspired by the Ritz Hotel.

During the war she had been commandeered as a military vessel, but remained in dock in Hamburg. In March, 1919, she was surrendered to Great Britain. In May, 1921, she was sold to Canadian Pacific, who renamed her yet again and refitted her to carry 459 passengers first class, and 960 second and third class. She was also converted to oil fuel.

This was only her second trip from Southampton via Cherbourg to Quebec.

Conditions were vastly superior to the insanitary, overcrowded steerage quarters on the pre-war immigrant ships. Of that category still in service, facilities had improved, with provision of rest rooms and basic meals. Now, though, there were lengthy forms to complete and immigrants must prove that they were financially solvent, or sponsored with jobs to go to.

The newly weds were determined to conserve their nest-egg as much as possible, and so had decided to travel second class. At least, Mattie thought, they had a cramped cabin to themselves and were not forced into segregated dormitories each night. So many fretful children and tired mothers! Not much chance of sleep there.

Griff's arm hugged her shoulders. 'Cheer up! This may not be the fastest ship, and she's not like she was in her heyday, but we'll be in Quebec within five days.'

Mattie looked over the rail at the heaving dark-green sea. 'I already feel sick,' she said faintly.

'You need something to eat—'

'I don't think I could.'

'Come on, let's go below, see what's on offer in the canteen.' He picked up their hand luggage. 'This is just the start of our big adventure!'

By the time they stopped off at Cherbourg Mattie was feeling less queasy. She'd made a friend, too, which helped. Grace Dowling was a few years her senior, with two children, a boy of nine and a baby girl in arms. They were in the adjacent cabin to Mattie and Griff's. Grace's husband, Edwin, had gone ahead to Canada while his wife remained with her sister for the birth of the baby. She confided to Mattie that this was her second marriage. Her first husband had been an officer in the fire brigade. He was killed on duty when their son Tommy was a toddler.

'Tommy knows that his dad was a hero. Things have been difficult. He was used to it being just the two of us. I had a good position as housekeeper in a big house at Newmarket where I was able to have Tommy with me. I met Edwin there. He was a jockey, rode some winners, but after he had a bad fall some years ago he was kept on as a stable lad. He isn't used to children, but he does try,' Grace said.

'My family home is in Suffolk too!' Mattie exclaimed. This was something they had in common.

Cherbourg proved disappointing – they didn't disembark, but waited while some cargo was unloaded and replaced by other commodities intended for Quebec.

'I wish it had been possible to visit Paris,' Mattie said wistfully, as she and Grace sat on deck in canvas chairs, shrouded in mackintoshes and scarves. A keen wind whipped their hair into disarray. Grace's tiny Lydia was cocooned in her shawl in her mother's arms. Griff was at the rail with Tommy, pointing out things of interest.

'I always dreamed of going to Paris too,' Grace observed, 'but that's over two hundred miles from here. We'll hear plenty of French spoken in Quebec! Griff's good with young Tommy – are you looking forward to a family of your own?'

'We've only been married a week, Grace!' Mattie quickly changed the subject. 'It's quite a coincidence we're both travelling on to Moose Jaw, isn't it?'

'I'll be very glad of your company. We first heard of the place when the Prince of Wales visited there, on his Commonwealth tour a couple of years ago. Do you remember that picture in the newspapers of him dressed like a Red Indian chief? He even drove a train part of the way to Ontario – a CPR engine, like the one we'll be travelling on shortly.'

'We'll be living out on the prairie, same as you. Edwin works on a large holding with horses. Our quarters are in the main house. I will be helping in the kitchen.'

'Can you manage that – with the baby to look after?' Mattie said, concerned.

'Easier, while she's small. I've always had to work, and the women out here are the same, it seems.' She glanced down at Mattie's smooth hands with their polished nails. 'I can see that *you* were not in service!'

'My parents ran the village inn, until just after the war. My mother had a woman in to do all the household chores in those days – my sister and I were not expected to do much in that respect. My first job was in the local post office, but for the past year I've lived with my cousin Sybil and her husband in Plymouth – Griff is his stepson. I was a drapery assistant in the family emporium. Griff was employed there too, in another department.'

'Your new life will be very different, eh?'

'I'm looking forward to it,' Mattie said firmly. 'Apart from the broken nails!'

They arrived in Quebec, on the northern bank of the St Lawrence River. Here were the termini for the Great Northern and the Canadian Pacific railways.

The harbour was vast and with so many people milling around, progress was slow. There was a formidable queue at the immigration office: papers had to be thoroughly checked after luggage was located and collected. Mattie and Grace took turns at carrying the fretful baby while Griff kept an eye on young Tommy. It was a chilly arrival in the new country; they'd been warned that winters were longer here, and summers shorter, but they'd left England on a balmy spring day. It was quite a shock to the system.

At least Mattie and Griff knew where they'd be staying overnight. Grace had to make her own arrangements. 'Come with us!' Mattie told her. She could see that Grace was fighting back tears, determined to stay strong for her children.

There was no time to marvel at the magnificent parliament building, which formed a perfect square, 300 feet in length, with towers at each end, or to give more than a cursory glance at the statues of Wolfe, Montcalm and other historical figures. Griff hailed one of the many cruising taxis and they climbed thankfully inside. It was already evening, and they were hungry and weary. Little Lydia had cried herself to sleep.

They left the grand buildings behind and drove along meaner streets where every building appeared to be a lodging place. The taxi drew up outside a three-storey house.

'Ma Smith's,' the driver announced. 'You'll be all right here. She's from the old country. She don't have to advertise; the word gets around.'

'She's not expecting *us*.' Grace said faintly.

'Don't fret, Ma'll fit you in,' he said confidently. 'You go up the steps and pull the bell while the young gent and I foller with the baggage.'

Mattie had pictured Ma Smith as comfortably plump and kindly. The woman who opened the door was tall and angular, with dark hair scraped back from a prominent forehead and piercing deep-set brown eyes. She was dressed in old-fashioned clothes: an ankle-length skirt in rather rusty black alpaca, and a jacket which buttoned up to her jutting chin. 'Here you are, then,' she greeted them. A searching look, a quick count, then her stern features were illuminated by a smile. 'More of you than I expected. Come in. We can stretch the supper, no doubt.' She took the baby and held her in the crook of one arm. 'Follow me. Up two flights, I'm afraid.'

The first bedroom was under the eaves. There was a double bed with brass rails, and a sagging mattress. However, the sheets were clean, if much darned, and there was a brightly patterned patchwork quilt. There was a plain pine washstand with soap dish, jug and basin patterned with blue cornflowers. The matching chamber pot was hidden in the cupboard below the marble top.

Mattie was looking forward more to bed than to supper. She blushed at her thoughts. She and Griff had slept in narrow bunks in their cabin – no honeymooning there.

Ma Smith indicated the next door along. 'The only one spare; it's small, but there are two single beds – can you and the boy manage in there, Mrs Dowling? I see you've got a rush basket for the baby. I'll have to make the beds up after supper – is that all right?'

'I need to feed the baby,' Grace said faintly. She sat down abruptly on the one chair in Mattie and Griff's room. She unwound the shawl and Lydia's pink, cross baby face was revealed. Her tiny hands flailed at her mother's bodice, with the tell-tale damp patches.

Mattie and Griff exchanged quick, embarrassed glances.

Griff said: 'You must share with Mattie, Grace. Tommy and I will take the other room.'

Ma took it in her stride, with just a slight raising of her eyebrows. 'Wear something warm in bed,' she advised. 'Gets mighty chilly at nights. It's a draughty old house. Well, I'll send me niece up with the hot water for you to wash, while I dish up the dinner. When you hear the gong, it's on the table. Some of the lodgers got no manners – they'll pinch bits off your plate, if you don't hurry. No need to dress up!'

Mattie tactfully made her ablutions while Grace nursed the baby. This is certainly not the place to dress up, she thought, so I'll borrow a pair of Griff's flannel pyjamas tonight. No seductive silk nightdress – one night of love is all we've managed since we were wed!

They sat at a long table in the dining-room. The thick glutinous stew had more carrots and onions than meat. Ma ladled it out from a blackened cauldron in the kitchen, on to tin plates. It was accompanied by mugs of strong, sweet tea. Bread was sawn in uneven lumps; salt was scraped with a knife from a big block. The best part of the meal was rice pudding, cooked in a great earthenware dish, dusted with nutmeg and served with cream taken from the top of the milk. There were fifteen people round the table, and Ma was right, Mattie had to avert her gaze from a youth opposite when he picked up his plate to lick it clean. As she did so, her half-eaten crust disappeared by sleight of hand.

The conversation was mostly incomprehensible to the new arrivals. They'd expected some of their fellow diners to speak French, but there was a Scandinavian element, too.

'Norwegian?' she whispered to Griff, who was also eavesdropping.

'Danish – Swedish?' he countered, with a grin.

Then they heard a precise Scottish voice, 'Make room for mother and child!' as Grace hesitated at the door, with her replete baby in her arms. She was escorted to a chair at the end of the table by a stocky, black-haired man in a kilt.

Grace managed a brief wave at her friends.

'Tommy,' she called to her son. 'If you've done eating, you can take Lydia.'

Tommy had been surreptitiously flicking pellets of bread across the table to another boy, of about his age. He sighed, but rose obediently to do his mother's bidding.

Chairs scraped the uncarpeted floor; the other guests were returning to their rooms. Mattie, Griff and Tommy were waiting for Grace to finish her meal.

Ma Smith joined them for ten minutes, with her own mug of stewed tea. There was a clatter in the kitchen – her niece Jeannie was starting on the washing-up.

'Going on to Moose Jaw, are you?' she asked, fishing out a tea leaf with her thumb.

'We are,' Griff agreed. 'Have you been there?'

'No. Wild in parts, they say . . . you'll be out of town, I reckon?'

'My Aunt Anna and her husband farm there. We'll be with them for a while.'

'Ah – it can be a lonely life on the prairie. A hard life, too. When my husband and I came here ten years ago, we thought we'd do just that. We took on this place to get a bit of cash behind us, like, but he died in the influenza epidemic in 1918, so we stayed on, Jeannie and me. She's getting married later this year.' Ma sighed. 'I get homesick for the old country now and then, but – I made my bed, and this is my life now . . . Reminds me, I got those single beds to make up. If you'll excuse me . . .'

Later, while Grace tucked Tommy into his bed, Griff and Mattie had a few minutes privacy to say goodnight in the other room.

'You're swamped in my pyjamas,' he whispered ruefully. Rather than undo the buttons, in case Grace returned quickly, he groped under the flannel jacket. 'You're wearing a winter vest!' he exclaimed.

Mattie giggled. 'Well, Ma said the temperature drops at nights ...'

'She didn't put it quite like that. Well, that vest has definitely cooled my ardour!'

She clasped him to her. 'We'll make up for it in a day or two!'

'An early start tomorrow, Mattie. We've still quite a way to travel,' he reminded her.

ELEVEN

There were not so many around the table at breakfast as there had been last night at supper. At seven o'clock some had already departed to work, or in hopes of obtaining a job of any sort. There were always long queues at the employment offices.

The Scotsman joined their family party, enquiring if they were refreshed after a good night's sleep. He introduced himself as Mungo McBride, the fiancé of Ma Smith's niece Jeannie. 'We met in Edinburgh, shortly before Jeannie left for Canada to be with her aunt. We kept in touch over the past four years. You could say we became engaged by letter! Like you, I am travelling on to Moose Jaw today. I have a teaching post, and lodgings arranged. I want to be established before Jeannie joins me and we are married.'

'We will be glad of your company,' Griff told him. He would not dream of saying so, of course, but he felt rather weighed down with the unexpected extra responsibility of Grace and her family. He had spent a restless night missing Mattie. Also, Tommy suffered from enlarged adenoids and snuffled and snored while he was asleep.

Ma Smith banged the side of each plate with the ladle in order to dislodge the helpings of thick grey porridge. She indicated a large sticky-rimmed jar. 'Syrup. Salt for Mungo.'

This was not the golden syrup Mattie sometimes had at home, in preference to demerara sugar, but maple syrup. She was not too sure that she liked the taste. At the Plough, and recently at Sybil's, she'd enjoyed porridge made with milk. Here, it was steeped overnight in water, then cooked first thing. Only added milk made it palatable.

Jeannie brought them their mugs of tea. 'Would you care for fried bacon and eggs? You need to travel on a full stomach, if you are not booked on the restaurant car. Ma will pack you food for the journey, if you wish it, but you can buy hot drinks at stopping points along the way. You'll need to carry a rug or two, in case the temperature drops very low while you are travelling overnight. But you save a lot going third-class.'

'Thank you for your good advice,' Mattie said gratefully. She looked at Griff. 'We'll all be glad of the extra breakfast, I'm sure, eh? And the food for the journey.'

He nodded. He read into Grace's hesitation that she was worrying whether she could afford further expense. 'For four, please,' Griff said. 'On my account.'

Mattie squeezed his hand to let him know she was pleased at his quick response.

'That will be added to the bill then,' Jeannie said.

Griff winked at Mattie when they observed that Mungo's plate had an extra egg and a whole slice of fried bread. 'Will I get the same privilege when you serve our breakfast?' he whispered in her ear.

Mattie gave him a look of mock reproof. '*You'll* be doing the cooking, I reckon.'

Mungo overheard this exchange. 'I must admit that I have never been involved in matters domestic. I am the youngest by several years of six, the only son; I was spoiled by my sisters, none of whom married, after my mother passed away. They had been educated at home by my father, who was a minister of the Church of Scotland. They determined that I should go away to school and then on to university, I am very indebted to them for that. Jeannie and I met when she joined the evening class where I taught geography. I learned that she intended to emigrate to Canada. I was bored with academia; the idea grew in my mind that I would do the same. So here I am.'

'Yes, here you are, but not for long,' Jeannie commented, as she collected crockery.

She looks like a younger edition of her aunt, Mattie thought, as she tucked in. She and Mungo don't seem, well, very romantic, but then, they must be nearer forty than thirty.

Tommy dipped his bread in egg yolk. He spoke with his mouth full, despite his mother's frown. 'Why aren't you wearing your kilt today'?' he asked Mungo.

'It was a special occasion yesterday, laddie. Today and travel is more suited to sober attire, eh?' Mungo's voice was high in pitch, his tone precise. It contrasted with Jeannie's Glaswegian accent.

'What special occasion?' Tommy asked.

'Tommy, It's rude to ask personal questions!' his mother reminded him.

'Indeed, he is just curious, and why not? I was asked to play my bagpipes at a luncheon party for some of the Scottish contingent in Quebec.'

'Bagpipes! Are you bringing them to Moose Jaw?' Tommy wanted to know.

'My pipes and I are never parted. But don't expect me to pipe you on to the train!'

'My mother plays the piano—'

'Tommy!' Grace was embarrassed. She patted Lydia's back, her head bent.

'Then we may play in harmony one day, perhaps,' Mungo said gallantly.

When she reflected on the journey in years to come, Mattie would remember the biting cold, the bleakness of some of the countryside, then the contrasting beauty of the landscape, as the rail car sped along the tracks. The great lakes were silvery in unexpected sunlight; snow still capped the hills and the tall pine trees, and blanketed rooftops of the townships. When they halted, in remote areas, to take on coal or water, it seemed to Mattie that they were in no man's land. However, they became aware that mail was being sorted continually while they were on the move, and that this was collected and delivered at rural and city stations *en route*. Passengers had the opportunity to stretch their legs at the city stations, to purchase food from cheerful vendors.

Late on the first evening, when they sat huddled in the rugs while Grace nursed her baby discreetly, they were surprised and delighted when they arrived at a country station to a warm welcome from the station master and his wife, with an urn of tea at the ready, ham sandwiches and buttered fruit scones. This repast was served in the waiting room, by a good fire. Griff, Tommy and Mungo later strolled along the platform, while Grace and Mattie made the baby comfortable in the rush basket.

When it was time to reboard the train they discovered another cheering development. The stove in the corner of their carriage had been lit, and a basket of wood chips provided. This heat was a godsend during the long night's travelling ahead.

A new day dawned. The men ruefully rasped their stubbly chins, the women shared a billy-can of hot water, heated on top of the stove, and had a perfunctory wash. There was a yawning line of people waiting outside the WC in the corridor. Only little Lydia had a change of clothes. Tommy was bored; he was reprimanded by Grace for trying to open the carriage window. 'D'you want us all to freeze?' she demanded.

Mattie had a crick in her neck. Not surprising, she thought, when she'd rested her head on Griff's shoulder all night. She'd been the first of their party to wake, and had observed Grace similarly supported by Mungo. Quite innocent, of course, she told herself, but just as well that Jeannie is not with us, or Grace's husband . . .

What a vast country this was, with scenery that changed continually. They glimpsed boats on busy rivers, rolling pastures, distant mountains. They would spend another night on the train and most of the following day, and they were all becoming very travel-weary. Grace was preoccupied with the baby, so Mattie, Griff and Mungo did their best to keep young Tommy happy, with a pack of battered playing cards and pencil-and-paper games.

There were more mail stops, then, at last, the signs that they were approaching a prosperous area: Regina! They had travelled almost 2,000 miles. The name was written large and black on the map Griff had purchased in Quebec. They were in Saskatchewan, Central Canada; in another hour or so they would arrive at Moose Jaw, which was some forty miles away.

'How did it get its name?' Tommy wondered.

Griff had been primed by Evie, who was fascinated by such facts. 'Apparently it's derived from a Cree name for a place. Did you know that the male moose is the largest animal in the world with antlers?' he asked.

'Bet it's got a very big jaw then, too!'

'At least it can't jaw-jaw like you,' his mother put in ruefully.

Moose Jaw had expanded considerably since the early pioneer days. The population was cosmopolitan and Mattie's and Griff's first impressions were favourable. They were impressed by the amenities on offer. The bustle of the place reminded them of Plymouth but, as with any city, Griff thought there could be a darker side, too.

Here, they parted company with Mungo, who was going downtown by taxi. They exchanged addresses and promised to keep in touch.

Mungo ruffled Tommy's hair. 'Maybe you'll be enrolled at my school – it would be good for me to see a familiar face.' He looked over the boy's head at Grace.

'Oh, I hope so!' Tommy said fervently. 'Then I could learn to play the pipes!'

They didn't have long to wait before Griff's uncle arrived to collect them and Grace was reunited with her husband. It was the first time Edwin, a small man as befitted a jockey, had seen the baby. Poor Tommy stood disconsolately by, not even acknowledged by his stepfather. He moved back to stand by Mattie and Griff.

Mattie hugged him impulsively. 'Well, we're off, but hope to see you again soon!'

'I wish I was going with you and Griff,' he whispered.

'Oh, Tommy, your mother couldn't do without you!'

'You don't know what *he's* like. He wants her to himself. He doesn't like me. I'm afraid of horses, he thinks I'm a sissy. He says I need toughening up.'

'I hope if we have a son one day, he'll be like you!' Mattie said stoutly.

Uncle Charlie, a long, lean man with a weatherbeaten face, wore his Sunday suit in their honour. His sparse hair was slicked down with lard and he'd trimmed his moustache. His welcoming smile revealed gaps in his teeth, and later he would cheerfully tell them that he had pulled troublesome molars himself with pliers.

He handed Mattie up into the trap. She tried to smooth down her crumpled skirt. She thought ruefully that her trousseau would likely remain in the trunk, but she longed for a hot bath and a complete change of clothes.

Fifteen minutes after passing through the nearby town of Morse, they rattled and jolted along a dirt track, iron-hard from the grip of winter and scored by wagon wheels.

Charlie indicated a small wooden building with an adjacent barn. 'Built that with my own hands when we first come here. I'd trained as a carpenter back home. When we laid claim to the land and got the papers signed, my son and I began work on the farmhouse. Still adding to that! That's the beauty of wood, eh? We'll be glad to have your company for a while; we miss our family since they moved to North Dakota. They're doing well, building their own homestead now. The sod house is still standing! When we retire, we aim to join them.'

The farmhouse was a pleasing sight with its gabled roof, smoke curling from the chimneys, and a veranda running the length of the house. There were outbuildings, a grain store, a brick well, an impressive vegetable patch, a plough-share in the drive and horses in the stable.

Aunt Anna came hurrying out to meet them, wiping floury hands on her sacking apron. Like Charlie, she had a ruddy complexion, but her abundant greying hair was bundled into a knot on top of her head. She was obviously strong and energetic.

'Here you all are, then,' she cried, almost lifting Mattie off her feet, in her embrace. 'Not much of you,' she told Mattie, 'We'll need to feed you up!'

'You sound just like my mother!' Mattie had a sudden rush of tears to her eyes.

'My dear, you're all worn out after all that travelling . . .'

'I feel – *frowsty*!' Mattie was crying now. 'I'm so sorry,' she gulped.

'Griff, you'll have to wait for *your* hug! Leave the trunks to Charlie. Let's take Mattie upstairs, then I'll fill the hip bath with hot water – a good old soak will help. But first,

I'll get Charlie to bring you a nice cup of tea. Supper will be served in an hour.'

The bath was behind a reed screen in the bedroom. The furniture was plain, hand-made, of unvarnished pine, like the floorboards. There were shaggy rugs beside the low bed and, as Mattie discovered, when she sat on the side to undress, the softest of feather mattresses. She was tempted to curl up on it that minute.

'I think I'll get in the bath after you,' Griff said. 'We can't waste all that hot water.'

Mattie undressed behind the screen. Anna had provided a big towel, a bath mat, and a bar of green soap. Mattie thought ruefully of the luxuries she had become used to in Plymouth, a proper bathroom, fragrant bath salts, hot water on tap.

She called out to Griff, 'Can you delve into the depths of my handbag? You'll find a small bottle of Mitcham lavender . . .'

She was immersed in the steaming water, leaning comfortably against the curved back of the bath, when a hand appeared round the screen, waving the scent bottle.

'Oh, bring it to me, please. I can't get out and drip everywhere.'

'I thought you wouldn't want me to see you,' he floundered.

'Don't be silly. We're married, aren't we? It's perfectly normal. Anyway, I was hoping you'd wash my back.'

'In that case—' The rest of him emerged. He handed her the bottle, with a bemused smile. As she tipped the contents in the water he added softly. 'You're beautiful, Mattie. I'm so lucky.'

'So am I. You really must stop being bashful. I may have held you off before we tied the knot, but now we've a lot to catch up on, eh?'

At Griff's urging Mattie had changed into the red woollen dress she had worn when they travelled to Suffolk to tell her parents the exciting news of their engagement.

'You may feel we have gone back in time coming here, Mattie, but I can't visualise you in shawl and clogs.'

'No, but I'll need longer skirts to avoid chapped knees,' she joked.

'Let your hair down, you're still a girl, not yet twenty, even though you're married.'

Charlie gave Mattie an appreciative wink when he saw her. Anna batted him on the head with a cork table mat. 'That's enough of that, old man!' she said.

Supper was quite a celebration. Roast lamb, floury potatoes, a domed Yorkshire pudding, mashed swede and finely sliced greens. They spooned on mint jelly, 'sent on by my sister in South Wales,' Anna observed.

'I've never been there, where my father came from,' Griff told her.

'It's a lovely place, my dear, with an unusual name: The Mumbles, near Swansea. Our father worked in the docks there. Your father was the only son, he joined the army and fought in the Boer war. You were just a baby when he died, so far from home.'

'And now, I'm far away from England, where I was brought up,' Griff said.

'Are your first thoughts that you are happy to be here?' Anna asked.

'Well, mine are, but Mattie must answer for herself.'

'It seemed the journey by train would never end,' Mattie said candidly. 'But, when I stepped inside here, it was such a relief – I felt I was at home!'

'The moment I saw you, Mattie, I fancied you were the daughter I never had.'

'Thank you,' was all Mattie could manage to say in return.

By ten o'clock they were in bed; Griff nipped the candle out, and Mattie snuggled down, not sleepy, but full of joyful expectation. His hands explored her smooth skin hesitantly at first, then, as he felt her response to his touch, his confidence grew. This was how expressing love for one another should be, Mattie exulted.

The frustrations and the fatigue of the days since their marriage melted away. They had arrived in their new country, and the start of a new life together.

TWELVE

When they ventured downstairs to breakfast at seven they found that they were the second sitting. Charlie was rounding up the sheep with the hired hand, Anna told them. 'They are taking some to market this morning. Charlie and Lee had their usual lamb chump chops, but I guess you'll prefer something less meaty.'

'We really don't mind, honestly, whatever is easiest for you to make,' Mattie said. 'My father used to rear lambs, but he gave that up, because of the watercress in the stream near the meadow. Something to do with liver fluke, I think, and the cress might become contaminated. Not that we had any problems with that.'

She was relieved that porridge wasn't on the menu! Scrambled eggs went down a treat.

'You must have a tour round outside.' Anna whisked away plates as soon as they were empty. 'We've two house cows, too many chickens to count and two farm dogs, Welsh collies, like the ones back home. You saw the horses yesterday. Treesa is already in the dairy, patting up the butter for me to take to market—'

'Treesa?' Mattie queried.

'My helper; doesn't say much, but she's pure gold. She's Lee's wife.'

'Do they live in?'

'Oh no, they come out from the Indian reservation. Most days they paddle their canoe over where the river narrows, then walk along the track.'

'You must allow us to help too,' Griff put in, 'while we're looking for jobs and a place of our own. It appears both of these are harder to find at this time.'

'That's true, but the way forward is to become mechanised,' Anna said. 'We have to hire a team of workers with their machinery at harvest time, and to transport the grain. We bought a generator at the start of last winter, and, oh, the brightness of electricity after the old lamps. Mind, when it breaks down, you'll hear old Charlie cussing in the basement. We're hoping to have a telephone eventually, but the linesmen have more important places to fix up first. I understand you drove a motor for your stepfather, Griff? Well, we've a tractor in the barn awaiting an experienced driver. Charlie is wanting a motor car next! When he appears, ask him about it, eh?'

'I certainly will,' Griff agreed.

Anna turned to Mattie. 'I'd be glad of your company to market, Mattie. Plenty of buying and selling to be done today. I take my own buggy, in case I hear my services are required and I need to get somewhere in a hurry. Griff might like to go with the men, but I'll warn you that if they have a good morning at the auction, they'll celebrate with an illicit beer or two, so the wagon sways on the way home, with the reins all slack.'

'Who might need you?' Mattie wondered.

'Didn't I say? I'm the local midwife, my dear. A family tradition – my mother and grandmother in Wales, you could say they inspired me. It's not for the money, most of my patients can't afford to pay the doctor either. He's a grand old chap, Doc Pedersen, mixes up his medicines himself, though the farmers are hardy and use their own home remedies mostly. He says we make a good team.' She looked at Mattie speculatively, 'We'll be here when your time comes.'

Griff, aware of Mattie's embarrassment, tweaked the long tail of hair she'd tied back with a moire ribbon. 'See, you're a prairie wife already!'

'That's enough for now,' Mattie said firmly. 'I'm not ready to be a prairie *mother*!'

Grace was still in her dressing-gown, in the bedroom, nursing Lydia. She was sobbing softly, but she wasn't aware of it. It had been a long night, and after six months apart, Edwin had been rough and demanding. She tried to tell him that she was still sore from the birth, a protracted delivery because Lydia had been in the breech position, that she was weary beyond belief, that all she wanted was a good night's sleep. He had grumbled when Tommy called out from his little room next door for his mother, only to have his stepfather tell him sternly to go back to sleep. 'Stop that snuffling, blow your nose!' he added. He had complained about the baby being fed on demand: 'We should move the cot into Tommy's room. You give in to their demands too easily, Grace. You must discipline yourself, and them.'

Discipline was obviously the order of the day in this big house. Being on the periphery of Moose Jaw, it was an imposing brick-built property, with modern sanitation and a large work force, both in and out of the house. The cook-housekeeper had shown Grace the well-appointed kitchen, and the boiler which must be kept riddled and topped up with fuel. Grace soon realised that her previous experience would be disregarded, she would have a lowly status here.

Now, she shifted the baby in her arms, murmuring 'Please don't take too long.' Lydia clung determinedly to her mother, as if knowing she would soon be transferred to her carrying basket. It was almost time for Grace to begin work.

The door opened and Edwin came in. Grace had been thankful when he left their bed at dawn and departed to see to his beloved horses. He didn't smile, but stared at her bared white breast, noting the baby's limpet grip. She realised: *he's jealous* . . .

'Is the boy ready for school?' he said abruptly.

'I – I hope so,' Grace said anxiously. 'He's downstairs having his breakfast.' She wanted to add, but daren't, I should go with him on his first morning at a new school.

'I'll collect him from the kitchen, then.'

'Have I got time to say goodbye to him – to wish him well?'

'Too late this morning. Don't mollycoddle the boy, Grace.'

When he'd gone, she cried in earnest, and the baby wailed, too, as if in tune with her misery. She pressed her lips to the fuzzy little head. She whispered, 'I should have taken heed of what my dear mistress back home told me, that Edwin wouldn't make a good husband, that he'd never get over the disappointment of losing his dream job, as a jockey. I was lonely, Lydia. I'd known real love with Tommy's father, he was a gentle, considerate man and our marriage would have stood the test of time. *You* are the reason I came to Canada to join Edwin, because I couldn't deny you a father . . .'

Edwin had arranged for Tommy to go to the nearest school. Conversation was brief. Tommy sat unhappily alongside Edwin in the high-wheeled trap and fixed his gaze on the flickering of the whip on the horse's rump. He clutched his lunch packet and his pencil case; Mrs Mack, the housekeeper, had proved to have a soft spot for small boys.

'Don't think you'll get it this easy in future,' Edwin told him. 'You must earn your keep, like your mother. You'll have to get over your fear of horses because you'll need to rise like me, before it's light, and your job will be to clear the stable muck. Then do all that again when you get back from school in the afternoon.'

Tommy said nothing, but his stomach was already churning.

The school was a single-storey building, adjacent to the church, with a small clock tower, and a swinging bell in a wrought-iron frame. The playground enclosed by the picket fence was already swarming with children, some of whom stared curiously at the small man in breeches and riding-boots, with an unhappy-looking boy in tow.

They went straight to the head teacher's study. He was nearing retirement, white-haired, with glasses slipping down his nose, and, Tommy noticed, a blob of porridge on his tie. Mr Duncan's voice reassured him: another Scotsman, he realised.

'Ye'll be all right laddie. Your teacher is new here, like you. I'll take you to your classroom and introduce you. I expect you wish to return to your work?' he asked Edwin. 'It's almost time for me to ring the bell – make your escape before the rush begins, eh? Collect young Thomas just after four.'

Tommy followed Mr Duncan to a lofty classroom with rows of double desks. The teacher was perched on his high chair behind a tall table.

'This is the top class,' Mr Duncan said, 'and this is Mr McBride—'

Before he could continue, Tommy blurted out, 'I hoped it would be you!'

Mungo smiled. 'I had best explain to Mr Duncan that we met in Quebec, and I travelled with you, your mother and your friends on the train to Moose Jaw.'

'Find a seat Thomas, and enjoy your day,' said Mr Duncan kindly, as he departed.

'Well, Tommy,' Mungo said, 'how are you settling in your new home?'

Tommy swallowed hard. 'All right.'

Mungo didn't probe further. 'There goes the bell – now I must become acquainted with thirty other children! Remember that I am Mr McBride in school hours, eh?'

Tommy nodded. He was glad to have a friend, even if he couldn't show it.

Treesa was short, with jet-black hair hanging in a plaited rope to her waist, and she was very pregnant. She wore loose, padded trousers, a beaded smock. She smiled shyly at Mattie, continuing the rhythmic patting of blocks of yellow butter, but she didn't speak.

'Would you like to lend a hand, Mattie?' Anna suggested. 'Wrap the pats in a sheet of greaseproof, then pack them in this cool box?'

'I'd be pleased to do so!'

'Take from the pile on the left. The ones on the right still have to be stamped. We have our mark, *Prairie Butter*, embossed on this wooden block. I'll do that.'

While she packaged the blocks of butter, Mattie glanced covertly at Treesa. The young woman's features were distinctive, with high cheek-bones, bronzed skin, aquiline nose and dark eyes which appeared hooded as she concentrated on her task.

Treesa spoke at last: 'All finish, Missus.'

'That's good. We'll load the buggy now. My husband has harnessed the horse. We have four baskets of eggs to take, too. Are you ready to leave, Mattie?'

Mattie nodded. Charlie, Lee and Griff had already gone, having called goodbye.

It was much more springlike today; the sun's rays glittered on the remaining rime, and they bowled along in the buggy behind other conveyances bound for market.

Mattie sat up front with Anna. Treesa, despite her bulk, climbed into the back.

'You all right, Treesa?' Anna enquired. 'Nearing your time, I believe?'

'Soon, Missus,' Treesa agreed equably. 'But not today.'

'Has she booked you for the confinement?' Mattie asked. She thought the jolting sitting over the wheels wasn't what Treesa needed, just now.

Anna was obviously amused. 'I wouldn't dare to poke my nose in, unless I was asked. Treesa has three sisters, with half a dozen babies between them, and a rather fierce grandmother who delivered them all!'

The market was already crowded and noisy. They had a small stall under a faded striped canopy. Anna quickly covered the unlovely wooden trestle with a spanking white cloth. Then she and Treesa put out the baskets of eggs and a sample pack or two of Prairie Butter. There was a shoebox till and a bag of coppers as a float.

'Here, wear this,' Anna told Mattie, tossing her a white apron.

Treesa, Mattie realised, had disappeared into the crowd. 'She's got things to buy for her family,' Anna said. 'I slipped her wages to her in advance this week. If Lee got hold of it first – well, it wouldn't go on such wholesome refreshment.'

'Do you do all your shopping here?' Mattie wondered.

'No, we only come to market to auction the lambs. Though I drive out here on Sundays to church, being in the women's choir.

'We buy in bulk, and our requirements are delivered to our door. We order clothes and household goods from the Sear's catalogue. We grow most vegetables and, as you know, we are well-provided with dairy products, flour milled from our own grain, meat and eggs. The trading post is nearer home, handy if you run out of something. That's the local post office for our community too.'

'Sounds rather like our village shop back home! I worked there when I left school.'

'Olive Henry – known to us as Ollie – is wanting an assistant, but you might consider that a step backwards, Mattie. Shall we call in there, when we finish here, after lunch?'

'Please! I want to work – to help Griff realise our dream.'

*

At first sight, Mattie wondered if Ollie was short for Oliver, not Olive, as Miss Henry, with close-cropped hair under a man's flat cap; lean figure encased in a thick, checked lumberjack's shirt, corduroy trousers with braces, and sturdy boots, had a gravelly voice to match. Mattie's hand was seized in a tight grip and pumped up and down.

'Nice to meet you, Mrs Parry,' Ollie boomed.

'Oh, Mattie, please!' Mattie tried not to wince.

'Still need help here?' Anna came straight to the point.

'Only if the right person comes along. Interested, Mattie?'

'Yes, but . . . I haven't told you anything about myself,' Mattie floundered.

'Being related to Anna is good enough for me.'

Mattie thought: I ought to make it clear I'm only a niece by marriage . . .

Anna gave her arm a reassuring squeeze. 'When can she start?'

'Why not leave her with me for the afternoon, so she can learn the ropes?'

'I'd like that,' Mattie put in, before they continued in this vein, talking over her head.

The telephone in the post office section was ringing.

'Excuse me.' Ollie went through to answer the call.

She soon returned. 'Well, that's a bit of luck, your being here, Anna. A message for you from the doc. Can you get to Taylor's farm as soon as possible? Myra's started her labour. Doc'll come if you need his help.'

'I'll drop Treesa off at our place first, then she can see to the men when they arrive back. Lee must carry her packages back along the trail, that's if he can walk in a straight line, eh? I'll collect you later, maybe much later – all right?'

Mattie wasn't too sure about that, but she heard herself say, 'Of course!'

'Let me show you where we keep everything, Mattie,' Ollie said.

It took Ollie some time to do this, especially with interruptions when customers arrived, sometimes two or three at a time. Mattie thought it was amazing what was on the shelves inside what, from outside, appeared a shack. Everything from shovels to sausages, dungarees to dog biscuits, she would tell Griff later. But she emerged triumphant from her first stint behind the post office counter. Ollie looked at her approvingly. 'I *knew* you were a good 'un, soon as I saw you, Mattie!'

*

The end of the school day was imminent and Tommy, who had spent a happy, stimulating day and shown his skill with dribbling and heading a ball during an impromptu game during the lunch-time break in the playground, now became apprehensive. Edwin didn't wait to see his teacher, or ask Tommy how he'd got on.

'Get in,' he ordered, leaving Tommy to scramble up over the wheel into the trap. He was still smarting from the ticking-off he had received earlier from Mrs Mack. She'd said, while Grace was busy with the baby, 'Your poor wife is still recovering from the birth, and all the travelling she's had to endure. I got it out of her that she has women's problems right now, and I shall ask the mistress to allow her a few days' rest before she starts work proper. You must back me up, it's the least you can do.'

Edwin wondered angrily how far Grace's confidences had extended.

He said now, 'Watch out as we go, you can walk to and from school tomorrow.' He expected the boy to be upset at this, for it was a couple of miles each way, but Tommy was relieved. There were still the afternoon chores to get through, though.

Tommy was surprised and pleased to see his mother when he went upstairs to get changed. Grace was resting on the bed, cradling the baby in her arms.

'Mrs Mack says I'm not to work until I'm properly fit. Isn't she kind, Tommy?'

'Mm,' Tommy agreed. The housekeeper had slipped him a sandwich, to 'keep you going till supper, my dear,' when he looked in at the kitchen for his mother.

Most of the horses in the stables were highly strung thoroughbreds. They were bred for racing. Fortunately, these were considered too valuable for Tommy to have any dealings with. This was a mechanised farm, but there was still the pair of great Shire horses, who were kept now for ploughing competitions. Tommy looked with trepidation at the huge hoofs, but he soon realised that these were gentle giants. Inquisitive, yes, but not liable to kick or bite. He'd never been involved with the horses in New-market, having shown fear of a mettlesome bay when he first went there.

A very old man, bent and rheumy-eyed, shuffled over and showed him what to do. He shovelled and scraped with a will, glad that Edwin was not watching.

The Shires had a small companion, a Shetland pony, long since outgrown by the children of the house. The pony had a thick, shaggy coat, more rust-coloured than black, and a glint in his eye. Tommy was trembling but stood still, as the old man cautioned, when the pony nosed impudently into his coat pocket. Mrs Mack had thought to put a couple of sugar lumps in there. The pony tossed his head, snorted, and crunched happily. Tommy even dared to pat his neck. The expected ordeal had proved nothing of the sort. He couldn't wait to tell his mother all about it. Also, he was sure she would be really pleased to hear that Mungo was his new teacher.

Anna found the farm gates open awaiting her arrival. She smiled to see Granny Taylor's ancient red-flannel bloomers fluttering on the gatepost, a sign which meant, HURRY! She did just that, glad that she had taken her maternity bag to market.

Mr Taylor was splitting logs in the yard. Myra was his second wife, and he had a grown-up family of four girls already.

'Thought I was past all this,' he remarked sourly. He jerked a thumb. 'Upstairs, first door you come to. I couldn't stand all the racket. It can't be long now, that's why I put out the red flag.'

His companion brought down his axe with a flash of the silver blade. He was a handsome young man, of mixed parentage, with jet-black hair and tanned skin. He said nothing, but Anna noted his compressed lips.

Poor Myra, some thirty years younger than her husband, gasped with relief when she saw Anna. She was obviously in some distress. Anna sent the young girl who was attending her to fetch hot water and towels.

She said soothingly to her patient, gently stroking back her hair from her damp forehead, 'It'll all be over soon, my dear. I can see the baby's crown . . .'

Ten minutes later Anna helped Myra's little son into the world.

'I can't look,' the girl whispered faintly. 'Is he . . . is he, like his father?'

'He is indeed,' Anna assured her. 'Mr Taylor will be delighted that at last he has a son.' She wrapped the baby in a towel, placed him in his mother's arms. The tiny boy had a thatch of black hair. She added, 'Most babies are born dark, but come the summer, he could well turn fair like you.'

'Thank you, Anna, *thank you*,' Myra said gratefully.

THIRTEEN

JUNE

Treesa and Lee had not been to work for the past four days. Anna guessed that the baby had arrived. Charlie grumbled a bit, saying Lee could have turned up on his own, that he was surprised that Treesa's grandmother had not given him a push in that direction.

'Luckily,' Charlie said to Griff, 'I had you, boy, to help me out. You done wonders with the Fordson tractor. I wanted one of those, you know, ever since I heard how useful they've proved to be, back home. The first ones were shipped out to Great Britain to get things going again after the war, when there was a shortage of horses and wagons as well as men. At last, *we* can catch up, over here!

'We were able to make the most of the fine weather, eh? We'll go into town after milking, to see a motor which has come up for sale. I need your advice. If I buy it, you can drive it back while I foller in the buggy.'

After the men departed Lee and Treesa appeared. Treesa carried her precious papoose on her back, leaving both hands free. Anna and Mattie ushered the new mother into the cosy kitchen for a cup of tea. Lee was despatched to the cowshed, clutching his mug. He didn't mind. 'Women talk,' he muttered, but with a grin.

'I have to go to work, too,' Mattie said regretfully. She was enjoying her new job, but wouldn't have minded the morning off to become acquainted with little Mai – named for Doc Pedersen's Swedish wife, who'd provided comforts for mother and baby.

'Holda baby first,' Treesa looked up shyly at Mattie. She'd laid the papoose on the table while she quaffed her tea. She lifted the baby out of her snug hollow and handed her to Mattie.

There was a strange fluttering in Mattie's chest. Mai didn't resemble the babies she'd had limited dealings with, like her plump nephew Robbie, or fretful, pink Lydia, Grace's child. Mai had peachy-gold skin, with dark eyes which seemed to follow any movement Mattie made. She gently kissed the baby's forehead.

'She's beautiful,' she managed, aware Treesa was awaiting her reaction.

Anna smiled knowingly. 'Pass Mai to me now, or you'll be late and Ollie will be wondering where you are.'

'Yes, I must go,' Mattie agreed reluctantly. She buttoned her jacket, and left.

The men had cut plenty of wood for the stove, and the water in the reservoir tank alongside was bubbling merrily. Treesa fetched the laundry basket. 'We do washing? I get tub? Turn mangle? Good wind for drying, Missus.'

'No scrubbing on the washboard for *you* today, Treesa. Did you get to lie in at all after having the baby?' Anna wondered.

'Women must work,' Treesa said reprovingly.

'And men must be allowed to admire a Model T Ford or two,' Anna said wryly.

The trading post owed none of its success to window-dressing, for goods were piled so high on the shelves that they covered over the small panes of glass. The interior was lit by hanging kerosene lamps. The overriding odour was of the oil, mingling with that of serviceable clothes, stiff with dressing; rubber boots, sacks of animal feed, a cart-wheel of strong cheese wrapped in muslin, and the side of hickory-smoked ham suspended on a stout hook, from the low beam. Fly swats were kept at the ready.

It was one of Mattie's tasks to lift the ham down on to the counter on request, to ease back an inch or so of the rind with a sharp knife kept specially for this purpose, then to slice thinly before weighing portions on the brass scales. The top slice was always greyish, and this was put aside to be made into sandwiches later for Mattie's and Ollie's lunch. This ham was mainly sold to the bachelor farmers, as those with womenfolk, whether wives, mothers or sisters, ate their own home-produced bacon.

The local self-sufficiency meant that Ollie did not stock staples, such as bread, milk and perishable foods. Most homesteads, however humble, had their ice boxes: the men cut blocks of ice from the lake when it froze in winter, dragged their loads home on sleds and stored the ice in an ice hut outside, insulated with straw, or in a dug-out cellar. Ice carts might deliver to townsfolk, but this service must be paid for. The rich had refrigerators, but most of the community had never even seen one of these.

The drought that had begun in 1919 continued in 1922. Old Wives Lake, south of Moose Jaw, was almost devoid of water. There were high winds and already it was predicted that this could be one of the driest years on record.

However, Ollie's store had everything needed for preserving produce, as Mattie discovered, including isinglass for buckets of eggs, as well as canning and bottling equipment.

It was a fairly slack morning, so they set the dented old coffee pot to boil on the primus stove 'out back' in the tiny kitchen area. It was Mattie's job to grind the coffee beans. If customers came, they announced their presence by ringing the handbell on the counter. They'd have time to look through the pile of old-fashioned sun bonnets which Ollie had on offer, now that it was summer.

Mattie and Ollie sat on three-legged stools which had price tags attached, so might be sold at any time. They sipped the scalding black coffee; nowadays Mattie could drink it without a grimace.

'How long have you lived here?' Mattie asked. It was difficult to judge Ollie's age, as well as her gender, she thought.

'Must be forty years. I didn't grow up in these parts; my father was a fur-trapper for the Hudson's Bay Company. He was not often at home; my mother said that was why I was an only child. She was the local teacher, so I got to go to school.'

'What was it like in that part of Canada?'

'You'll think it cold here when winter strikes again, but *there* – you had to be tough to survive. My father deserted us when I was ten. I believe he went to California, had a new family, but I don't know. Mother decided we'd pack up and find a more hospitable place. I was sixteen then. She thought I might have more chance to find a man and get married on the prairie. But I had no inclination in that respect. We set up in the trading post, and four years later Mother died. I'm still here, as you can see. I think she would have been pleased . . . More coffee, Mattie?'

'Better not,' Mattie said, as the bell clanged. 'I'll go, shall I?'

The Tin Lizzie was in good condition and Charlie seemed impressed as he circled it a few times, while the garage owner extolled its virtues. When he learned that Griff was an experienced motorist, he said: 'I can leave it to you then, boy, to show old Charlie how to handle her – she's a bit temperamental, like all women. I gotta customer honking his horn for gas. Take your time. Go for a little drive, if you want.'

'He ain't usually that obliging,' Charlie said suspiciously.

'I'll tell you why,' Griff told him. 'These motors are the very devil to get started.'

Charlie took his time, as the garage man suggested. 'Magneto ignition – you say, this here lever is to do with the spark?'

'Shove that up – that's it. Now, look right and pull that lever *down* – cautiously, mind – that's the gas – next, turn on the ignition while I put the gear into neutral.'

'Is that it?' Charlie asked hopefully.

'Not quite,' Griff admitted. He wondered how he could explain the dangers of cranking up the car, after blocking a front wheel to prevent the Tin Lizzie creeping forward when it throbbed into life. There was a great deal more to tell, including the possibility of an electric shock. Charlie couldn't be taught to drive in one easy lesson.

'Still here then?' The man was back. 'Decided to buy her?'

'You get her started, ready to drive off, and Griff'll hop in. A dollar deposit now and if he arrives safely, we'll come back tomorrow and pay you in full. All right?'

They shook hands on it.

The journey back to the farm, cruising at around fifteen miles an hour, was without incident until the car began to bump along the dirt track. The old horse, of course, knew every pothole along the way, as did Charlie; the buggy overtook into the lead when the Tin Lizzie hit a hole and tipped sideways, with Griff clinging on grimly to the steering wheel. It was fortunately only a half-somersault, as the car bounced off the stock fence, righted itself and Griff scrambled out, mercifully unscathed.

Lee appeared as if from nowhere; he'd actually been having a smoke under a tree. 'You all right?' he asked, as Charlie reined in the horse, jumped out and walked back.

'I am, but I don't know about the motor.' Griff inspected the car. 'A couple of scratches, no dents, thank goodness.'

'We've got some black paint, don't worry. So long as she still goes,' Charlie said. 'Leave her where she is for now. You've had a shock. Damn motor can go back to the garage tomorrow – chap didn't warn us this might happen.'

'It was my fault. I haven't driven on this sort of surface before. Look, if you feel you'd rather not buy it, why don't I? I've learned my lesson, after all!'

'Can you afford it? I'm sorry I can't pay you for what you do, but—'

'I don't expect you to – I'm just glad to earn our keep, Charlie! You've helped me realise that this is not the right time for us to chance setting up on our own. However, the car will be an investment; we'll need transport when we move on . . .'

'Not going yet, boy, I hope. We've got used to having you around,' Charlie said.

During the summer, the church ladies' sewing-circle met on Friday evenings at the farm. They sat out on the veranda and chatted while they sewed. At 8.30 they folded their work: garments for the missionary box and layettes for babies of needy parents in the parish. Then Charlie would appear, beaming, with a tray of glasses, a big jug of home-made, iced lemonade and oatcakes.

When Mattie was asked to join the working party, she hesitated. 'I'm not very skilled at sewing, Anna.'

'Look, my dear, we use the simplest, free materials. We save our flour sacks and boil them white. You'd be surprised what we can make from 'em! Pillowslips, petticoats and underwear, children's nightdresses, tea towels, and hankies, from the scraps. It's the embroidery that makes them special. You can do daisy-stitch and a french knot or two, surely? And you must have learned to hem!'

'Not without sore, pricked fingers,' Mattie admitted ruefully.

'Persevere with a thimble! Making do and mend is what we learned to do in the old pioneering days. They say times will be as tough again, so best be prepared! You'll meet a few neighbours; you'd like that.'

So Mattie joined the group. She actually enjoyed sewing the soft cotton and making the garments pretty with embroidery.

Her first success was a tiny gown for Mai. With much encouragement from Anna she edged the cuffs and neckline with fine lace. One of the older ladies had hands twisted with arthritis. She couldn't sew because 'my fingers are too stiff', but she collected scraps of lace and pieces to appliqué to share among her friends as her contribution to their efforts.

Mattie wrote to tell her family of her prowess. Evie wrote back:

This will all come in very handy when you have a baby of your own to dress! Robbie is running about and talking now. There is a lot of whispering between Mother and Fanny – so I think there will be an announcement shortly.

Ronnie is busy studying at nights to better himself. The station master retires in a couple of years' time and Ronnie is the right age for promotion.

In September I'll be on course for matriculation! We have to work really hard at the grammar school.

I am sorry to be the bearer of bad news. Christabel's mother is very ill. She is in hospital, but there is not much hope . . .

Mattie read the letter out to Griff, omitting the bit about 'a baby of your own'. She knew he was keen to start a family, but they were still considering their future. If they stayed over winter here, Griff said he would have to get a job in town, or their savings would dwindle rapidly. They had to adapt to their circumstances. There was more chance of succeeding if they bought land and by a miracle struck oil. They were heading for a world-wide recession: the papers were full of gloom and doom.

'Christabel must miss you, Mattie,' he said quietly. 'You were good friends.'

'We still are, but you were her friend before me,' Mattie reminded him gently.

'Will you write to her from both of us?' he asked.

She nodded, not trusting herself to say more, in case she cried.

FOURTEEN

It was Mattie's birthday at the end of July.

'We usually have birthday picnics at the lakeside,' Anna said, 'but in this heat, with everything so dry – just look at the yellow grass! – and all that dust blowing in the wind, not enough water to paddle in, and the poor, stricken wildlife we're bound to come across, we might as well sit in the shade under the veranda and invite your friends to join us there, for tea. We'll make some ice cream, shall we, and a big chocolate cake—'

'With glacé cherries on top, and cream inside?' Mattie was excited like a child.

'If that's your favourite, it shall so be! Now, who would you like to come? You won't mind waiting until Saturday afternoon, will you, then Charlie and Griff can join us.'

'I'd like to invite Grace, Tommy and Lydia. I'm not sure about Edwin. He didn't appear pleased to meet us when we all arrived at Moose Jaw. We hardly had a chance to say goodbye to them. Oh, would Ollie and Treesa come, d'you think?'

'Treesa would insist on serving the refreshments. As for Ollie, she's not one for social gatherings, but I'm sure she'd like to be asked, even if she declines.'

'Just a small party, that will be good, Anna.' Mattie thought wistfully of past birthdays, before she came to Canada, at home, with her family, especially Evie, and more recently with Sybil, Christabel and Griff in Plymouth.

'You still have dear Griff and happy memories of family gatherings,' Anna observed, sensing Mattie was experiencing a pang of home-sickness. 'Your party will be the calm before the storm, I reckon, Mattie.'

'Is bad weather on the way?' Mattie asked anxiously.

'Not in the usual sense, like rain or even snow! But harvesting is about to start, and what with the drought and blight spreading on the crops, it's a worrying outlook.'

Mattie wore the pretty dress Dolly had made for her to wear on the emporium outing. As she regarded herself in the long mirror in her bedroom, fingering the coral necklace which was Griff's birthday gift to her, he came up behind her, smiled at her reflection, spanning her waist with his work-roughened hands.

'Mind you don't snag the cotton,' she teased him.

'I've toughened up since we came here. *You*'re more shapely . . . and irresistible . . .'

'Enough of that,' she returned, firmly removing herself from distraction, 'our guests will be arriving any minute!'

'I just wanted to say – I'm sorry things haven't worked out exactly as we planned.'

She had turned to face him now. She reached up and gave him a kiss. 'Maybe not, but we're very lucky to have been made so welcome by Anna and Charlie.'

'I feel like part of a real family again. No regrets about coming to Canada, then?'

'None at all. We'll get by,' she said firmly.

Mattie was determined to be cheerful, despite receiving sad news along with the birthday post. Dolly had passed away soon after she was admitted to hospital. Christabel was leaving Plymouth, the unrewarding job, to 'change my life' as her mother had hoped she would. Sophia and Will had invited Christabel to stay with them at the Plough in Suffolk for a while, while she considered her future.

Evie wrote:

She is repeating your journey in reverse! Walter will meet her in London, and she will stay at Mitcham overnight. He is due for his annual holiday, so he'll accompany Christabel here tomorrow. I know you'll be glad to know she will be with us. She has become a good friend, because of you.

I find it hard to believe you are 20! I can't imagine marrying so young, if at all. Have a lovely day – I will be with you in spirit!

Fanny had her birthday last week and announced
that they are expecting a new baby next spring –
they were married a month after you!

Now, glancing out of the window, Mattie exclaimed, 'Oh
good, Grace is here!'

Grace, looking younger and trimmer in a pretty blue
cotton frock and wide-brimmed hat, told them proudly,
'Tommy drove us over in the buggy.'

Tommy, who appeared to have shot up a few inches,
grinned widely. 'I'm not nervous of horses any more – you
should see the *huge* pair I help to look after. There's a pony
too, called Nipper – that's what he does to the seat of your
pants if he can't find a sugar lump in your pocket! Ted, the
man who is in charge of them, says the big old boys are
sort of retired – like him! But he still takes them to ploughing competitions and they often win. I help Ted with their
grooming, plait their manes and tails before shows. Ted
taught me how to handle the buggy.' Ted was obviously his
hero, not Edwin.

'Oh, I'm really glad things are working out for you all.'
Mattie gave Grace a warm hug. Anna whisked Lydia away
to the shade of the porch, while Griff helped Tommy to
unharness the horse in the stable.

'For Tommy, yes. He quickly learned to keep out of
Edwin's way. That's not possible for me. I have to make the
best of things, but I'm not going to kowtow to *him*.'

'Good for you!' Mattie approved. As they walked toward the house, she added, recalling the rapport between Grace and Mungo on the train, 'Any news of Mungo? Has Jeannie joined him yet?'

'He's Tommy's teacher at school! As for Jeannie, I've only just received a reply to my letter, letting them know we'd arrived here.'

'Oh, what does she say?'

'It was short and to the point. She's decided to stay in Quebec with Ma. She said, "The engagement is off, but fortunately neither of us is broken-hearted!" She hopes we will keep in touch.'

'Have you seen Mungo at the school?'

'No. After the first day, Edwin decreed Tommy could make his own way there. It's not so bad, because he has another boy to walk with, the son of a Chinese worker on the estate. His friend is not from the town, which is a relief.'

'Oh, why is that?'

'Surely you've heard the rumours about the secret tunnels under Moose Jaw?'

'No . . .' Mattie was mystified.

'They say – whoever *they* are! – Chinese illegal immigrants live in the tunnels, and are involved in smuggling supplies of liquor by rail over the US border to beat prohibition. They are organised by gangsters from Chicago. It's called the *Soo Line*. Or so they say . . .'

'No wonder Anna tells me not to venture into Moose Jaw by myself, especially to River Street, which she says is notorious, but hasn't explained why!'

Then Grace confided: 'Tommy brought me a note from Mungo. He would like me to play the piano at the end of term show. I haven't mentioned it to Edwin yet, but—'

'You're going anyway?' Mattie guessed.

'Yes, I am. Mrs Mack, the housekeeper, she's been good to me, will look after Lydia, I know, so there's no reason for me to refuse.'

'Be careful, Grace,' Mattie warned her, then wished she hadn't. It was none of her business, after all.

Grace gave a little shake of her head as they stepped up on to the veranda. It was hard to deduce what she meant by that.

Treesa scooped ice cream from the bucket, and served it in little glass dishes.

'Your boy already ate his up!' she told Grace. 'It took a long time to make!'

'Lydia looks quite big beside Mai.' Anna now had a lap-ful of babies.

'She's five months old, already determined to sit up,' Grace said proudly. 'But if she decides to crawl early, she could cause havoc in the kitchen!'

'Charlie made a playpen for our son at that stage,' Anna said. 'It's still stored in the barn. A good clean, and it's yours, if you want it.'

'Best place for baby is on mother's back,' Treesa put in. She didn't hold with prams, or penning babies in. 'She not a lamb.'

Grace unwrapped Lydia's bottle and ascertained that the milk was the right temperature.

She caught Mattie's look of surprise. 'I had to wean her. Edwin – insisted.'

'Ah,' Anna observed. She could guess the reason why.

'Can I go with Charlie and Griff to feed the animals?' Tommy asked.

'Why not? Be back in time for the birthday tea! There's chocolate cake . . .'

'It'll give you a chance to jaw-jaw!' Tommy grinned.

'Cheeky child!' Grace called after him, then, 'He's right, though, eh?'

Back home in England, Evie and Walter were picking watercress for tea. Christabel declined their invitation to accompany them, pleading a headache and sore throat. Sophia fussed around her, pulling the curtains in the bedroom she shared with Evie, and making her a comforting brew of hot water, lemon juice and honey.

'You have a nice nap on the bed, dear, and don't forget, I'm here to listen, if you feel like confiding your troubles to me . . .'

'You're so kind – thank you.' Christabel sipped the mixture, to please her. 'I really decided not to go along, knowing that Evie thinks of Walter as *her* special friend.'

'My dear, he's her cousin, that's all. And it should stay that way. He's too old for her, and she's far too young for him. Perhaps I shouldn't say, but I will! *You*'d be a good match for him . . .'

How could Christabel explain that she'd discerned a hint of jealousy in Evie's greeting yesterday? Young love, as she knew from experience, could be unsettling. She had, after all, been barely sixteen when she fell for Griff. She and Walter had immediately been at ease with each other, but nothing more, she thought.

'Well, I'm off, to ice a cake. Fanny's baked some Suffolk rusks, bless her, but we must celebrate Mattie's birthday with her favourite chocolate sponge, even though she's not here to share it.'

Evie and Walter plumped down on the parched grass by the stream. His forehead glistened with sweat. He pushed his straw boater to the back of his head.

'Why don't you loosen your tie, Walter – or better still, stuff it in your blazer pocket. Phew, it's hot, isn't it? I should get a nice tan out here in the sun, today.' A trifle too innocently, she pulled her skirts well above her knees.

'Do cover yourself up.' The sharpness of Walter's tone surprised her.

'What – you think I'm being improper?' she asked in an injured tone.

173

'You must behave like a young lady now.'

'You sound really pompous!' She giggled, but rearranged her dress.

'Your mother . . . told me not to encourage you, Evie.'

'I don't know what you mean?'

'I think you do. It made me think. I'm very fond of you, of course, but in a brotherly – or rather, cousinly fashion. I'm hardly Rudolph Valentino!'

'Who's he?' She jumped to her feet. 'Why are you looking so serious? We came to pick watercress for tea, that's all – come on!' She shed her shoes and stepped into the shallow, sun-warmed water. She didn't look back, aware that he was following her, but not intent on catching her up. It's just as well, she thought, I don't want him to see me blubbing like a baby. The girls at school giggle about their 'pashes', mostly for teachers or prefects. I *would* be different, having romantic notions about an older man . . . I wish Mattie was here, so I could confide in her.

Grace was ensconced at the piano to one side of the stage in the hall, which was attached on the other side from the school, of the modern Presbyterian church. Most of the congregation over middle age had been involved in some way with its erection, and subsequently with the building of the school. As the rows of seats filled up, she took a deep breath, and began to play the opening music, selected by Mungo. There was a background buzz of conversation before the lights were dimmed, so she wondered if anyone was listening. She stopped playing when there was a sudden hush at a skirl of bagpipes. Mungo strode down the aisle, resplendent in his kilt, the MacBride and MacDonald ClanRanald tartan, predominantly blue and green, striped with red, the pattern accentuated by white lines.

He turned to address the audience. 'Time for curtain-up! We're ready, Tommy!'

The curtains were jerked apart, rather than up, and a red-faced Tommy was fleetingly revealed hauling on one side, his diminutive friend Ho Wang on the other.

None of the acts took long, and followed smoothly on, one from the other. The curtains opened, then closed, opened again to a change of cardboard cut-out scenery. A small boy, the tip of his tongue protruding in concentration, juggled four balls; an even smaller boy sang in a pure treble; two girls in old-fashioned bonnets sang 'I'll be your Sweetheart' with great fervour; a lanky lad impressed with a reading from Dickens. Leading up to the interval, handbells were rung by the school team. All eyes were on the youngest member, who came in belatedly with the final 'dong!'

'You've earned your cup of tea.' Grace looked up from the piano keys to see Mungo smiling at her.

'Thank you, just what I could do with,' she said gratefully.

He pulled up a chair beside her. 'It's going very well, I think. I thought I'd take the chance to talk to you on your own, Grace.'

She was flustered. 'What is it? Tommy hasn't misbehaved, has he?'

'Goodness me, no. He is playing a vital part with the curtain pulling. He and his friend were too bashful to stand centre stage.'

'I heard from Jeannie . . .'

'Ah, then you know we are not to be married, after all. Did she tell you why?'

'No, of course not. That is private between the two of you.'

'I wish to explain. I had to tell her that I had fallen in love with another woman. She very generously said she understood.'

'Oh – you are to marry someone else, then?'

'No, Grace, it isn't possible. She . . . is already married. Can't you guess who she might be?'

'You haven't known her long enough to know how you feel!' she said in a rush.

'I see you have guessed my secret,' he said wryly.

'But you haven't guessed mine!'

'You mean, you feel the same way about me?'

'Yes, I do! But we must both forget this conversation, Mungo.'

He rose, took her empty cup. 'We should join the others backstage, I think.'

The steam-powered threshing-machines had arrived to harvest the grain. This was always a community effort, the prairie farmers joined forces, to work each farm in turn. The Fordson tractor came into its own now, but the Shire horses and wagons still had an important role to play in carting the grain from the fields.

Mattie took a couple of days off from the trading post to help Anna and Treesa feed the workers. Ollie presented her with a practical outfit to wear: blue denim dungarees and what Griff dubbed a lumberjack shirt.

'Wear these, then the men won't get any funny ideas, my dear! They get through a lot of home-made root beer at the end of the day.'

Not only that, as Mattie discovered, as she rolled great mounds of lardy pastry to cover pie-dishes full of diced mutton, onions, carrots and lashings of good gravy. When these were cooked, into the oven went more pies, plump with last autumn's canning of plums, with sugar to caramelise on each well-egged top crust.

During the day there were elevenses and fourses – the bread and cheese wrapped in clean cloths, and the bottles of cold tea to be taken out to the men labouring in the heat of the day, to keep them 'well oiled' as Anna put it. When the weary, hungry workforce filed indoors at dusk there was plenty of hot water in a basin in the kitchen sink, a big bar of soap for them to wash their hands, with a decent towel to dry them on. The women were red-faced and perspiring from the heat of the stove, but welcomed the neighbours to the harvest supper.

Later, there was a sing-song, and Mattie shared the big rocking chair with Griff. He whispered, as his arm tightened round her shoulders: 'At least I know what you're concealing under your lumberjack clothes!'

'Has it been a good harvest after all?' she asked.

'Charlie seems satisfied. If we can hang out here for another couple of years or so, he says, why don't we apply to go as a family unit to North Dakota? I'll get a job in town in the winter months. What d'you think?'

'It seems a good idea to me,' Mattie said.

But that was before the snows came, and winter would seem unending before suddenly it was another spring.

PART TWO

PART TWO

FIFTEEN

NORTH DAKOTA – CHRISTMAS 1925

They arrived in North Dakota – where the gopher that small, burrowing rodent with chisel-like teeth, and cheek pouches, had given the state the sobriquet 'Flickertail' – in late spring, after planning the route the preceding winter. They jolted along gravelled highways in Tin Lizzie, piled high with luggage and rattling alarmingly. They stopped off at country schools to use the outdoor facilities, and patched blown tyres on the roadside. Griff said getting the inner tube back was like wrestling a snake.

Mattie's first impression of the prairie homestead over the border was that it was an enchanted place. This was a small, scattered community, with a couple of stores, a church and one-room school, some thirty miles from the urban sprawl of Minot. Here, wildlife was abundant, with grouse, prairie chicken, geese, ducks and swans, good hunting in season; the climate was dry, cool and invigorating. As spring gave way to summer, the temperature rose without the air becoming humid. Nights were always cooler.

Their nest-egg was no more after the down payment on their small holding, which the original owners had built from scratch. To prove their claim these pioneers had been required to erect a house, fence their land, dig a well (aided by dynamite) and irrigation ditches. Twenty years on, Griff and Mattie took on the thriving herd of dairy cows, a wagon with a pair of sturdy cobs and an established milk-round. Some of the acreage was leased to a neighbour, which provided a modest income. However, Griff continued to work part-time, in the office of a local garage.

Anna and Charlie travelled on to the Red River of the North, a fertile area, to join their son in a new venture, backed by the sale of the farm at Moose Jaw. They were now part of the Bonanza Farming Community, growing a profitable commodity: sugar beet.

All summer, Mattie worked on her first garden. They'd been left a legacy of soft fruit bushes; these yielded pounds of delicious berries which she canned by the open kettle method, for the hard weather ahead, while Griff ploughed ground for vegetables. Flowers bordered the paths, and a yellow rose reminded Mattie of home. During the clement weather she decorated the rail of the front porch with potted plants.

Until recently, she'd assisted Griff with the milking and accompanied him on deliveries. Anna and Charlie's grandson Bert was driving his grandparents over to spend Christmas with Mattie and Griff. In January, Bert would stay with them for a few months to help out generally before going on to college.

The reason for this was that Mattie was heavily pregnant. The baby was due during Christmas week. Anna was keeping her promise to be with her, even though they were no longer in Moose Jaw with Doc Pedersen on hand.

'I'm a lady of leisure,' Mattie sighed, but she determined to do her bit towards the festive fare. The laying hens they'd invested in soon after their arrival were now clucking in the barn and enjoying time off too, so she took four precious eggs from the brown pottery crock in the pantry, studied the cookery book which Hilda had given them as a wedding present back in Plymouth and, with some trepidation, stirred up her first Christmas cake. The dried fruit was soaked first in marrow brandy to plump it up. Griff remarked appreciatively that you could get tipsy inhaling the fumes from the mixing bowl.

*

'Put on your boots,' Griff said on Christmas Eve. 'Something to see outside . . .'

Mattie was reluctant to leave the blazing log fire. Her stockinged feet rested on a footstool, her mending basket was to hand. The living room was the hub of the single-storey wooden house. She'd garlanded the room earlier with home-made paperchains, and a branch or two of Douglas fir. There were two bedrooms off this room. The kitchen was tacked on at the back of the house, under a tin roof. No space was wasted. A ladder led to a spare bedroom in the loft. This would accommodate Bert. There was not much headroom, but there was a comfortable bunk. The privy was adjacent to the wash-house with its own wood-burning copper. Tin tubs were housed here, together with the mangle.

'You've spotted them coming?' she queried.

'No sign of them yet . . .'

Griff slid the heavy boots on her feet, laced them up. He held out a warm blanket. 'Put this round your shoulders.'

She stood up and allowed him to tuck the folds around her. 'I don't want to be outside too long – it's freezing,' she said.

The drift of snow in the yard crunched underfoot. 'Look!' Griff told her.

Mattie caught her breath in wonder. She was witnessing her first prairie winter sunset. A dark tangle of undergrowth was poking through a powdering of white, the fence poles silhouetted against a spectacular sky heavy with snow clouds. Beyond lay the prairie and a ribbon of glorious crimson on the horizon streamed from the sinking sun. Mattie wished she could see the creek reflecting this, but it was too far off.

She must have swayed on her feet, for Griff's arms were instantly round her, holding her close to his chest. 'Are you all right? Not too cold?'

'I'm all right,' she said. 'Turn me round, so I can take it all in, again.'

As she leaned back against him, she whispered. 'Feel the baby kicking, Griff – he's aware something important is about to happen ...'

'Being born, you mean? Mattie darling, it might be a girl, you know ...'

'I'm not due for another four days – nothing must happen until Anna is here!'

'Well, listen, isn't that the sound of a motor in the distance?'

'Now I can relax,' Mattie said, '*He* can come as soon as he likes!'

They sat around the big table, warmed by the crackling fire, eating the simple supper Mattie and Griff had prepared earlier – thick slices of gammon, a pile of buttery mashed potato, crusty new bread and more yellow butter. Mattie proudly offered sauerkraut, made by a German neighbour, and her own pickled onions.

'Like ping-pong balls!' Bert said, spearing a couple with his fork to eat with relish. He was not very tall, but thick-set and obviously had a good appetite.

'How are you, my dear'?' Anna asked Mattie. She'd noted the flickering of discomfort on Mattie's face, the biting of her bottom lip.

'Weary,' was all Mattie would admit. She'd eaten little herself. Her hands strayed to her middle, rested on her bump. The baby was quiet now.

'We can clear up here,' Anna said. 'Why not go to bed, rest up for tomorrow?'

Griff helped her to her feet. 'Anna is right, you need to lie down, Mattie.'

'You must come back to entertain the family, then,' she insisted.

'I will,' he assured her.

Mattie was restless. She flung the feather-filled ticking back, tried to sort out the tangle of sheets. Griff heaved a gentle sigh, swung his legs out of bed, and turned up the oil lamp. They used these to conserve electricity from the generator. He squinted at the clock on the bedside table. He was used to rising early. Christmas morning would be no exception, he thought wryly, with the cows to be milked. No doubt Bert and Charlie would help him and Anna would see to breakfast, the traditional ham and eggs.

'Not even three o'clock,' he said aloud. 'You awake, Mattie? Happy Christmas.'

'Of course I'm awake!' She sounded truculent. No return of his greeting.

'Are you all right?' he asked anxiously, feeling her forehead.

She thrust his hand aside. 'I haven't got a temperature! I'm having a *baby*, Griff!'

'You mean—?'

'*Yes*! Don't get back into bed – fetch Anna!'

Anna, wearing a flannel wrap and with her hair hanging in long grey plaits down her back, took it all in her stride. Charlie and Bert, she said, would see to the milking; Griff had his fatherly duties to perform. These included resurrecting the fire, boiling water, making tea and rubbing his wife's back when called upon to do so.

Mattie wasn't behaving as he'd naïvely thought she would. She was in agony, and she didn't care who knew it. After one piercing shriek, when Griff murmured, 'Never mind!' she replied, through gritted teeth, 'Only a man would say that!'

Three hours later, Anna, concerned that the second stage of labour was delayed, passed a note to Griff, not wishing to alarm Mattie. *Time to fetch the doctor.*

It was freezing outside, so the motor took some time to start. Griff gave it a kick up the backside in exasperation. Tin Lizzie coughed irritably, then obliged. The doctor's house was in the main street. Griff banged so vigorously on the door that lights went on in several upstairs windows in nearby properties.

Doc appeared in his nightshirt and slippers. 'Come in,' he said laconically. 'Give me five minutes.'

Griff waited by the Christmas tree in the hall. From behind a closed door emanated excited voices. Doc's children were unwrapping their Christmas gifts. His wife emerged, yawning, with a paper crown on her head, to present the doctor with a warm woollen muffler. 'Your present from your mother, dear – she told me what it was, so I unwrapped it for you. Put it on! Good luck with the delivery,' she added, to Griff.

When they arrived back at the homestead, they found Mattie sitting on the edge of the bed. She had an announcement to make. 'I've decided not to have it today!' she said firmly. Anna's eyebrows twitched expressively.

Doc sat down heavily beside her. He still wore the scarf, powdered with snow. 'Is that so? The pains have subsided? Time to get you on your feet, my dear. Griff, hold her firmly and help her to walk round the room . . . back and forth, that's it . . .'

'Ouch!' Mattie exclaimed, leaning on her husband and panting at the exertion.

'The force of gravity; it often does the trick,' Doc said.

'I want . . . I want to—' Mattie gasped, before she doubled up with a contraction.

Between them they got her back on to the bed. Griff gripped her hand.

'You wish to stay?' Doc asked, discarding the scarf and rolling up his sleeves. Griff nodded. 'First, fetch me hot water, soap and towels. Anna, ease her into position. Now, young Mattie, no more yelling, save your energy for giving birth.'

The pain swamped her, receded, then returned. At its height, a cloth soaked in ether and pressed to her nostrils afforded blessed relief. Mattie made one last desperate effort. She was unaware of the drama about to take place as Anna, guiding the infant into the world, exclaimed: 'Quick! The cord's tight round the baby's neck!' Doc was leaning over Mattie, checking her pulse, so it was Griff who responded instinctively. Then Mattie heard cries, which grew louder by the minute.

'Darling, you've done it!' Griff was sobbing; she didn't understand it. A little bundle, wrapped in a warm towel, was placed in the crook of her arm.

Mattie was suddenly wide awake, trembling at the magnitude of what had just happened. She looked down at her baby's puckered, red face. The protesting ceased.

'Hello, baby,' she whispered. The small head was still greasy with vernix as the baby had not yet been bathed.

'Well?' asked a jubilant Anna, 'have you chosen a name?'

Griff said quickly, 'Mattie was sure the baby would be a boy ...'

Mattie smiled tremulously. 'You're trying to tell me it's a girl, aren't you? I really don't mind – so long as she's all right. You choose, Griff.'

'Would you mind, Mattie, if we called her after my mother? Megan Myfanwy.'

'Megan Myfanwy – our Christmas Day baby,' Mattie said softly. Tears of relief rolled unchecked down her cheeks. 'I could do with a cup of tea . . .'

'Couldn't we all!' said Anna, with feeling.

Christmas dinner was served late that afternoon. The turkey was dryish, with crispy skin, as Anna had been too preoccupied to baste it, but Charlie carved the best white meat for Mattie, and Griff plumped the pillows behind her, tucked a new flour-sack napkin embroidered with holly sprigs round her neck, then placed the tray carefully on her knees. 'Christmas dinner in bed – we're spoiling you today!'

'Oh, does that mean I'll be up and at the chores tomorrow?' she joked.

'Anna will decide how long you lie in,' he said firmly. 'You had a rough time.'

'I don't think I could go through that again in a hurry,' she admitted.

'Worth it, though, wasn't it?' He looked in at the baby, in the cradle.

'Of course it was! You'll send the family a cable as soon as you can, promise?'

'Promise. I'll ask your mother to let the rest know . . .'

'They won't be worrying too much with Christabel's wedding on Boxing Day!'

'Christabel and Walter have had a long courtship,' Griff observed.

'I'm so happy for them both,' Mattie said. 'I think Walter made his mind up to marry much quicker than she did, but I can't imagine him being a romantic, like you! While she was in Suffolk after losing dear Dolly, back in Mitcham, he studied all the situations vacant in the papers – that's how she got that good position in one of the best London stores! Aunt Mary took to her, and invited her to live with them!'

'Evie is to be a bridesmaid again, eh?'

'I guess she needed a new frock! She's in her last year at school, and will be off to college to train as a teacher in September.'

'See, despite the hard times, they are all doing well!'

'Mmm, Ronnie and Fanny – three boys now! – moving into the station master's house. Mother and Dad busy with bed-and-breakfast again, now that they get so many visitors touring round East Anglia by motor car . . .'

'The only ones we haven't heard from for a while are Sybil and Rufus,' he said.

'I hope everything's all right there,' Mattie said. She had a niggling feeling that something could have happened, but they were still on the farm, as far as she knew. Rufus was now managing his in-laws' affairs, and Sybil was involved with the local operatic society.

'Shall I take the tray?' Griff asked. Mattie nodded. 'Then you have a nap, like Anna and Charlie intend to. Bert and I are going to tackle the washing-up before we go back to the cowshed!' He paused at the door. 'D'you know where my old sketch book might be? I've got an inspiring new subject – Megan!'

'Try the bottom of the wedding trunk,' said Mattie before she closed her eyes.

SIXTEEN

The exterior of the Amy Able Ladies' College in Lincolnshire presented a somewhat grim appearance to the new intake of students about to pass through the portals. The majority, which included Evie, were in receipt of bursaries from various charitable trusts.

Evie had been interviewed at her school, in March. A formidable woman in a black gown, with a mortar board, sat alongside the headmistress in her study. The first remark she addressed to Evie was a disapproving comment on her appearance. 'I see you follow fashion, with that shorn hair. *Long* hair, suitably restrained, is required by our young ladies.'

Evie had been warned by kind Miss Jackson, who still resided at the Plough, that she must refrain from answering back. She bit back the retort that with curly hair such as her own, the only solution to controlling it was to keep it short.

When she remained silent, the headmistress said, 'Eveline will, of course, grow her hair from now on.' She smiled reassuringly at Evie.

'You are required to provide your own linen, two of everything. Clothes – no uniform as such, but you may continue to wear your gymslip, provided the hem reaches well below the knee,' the college professor went on. 'Stockings, at all times – and a hat whenever you are outside the college. You need a tunic or divided skirt, long socks and gym shoes for netball and hockey; physical exercise is essential for mental as well as bodily health.

If you are accepted, you will be given a list of books you must buy. There is no objection to your purchasing these second hand. We have an extensive library, thanks to our generous benefactors, and you should use that facility for extra study and research.

You will be expected to attend services regularly in our chapel. You are required to undergo a medical examination with your own doctor before your place is finally awarded; we have a matron on the premises to look after your general well-being. We can cope with minor disabilities, but the aim is for our young ladies to be stoics.

Evie couldn't help thinking that the Amy Able didn't sound very charitable!

Ronnie had accompanied her on the train to her destination, where a station wagon arrived to collect Evie and other students, and to convey them and their luggage to the college. She said goodbye to her brother on the platform.

'I wish you could come and see me settled in, Ronnie, but we are not allowed visitors, especially men! *No followers*, it states on the prospectus!'

'You'll get by, Sis,' he told her. He looked very personable in his uniform, and Evie caught one or two envious glances from other girls who were without an escort.

'Give my love to Fanny and the boys,' she said. 'Tell Mother to write to me soon!'

She turned and waved to him before she climbed aboard the wagon.

Ronnie hoped fervently that his young sister would be all right. She looked forlorn, her hair screwed back unflatteringly off her face in a fuzzy bun, under that pudding-basin felt hat. Three years! Incarcerated in what sounded like an institution.

Evie stood back from the main body of students in the hall. There were plaques on the oak-panelled walls, detailing the alumni of the Amy Able College. She regarded the picture of the founder in its gilded frame, painted some forty years before. Dr Able's gimlet gaze made her feel uneasy. Ahead of the group was a wide sweep of stairs with polished balustrades. There was a pervading odour which reminded her of the museums she had visited from time to time with the school, in the course of her studies. Here too, were DO NOT TOUCH and QUIET! signs.

The girls whispered together, rather than chattered, while they waited for a guide to greet them and take them to the dormitories.

'I must apologise for keeping you waiting.' They were startled by a cheerful, ringing voice. It was a pleasant surprise to see a smiling face, and a young woman not many years older than themselves. 'The porter will bring your trunks up; you can carry your hand luggage. First, I shall call out your names and tick you off, to make sure you are all here. Then please pair up, and follow me.' She waved a foolscap list at them.

'May I walk with you?' a tall fair-haired girl with glasses, asked Evie.

'Yes, of course! I'm Evie Rowley, and you are . . . ?'

'I'm Rhoda Jefferies. I brought my hockey stick. Did you?'

'I haven't one. Still, genteel sport will at least be outside, not in this mausoleum!'

'Shush!' Rhoda warned her, but it appeared from her wry smile that she agreed.

The dormitories upstairs were either side of a long corridor. Evie and Rhoda were allotted beds at the far end of the first room. The narrow iron bedsteads with biscuit-like hard mattresses awaited the new occupants' linen, marked with their names. The distance between the beds was the width of the bedside lockers. Each girl took the locker to her right. Trunks were placed at the foot of the beds to be unpacked. There was a linen press on the opposite wall. Clothes were hung on curtained rails. Cupboards were shared.

There were communal washrooms for each dormitory, with WC cubicles, basins and a single, screened bath. A sign read: DO NOT WASTE HOT WATER.

'You are allowed a weekly bath. You must adhere to a strict rota,' their guide, Miss Vanstone told them. She added, 'Nothing to stop you having a strip-wash daily, eh?'

The first thing Evie did was to take her family photograph from her bag. Rules stated that only one picture frame was allowed on the locker, so she'd made a montage of snapshots of her parents, her young nephews, and Mattie with Megan. On the back of this photograph Mattie had written: 'Megan looks like *you*, we think!'

'When you have made your beds and tidied yourselves, come downstairs in an hour's time. Two senior students will be waiting to take you to the dining hall, where supper will be served. Afterwards, there will be a short talk in the assembly hall, welcoming you to Amy Able, before you retire for the night. Lights out at 9.30 p.m.' Miss Vanstone looked round at them all. 'Any questions?'

'When do we begin our studies?' Rhoda Jefferies asked.

'Tomorrow, after you have familiarised yourself with the building and received your schedule.' Miss Vanstone left them to their chores.

'I'm not sure I'm going to like it here,' Evie observed to Rhoda.

'So far, to me it doesn't seem much different from boarding school,' Rhoda said. 'My parents are missionaries out in Africa, and I was sent back to England at six years old. Some of the girls I was at school with had nowhere to go in the holidays, so they had to stay at school. I was lucky, my aunt was my appointed guardian and I was able to spend Christmas and the summer with her family.'

Evie realised she was still wearing her hat. She took it off and flung it on the bed. 'Oh, I hate wearing this monstrous thing! I feel like jumping on it!'

'Why don't you, and relieve your feelings? It would bounce back into shape! Your hair – d'you always wear it like that?'

'Of course not! We were told we had to restrain our locks, weren't we?'

'Look,' Rhoda said sympathetically. 'I took that to mean tying it back or plaiting, not torturing it into a bun! It doesn't suit you at all. Where's your comb? I'll arrange it for you.' Evie's hair tumbled round her shoulders. 'Gosh, you have beautiful hair! Not greasy and straight, like mine. But . . . got a rubber band? Must obey the rules.'

'You sound like my sister! Mattie could always get round me, make me feel better. I still miss her, even though she left home five and a half years ago. She's married now, lives in America, though she went to Canada first, and she has a baby, Megan.'

'Is that them in the picture? I envy Mattie's blonde bobbed hair, too!'

'She wrote that her hair came out in handfuls after she had the baby, and the only thing to do was to get it cut, to help it recover! Actually, it really suits her. She looks a modern girl again. She was very fashionable at my age, but she has to wear practical clothes, living on a farm. Dungarees and heavy boots in winter!'

'I'm an only child. You are very lucky to have a sister. I'll help you make your bed up, then you can help me.'

They sat at long refectory tables to eat their simple but satisfying supper after saying grace: cheese-and-potato pie, nicely browned on top, with a fresh green salad. Baskets were piled high with warm rolls, butter was apportioned on a plate; there were jugs of water. When the main course had been cleared away, there was a choice between slices of Madeira cake, and apples picked from a small orchard in the college grounds.

'At least they've got a good cook,' Evie remarked to the girl sitting on her right. She was feeling better about things now.

'Mmm. No second helpings though!' the girl, Noreen Carter, said ruefully.

'Everything is worked out mathematically, I think,' Rhoda put in. 'Measured before it goes on our plates! Did you realise that there was only one roll each, and few small apples left?'

The tutor in charge clapped her hands. The girls looked up.

'Please follow me in an orderly fashion to the assembly hall. Cups of cocoa will be served to you there. Our principal, Dr Anne Withers, is waiting to welcome you.'

Dr Withers was a petite woman with a round, rosy face, a mass of untidy light brown hair escaping hopefully placed hairpins, twinkling blue eyes behind spectacles which she constantly adjusted on her nose, and a Yorkshire accent. She was informally dressed this evening, no doubt to put the students at ease, in a tweed costume.

Evie recognised her companion on the stage, who was sitting at the piano, as the one who had interviewed her, Miss Bates.

'Good evening and welcome to you all!' said Dr Withers. 'Before the cocoa arrives and we have our chat, will you please all stand for the college hymn. I imagine it is one you know, but as you will see,' she tapped a nearby stand on which was pinned a large sheet of paper with words written on it, 'here is a prompt. Are you ready, Miss Bates? To the tune of *St Patrick's Breastplate*.'

Miss Withers seemed oblivious to the squirming embarrassment of adolescent girls at the mention of 'breastplate.'

Rhoda, despite her parentage, was unabashed. She whispered to Evie, 'Needed by one or two of the well-endowed girls here, I think.'

It was Evie's turn to say, 'Shush!' as Noreen's figure was plump and unrestrained.

Back in the dormitory they undressed and tried to get comfortable in the hard beds. As there was only one pillow, it wasn't possible to sit up and read. Anyway, Evie was suddenly aware of just how tired she was after a full day.

She glanced over at Rhoda's bed. 'Goodnight. I can't wait for lights out . . .'

There was no answer for a bit, then Rhoda said, 'I was saying my prayers. Goodnight, and I'm so glad to have made a friend already.'

'So am I,' said Evie. She closed her eyes. Time to say a prayer herself, she thought; she'd lapsed in that respect since childhood. 'Dear God, please take care of all my family,' she managed before she fell asleep.

There was a rush for the washroom facilities at seven o'clock the next morning. By the time Evie had managed to get to a basin the hot water tap produced only a tepid stream.

'Just be glad we're females and don't have to shave,' whispered Rhoda in her ear.

'Shush!' Evie said again, for Noreen had tagged along with them, and was at the basin on her other side. Noreen had a dark smudge above her upper lip. She thought: when I get to know her better I'll advise how to disguise it, with a dab of hydrogen peroxide. She can tell Matron she needs it for a mouth ulcer. Those beauty tips Mattie passed on from Sybil may come in useful for others here, if not for me . . .

Breakfast was at eight o'clock. A boiled egg, one slice of bread and butter, thinly spread, apiece and a cup of tea, much weaker than Evie was accustomed to drink. Then it was off to the assembly hall again, where they were given their schedule of studies, followed by a tour of the college.

Despite her initial misgivings, Evie began to warm to her surroundings. There were plenty of specialist areas, like the gymnasium, with its climbing ropes and parallel bars, vaulting horse and wall bars. In charge here was a human dynamo in a green tunic, a wiry, small woman with a bellowing voice like a sergeant major on parade. She looked the students up and down and obviously thought them a weedy lot. Miss Vanstone, again their guide, introduced them to Miss Dodds.

'Some of you need to lose weight,' she said disparagingly. She pinched a fold of Noreen's waist. 'Don't tell me *that*'s muscle.'

Evie saw Noreen's eyes brim with tears. As they moved away to the next location, she told her, 'Better than being all *gristle*, like Miss Dodds! Anyway, we'll all lose a few pounds on college rations – I didn't dare ask for more bread and butter!'

The art room, with easels and a pottery area, was colourful with students' paintings on the walls. The science lab was well-equipped. Its counterpart, the domestic science kitchen, had pine preparation tables, and gleaming saucepans.

All these designated rooms were in the west wing; the classrooms were on the other side of the quadrangle. The new girls would be taught in the first two rooms, thirty to each class. During the first year they would continue their general education at an advanced level. The second year they would be assessed again and split into several groups. Some would opt to teach children under the age of eleven, others would prefer to specialise and teach specific subjects in senior schools.

Evie's main subjects would be English and history. Rhoda had a preference for mathematics and science. Evie found herself in a class sitting next to Noreen, whose strengths were art and English. She would only meet up with Rhoda for music lessons, which took place in the assembly hall, in the gymnasium, and at mealtimes.

At lunchtime they were given a light meal because the Amy Able dictum was: 'Heavy food in the middle of the day is to be avoided. Full stomachs make for afternoon lethargy. Minds should be sharp at all times in order to learn.'

'I hoped we would be in the same group,' Evie said disconsolately to Rhoda, as they ate steamed fish with a modest amount of mashed, unbuttery potato, and peas.

'So did I. Never mind. We can still be pals. Wish hard that we are about to receive suet pudding and treacle!'

'No such luck. Here come the prunes and custard . . .'

'Oh well,' Rhoda was invariably cheerful, 'at least we can count the stones and see who we'll marry. Rich man, poor man – you can stop at rich man, for me! Though of course I know that my destiny lies in the mission field – my parents expect it.'

'Well, I aim to be a dedicated teacher – my parents made sacrifices to keep me on at school, and so I should pursue a career.'

'You might change your mind, Evie.'

'Not much chance of that happening, while we're here!' Evie said, with a mock sigh. 'I haven't seen a single man unless you count the caretaker, and he only comes out when he thinks *we*'re not around!'

SEVENTEEN

1930

'Today is special, it's Mayday,' Gretchen observed, as she fixed a big satin bow to Megan's short black curls. The ribbon matched her yellow frock with the smocked bodice, which Mattie had made for her to wear now the weather was warmer. As she sewed she recalled herself as a child, dancing round the maypole at the village school, clutching one of the yellow streamers. It was still a favourite colour.

Gretchen Larsen, the youngest of seven children born of Norwegian immigrants, kept an eye on Megan while her mom and dad were delivering their fresh, farm milk and other dairy commodities, like butter, cream and cheese.

Despite the depression and the Wall Street crash last October, when even the small branch of their bank had been besieged by angry customers, Mattie and Griff had kept going somehow and were at last cautiously optimistic.

As Griff said then, 'The bank is only paying out ten cents to the dollar – just as well we hadn't paid in last month's takings before it happened . . .'

Bigger businesses than their small enterprise had been ruined, and many were deep in debt. Most relied on the barter system – exchanging grain for sacks of flour and other commodities for a share in a pig. Small family farms strove to be self-sufficient.

Megan, almost four and a half years old, was a fidget, as her Auntie Evie had been at her age, so her mom often told her. 'You look like her, too!' she would add. Now, she wriggled free of Gretchen's grasp, grabbed her shoes and demanded, 'Want to go outside!'

Gretchen snatched the shoes back. 'I was about to tell you, only you don't stay still long enough to listen, that this is the day we go *barefoot*. It's traditional.'

Megan was puzzled. 'Why? What's that?'

'We go barefoot today, and all summer, some of us, to mark the end of winter.'

'Mom says you'll hurt your feet with no shoes.'

'Well, Mom isn't here, and I've taken my shoes off too, see, and I'll keep a good eye on you outside to see you don't step on a rusty nail or in a cowpat.'

Megan brightened up at that; she enjoyed poking the steaming crust of those big blobs. She wouldn't mind treading on one of those, she thought. Besides, Dad had whispered this morning that she might pick her mom a bunch of flowers. 'Let's go, then,' she said, reaching up to rattle the latch on the kitchen door.

Mattie's garden was burgeoning. They usually had a surplus of vegetables in season due to her diligent planting. These were shared with their neighbours. Big families were given jugs of free skimmed milk and crab-apple jelly made by Mattie from the little sour apples from the tree in the yard. In return, their friends were generous with the little they had to spare. They kept each other going that way. Every family made the most of all the abundant wild fruit, families foraged for chokeberries (again so tart, with huge pips, that just the juice was used to make jellies), wild currants and juneberries, which were dark blue with tiny pips, and sweet. The children ate nearly as many as they picked.

There was a little clump of violets in the plot, like the ones Mattie had loved in her mother's garden. Megan trod, cautiously at first, on the gritty path, then confidently, on the grass verge. She picked the violets and Gretchen added some longer-stemmed white daisies with yellow centres. They stuck them in a glass jamjar half-filled with water, but forgot to place it in the shade, to collect on their way back from their walk.

Gretchen took Megan's hand. 'We'll go through the fields to the creek. I'll tell you a story or two. We'll have a paddle, and wash the dust off our feet.'

She didn't know it, of course, but this was to be one of Megan's earliest memories: swinging hands with Gretchen and wincing now and then when she trod on a hidden stone, but not saying, because she was listening to Gretchen's Norwegian tales. 'Ten times more snow in winter than we get here! My parents used to ski to school and they fetched shopping on a sledge...'

The sun was warm on their bare heads, but the wind whipped around, as it always did, unchecked across the miles of wide open spaces. The satin bow slipped from her curls, dropped to the ground and nestled in the long grass which edged the crops, lost for ever. The water in the creek was clear enough for them to see tiny, silvery, darting fish, but still cold enough to make you catch your breath. Megan wished she had long legs like Gretchen, because the water came almost to her chubby knees.

Gretchen was sixteen years old. This was her first paid job. With her round face, snub nose and long plaits she appeared young for her age, but she was very capable.

They were away from the house longer than they intended. Mattie came up the path to meet them, clutching the jar of wilting flowers. 'Where on earth have you been!' Then, seeing their bare feet, 'No shoes? What are you thinking of, Gretchen?'

'Day to go barefoot, Missis,' Gretchen said simply. 'The violets are for you.'

'Oh dear, I forgot,' Mattie said. 'Thank you.' She suddenly recalled the scolding she'd received from her own mother when Evie slipped up in the stream one day while they were gathering watercress. She must make amends, as Sophia had done when she realised she'd overreacted.

'Come along, let's make some griddle-cakes and have them with maple syrup.'

How Mattie sighed in the warm weather when stubborn Megan insisted, 'No shoes.' Megan only gave in on Sundays, when she went to the afternoon service in the little Lutheran church with her mom, accompanied by Gretchen and her family.

Mattie thought the church looked something like an illustration from a children's fairy-tale book. It was a simple design, painted white with fascinating small windows – diamond-shaped, oblong, rectangular and square. There was a tower rising above the central building with a conical roof topped by a beautiful gleaming cross. It appeared to be in the middle of nowhere, with the prairie stretching out on either side, and during the winter this impression was intensified when the ground was blanketed with snow. This covered the cemetery too, beyond the palings.

The main body of the church was furnished with pale pine; there were chairs rather than pews, a font made by local craftsmen, a polished wooden cross, and a little organ which was worked by bellows.

Megan sat between her mother and Gretchen, turning the pages of her hymn book when they did, though she sometimes held the book the wrong way up. The service was conducted in English, though most of the congregation were Norwegians, like a handsome lad called Chittle, which mom said was nothing like the spelling of his name, Kjetl. He had his eye on Gretchen, she added with a smile.

Griff, having finished the chores, would be there when they emerged from the church, to drive them back to the farm.

One particular Sunday, at the beginning of June; they arrived home to find a surprise visitor. It was Bert. He had taken his final examinations at college, and was now looking for a job. Even though he was about to become a qualified engineer and had applied to the Great Northern Railway, so far he'd had no luck.

'Thought I might help out here till then – that's if you'll have me?' he asked.

'You must have read my mind,' Griff told him. 'If only Bert was here, I thought, Mattie would be free to put in action a plan she's been set on . . .'

'Oh, what's that?' Bert said, gulping hot tea from a big tin mug, which had hung in the pantry awaiting his return. He was unaware that young Megan was staring, fascinated, as his Adam's apple bobbed up and down in his throat.

'I'd like to take up an offer from the grocery store. To make and sell my ice cream two or three times a week on the premises, during the summer. They have a big freezer there. We would need to invest in an electric machine, with paddles to whip up the mixture in a bucket, much smoother than by hand, but we would use our own milk, cream and eggs.'

'Mattie is already famous locally for her delicious ice cream,' Griff put in.

'Don't think about it – do it,' Bert advised.

'All right, I will!' Mattie said.

'Well, how're the cows doin'?' Bert asked. He held out his hand to Megan. 'Pull me out of my chair, eh, and we'll go and see, shall we?'

Giggling, Megan pulled at his hand and he instantly sprang out of the chair. 'Strong girl you got there, Griff.'

'Gretchen's stronger'n me,' Megan told him.

'Who's Gretchen?' he asked, as they went out and along the track to the meadow. The cows were now allowed out of the big barn – it had been a long winter, spent inside.

'She looks after me while Mom's at work.'

'Got a job and a half then, I reckon,' Bert observed. He had slung his camera case round his neck before they came out. 'Had your picture taken lately?' She shook her head. 'Well, let's see if I can get a good one of you today.'

Megan was a trifle nervous of the cows now that they were not confined. They lifted their heads from grazing the grass and stared at the little girl standing on the bottom rung of the gate as the young man with her, pushed it open, waited for her to jump down, and then secured it again.

Three of the young heifers decided to meet them half-way. Their jaws moved rhythmically as they chewed the cud. Their long eyelashes flicked at the flies.

Megan tugged at Bert's sleeve. 'Lift me up!' she demanded. He obliged, encouraging her to stroke the head of one of the Red Poll cows. Then he said, 'Here, sit on her – she's a gentle gal – she won't throw you off. We got friendly when I visited last fall. I'll take a quick snap.'

'She's got a bony back,' Megan said, cautiously feeling it. But she wasn't frightened because Bert was calm, and so were the cows.

She was still wearing her best Sunday shoes, but she got her wish to tread in a cowpat, and then wished she hadn't, because despite Bert's best efforts to clean her shoes in the grass, the stains and the smell were evident when they went in the house. Luckily, her dad saw she was in trouble and quickly removed her footwear before her mom could scold her. Bert rubbed her feet with a damp rag.

Gretchen walked over with a covered dish sent by Mrs Larsen for their tea. She'd heard along the prairie grape-vine that the Parrys had a visitor.

Mattie introduced Bert to Gretchen and the two greeted each other shyly.

'Stay for tea, Gretchen, then you can take back the empty plate, and Bert will walk you home,' Mattie said.

Griff caught up with her in the pantry. 'Matchmaking already?' he teased.

'Nonsense,' she said unconvincingly. 'She can tell her mother how much we enjoyed her honey cakes if she sees us eat them.'

That night, when her mom tucked her up in her bed, Megan said sleepily, 'I wish Bert could stay for ever! He's got his own room, up in the roof, hasn't he?'

'Yes, but he needs a proper job. He deserves it, after all his hard work at college. He won't be able to play with you all day, Megan. Not only is he going to help Dad with the cows, and the deliveries, he'll be working part-time at Harry's garage too. Still, Gretchen will be able to bring you along to the stores for an ice cream when I'm busy there – that'll make you happy, I know! Goodnight, Megan dear.'

'Goodnight,' Megan said, snuggling down and thinking of vanilla ice cream cones.

Evie had graduated the previous summer; she sent Mattie and Griff photographs of the occasion.

'Rose between two thorns,' Griff observed, for Evie had matured into a strikingly attractive young woman and her companions, Rhoda and Noreen, looked much more like the schoolmarms Mattie remembered from her schooldays.

'They both have nice smiles,' she observed kindly. 'And Evie says the three of them will be friends for ever . . .'

However, Evie was evidently keeping in touch with her friends by letter, as she did her sister. It had taken her some months to find a permanent position. After a spell at a poor school in a slum area in the East End of London she'd returned home, to a post as a junior English mistress at her old school. She wrote to Mattie:

It seems as if I have never been away! Miss Jackson – yes they are still with us at the Plough – gives me a lift to school in her little car. I help with the netball team and enjoy the friendly matches with other schools. I have a very enthusiastic English group. We are rehearsing A Midsummer Night's Dream for an end-of-term performance . . .

Mother and Dad are well, and busy with visitors. Ronnie, Fanny and the boys send their love. Fanny is expecting again after all this time. They are hoping for a girl. How about you? I do wish I could see that lively little Megan – is it a compliment, when you say she takes after me?

I haven't heard from Christabel lately, have you? It doesn't look as if she and Walter will have a family.

Oh, did you know that Griff's stepfather has had a stroke? A full recovery seems unlikely, Sybil says . . .

'Well, "how about you?" ' Griff quizzed her as she sat at the breakfast table, drinking the first cup of tea of the day. Shortly he would be pulling on his boots and making ready for the early milking; they could hear Bert moving about up aloft, doing the same. Megan was still asleep in bed; Mattie would not leave the house until Gretchen came.

Mattie put down her empty cup, folded Evie's letter and slotted it back into the envelope. She was well aware of what Griff was getting at. He thought they should have a brother or sister for Megan before she went to school.

'Oh, Griff, you know we agreed to wait until we could afford fulltime help with the farm and the dairy – and now—' She paused, shaking her head.

'You've committed yourself to your new venture,' he concluded. Mattie and Megan, he thought, were the most important people in his life.

'Yes I have.' She rose, moved swiftly towards him and hugged his shoulders as he heaved on a boot. 'You know how much I love you – want to please you, but—'

'You *do* please me,' he said quietly, making her blush. Theirs was still a passionate union. The only time you disappointed me was when you cut your hair, but now, I like it.' Her hair was thick again, curving round her face in a shining bob.

'It's the only part of me that's fashionable nowadays! Which makes me think of Plymouth, and Sybil and Rufus. I do hope things are not as serious as Evie thinks.'

The cable came less than a week later: REGRET SAD NEWS. RUFUS PASSED AWAY TWO DAYS AGO. WRITING SOON. LOVE SYBIL.

'I'm glad they resolved their differences,' Griff said to Mattie, 'and enjoyed a few happy years together.'

EIGHTEEN

SEPTEMBER

Christabel and Walter were spending the weekend at the Plough. Fanny and Ronnie's new baby daughter was to be christened on Sunday. Evie and Mattie were little Sophy's godmothers, Christabel was standing in as proxy for Mattie. This made good sense, as Walter was the baby's godfather.

Sophia was thrilled to have the baby named after her. Will gently reminded her that she mustn't neglect their three grandsons, on whom she had doted until now.

'Let Evie hold her, she's used to babies, unlike me,' Christabel whispered in Fanny's ear, as parents and god-parents walked to the font for the baptism.

The baby was asleep until the holy water was poured over the crown of her head. By then, she'd been passed, wrapped in her crocheted cobwebby shawl, to the parson. She gave an indignant yell. Everyone present approved her reaction – part of the tradition. Duly named, and dried, Sophy was returned to her proud parents.

'Mattie should have been here,' Christabel said to Evie, as they walked back to the house together. Christabel clicked along in high-heeled shoes, while Evie strode out in her comfortable T-bar-strapped sandals.

Evie glanced at her. Christabel was very much a city girl, she thought, with Marcel-waved hair, smart grey flannel suit with velvet cuffs and collar, a wide-brimmed hat and sheer silk stockings. Quite a contrast to herself, in her good school skirt and plain cream blouse. 'All good experience. Has it inspired you?' she asked frankly.

'No ... Walter's mum keeps dropping heavy hints, but ... you can't have two women in one kitchen. The truth is, Evie, despite the recession, I'm really doing well in my current job, and I'm in line for promotion. I'd never have achieved that at the emporium, in Plymouth – though I'll always be grateful to Mr Fullilove for giving me my first chance. There is another reason, which I hope will show that I am not altogether selfish—'

'Oh, Christabel, I'd never think that of you!' Evie interrupted. 'I know how you cared for your mother and put her first, taking on responsibility at an early age—'

'Doesn't that sound like you, too, Evie? I don't regret those years, for one moment. But my mother's doctor warned me that her illness could well be inherited, if not by me, perhaps by a daughter, if I had one. I discussed it with Walter, and we agreed, we shouldn't risk it.'

'Well, I'm glad you were able to talk about it. How is Walter doing at work?'

'He finds selling insurance dull at times, but it is a job. Badly paid, but necessary. We are lucky to be in full employment. How about you?'

'I know I am in the right profession. I'm happy!'

'I wish you could find a partner in life – someone like dear Walter, or Griff!'

'As they are both taken there's not much chance of that!' Evie smiled.

Christabel stumbled, held on to her friend's helping hand. She guessed that Evie still carried a torch for Walter, as she did for Griff, despite her contented, loving marriage. Neither of us will say, she thought, but it brings the two of us closer together.

The papers back home were full of 'the gathering storm' in Europe. On the prairies summer storms at night were frequent, as they were to be all through the thirties, rolling in from the west around dusk, causing fear and havoc until the early hours. The sky was rent by the electric zig-zag of forked lightning and the thunder exploded like gunfire, reminiscent of trench warfare to any veterans. The sheet lightning, however, without the rumbling thunder, was even more terrifying and unexpected.

Bert came down white-faced from his loft room one morning. 'I couldn't help thinking: my bed is against the chimney wall and that lightning might flash down the flue and strike the iron bedstead,' he said. 'My, I was *quaking*!'

'Megan came rushing into our room and dived under our covers,' Mattie said ruefully. 'I guess it's my fault because my mother was terrified of storms too, and I feel compelled to carry out the same rituals as she did, when I was a child. Covering the mirrors and making sure all the cutlery is shut away in the drawer . . . Scissors, too. Anything made of shiny metal, Mother said, could attract the lightning. We were told to keep away from water, even the washing-up! All the windows and doors were shut.

'Mother was certainly right about one thing, when she said, "A storm will turn the cream." I don't suppose I will be making ice cream today, eh?'

'Ooh!' Megan said reproachfully.

Griff was rubbing his tired eyes. He hadn't had much sleep either. He'd ventured out a couple of times to check the cows, and to bring the terrified yard dog into the kitchen. 'This darn drought worries me – if we don't get some rain soon to dampen things down, there'll be dust storms. The wind will see to that.'

He and Bert ate their porridge standing up and, after gulping down their tea, they departed to see if there was any damage to the barns.

They were lucky on this occasion, but Gretchen reported later that Kjetl's father had not been so fortunate. 'Their big barn was struck – no lightning-rod conductor, he says. It didn't catch fire like another of their barns did a few weeks ago, when they had to rescue the horses and my dad and the boys rushed over to help put out the flames. Anyway, this time the flash hit a rafter and travelled down a stud against which Kjetl's dad had leaned his pitchfork. It split the handle clean down the middle. At least the women didn't have to form a human chain with buckets to douse that! Kjetl's dad said that handle was over twenty years old, and had been good enough for another twenty!'

Megan was not the only one who missed Bert when his patience was rewarded with an offer of a four-day working week as an engineer on the railway. Gretchen kept asking, 'Heard how Bert is getting on?' so Mattie copied out his address for her and suggested, 'Why don't you write and ask him yourself?'

This coincided with the onset of colder weather and a slump in the sales of ice cream, so Mattie resumed her dairy duties and deliveries. Tin Lizzie conked out and Harry at the garage, advised Griff to part-exchange her for a nippy little truck, which had room for a couple of passengers on the front seat, and would transport their products. Mattie learned to drive in a week. The wagon horses still had a role to play on the farm.

Megan liked visiting the garage. It was a square building which Harry had put up himself next to the general store. He lived in an apartment over the store, which had originally belonged to his parents. On the fore court was a single gas pump, and when Harry was in the pit examining the underside of a motor, and a horn sounded, Griff would leave his desk in the cramped office at the side and 'fill 'em up', as he put it.

'Don't touch that,' he warned his inquisitive daughter, whether it was the spike on which the bills were impaled, or the precarious pile of oil cans in a corner.

The rafters were used as repositories for various bits of small equipment. Harry, a kindly, middle-aged chap who wore greasy overalls and a flat cap, was amazingly athletic. He climbed a swaying ladder to retrieve items and sometimes swung perilously by one hand or hooked his knees round a rafter to reach what he was after. Harry was a jolly bachelor, but he had a twinkle in his eye when ladies were around. He was light on his feet at the church social dances, so he was popular in the Paul Jones. He hadn't married, he said, because, 'Who would put up with all the dirty washing, and all the noise, oil spills and smells?'

Megan agreed that the smells in the general stores, from sacks of meal to jars of mint humbugs were nicer! Her favourite thing was watching Mattie press dollops of yellow ice cream into cones. She waited her turn, until the queue of kids was satisfied.

The hamlet was expanding all the time, with more folk settling and building there. It was fast becoming a small town, with a bandstand and a war memorial, in the form of a cross, dedicated to those who died in the Great War. Half a dozen men were honoured belatedly. The local newspaper opened a one-room office, with a barber's shop above, and Harry's nephew had smartened up an old property into a café, which was proving very popular.

There were no evergreens on the prairie, but plenty of deciduous trees, many of which reminded Mattie of home, like ash, box elder and willow. The willows, together with cottonwoods, were always near water. Mattie loved to watch the lofty silver maple trees in her garden, planted by their predecessors, from her kitchen window, when she was standing at the sink. Silvery leaves shimmered, twirled and danced in the breeze, as if in time to the music from the wireless. Mattie thought that a wonderful invention!

There was one last foraging expedition to gather wild fruits that fall. Griff and Mattie hurried through their morning chores in order to keep their promise to Megan and Gretchen to take a picnic lunch up the hillside.

'Why? Why'?' Megan demanded to know, when she saw things that caught her imagination on their walk to Hickory Hill, known as Old Hick. She pointed out the rock piles which appeared to have been placed haphazardly on the outer edges of the fields.

'Ask Dad,' Mattie said, with a sigh.

Griff told his daughter. 'I'm not sure if you can understand it yet, but you will, when you learn about it at school. There were ancient glaciers – I'll show you a picture in a book when we get back home – and these great blocks of ice melted and the rocks were left. The settlers had to dig them out of the ground before they could plough it. That's how they got piled up like this.'

Gretchen had been listening attentively too. 'You know my friend Kjetl? Well, he was ploughing with the horses once on his dad's farm and the plough hit a *huge* rock and he was thrown in the air, but somehow he landed back in the seat and not on the ground. Every bone in his body was jarred. His dad said the same thing had happened to him when he was a boy, so lightning *does* strike twice in the same place—'

'You said it was the plough, not lightning!' Megan interrupted.

'Something I *do* know,' Mattie said now. 'The Indians found a lot of uses for these rocks before the settlers piled 'em up. They made hammers, axes, and ground seeds with the rocks. My friend Treesa, at Moose Jaw, told me that. When the Indians moved from place to place, before the pioneers came, they used the stones to hold down the edges of their tepees. I haven't seen one yet, but they say there are circles of stones to show where they camped.'

They had arrived at the slopes. Nimble Megan ran ahead, pausing only to pluck a few currants still clinging to the shrubs, and eating them, because she couldn't wait for Gretchen to come up with the basket.

'Don't touch that prickly cactus!' Mattie called out in warning. She knew her daughter would find those smooth oval berries tempting now that they had turned from green to a ripe red.

'You *can* eat 'em,' Gretchen asserted, 'but they're all sticky jelly inside and full of seeds. Don't worry, Missus, I heard Megan yelp when she got too near them spines . . .'

Megan knew better than to pick the little wild plums. The locals said they were poisonous, but Mattie suspected that they were tasteless, with tough skins like the ones back home. They weren't worth canning. 'Leave them for the wildlife,' as Mattie said.

They ate their cheese-and-pickle sandwiches and ginger cake and drank tea from the flask. Megan was reprimanded for throwing her crusts into the bushes. She had an answer, of course. 'I'm feeding the wildlife, Mommy.'

While Mattie and Gretchen cleared up the remains of the picnic, Griff and Megan went exploring further up Old Hick.

'When the snow comes,' Griff told his daughter, 'We'll come up here with a sledge and slide down all the way to the bottom!'

'Promise, Dad, *promise!*'

'All right, I promise. But in return, you must help your mom fill the baskets, eh?'

He watched as she hurried ahead, to fulfil her part of the bargain. Megan will be five this Christmas, he thought, and it won't seem long before she starts school, after that. Maybe I'll never have a little son to work with me on the farm, but Bert was right, when he said Megan is a girl and a half! She takes after my lovely Mattie, of course . . .

Griff felt in his inside pocket for his sketchpad and charcoal. He was in the habit of 'capturing the moment' where his daughter was concerned. They had quite a gallery of sketches pinned to the living-room walls. Mattie had been inspired by these to write a diary of 'the dairy on the prairie' as she called it. 'One day,' she said, 'we'll put our pictures and prose together and make a book!'

Later, when they were in bed, and Megan was fast asleep, still with traces of purple from the squashed berries on her hands and round her mouth, Mattie said, 'They are just like indelible ink! You need several good washes to remove them,' Griff hugged Mattie close and whispered: 'It was a good day, wasn't it? One for the diary!'

'Mmm,' she agreed.

'D'you ever regret coming here, Mattie?'

'Never,' she said firmly.

'We haven't been able to keep our promise to visit home. It'll be nine years next spring since we left Southampton, after all.'

'They understand, Griff. We can't afford to take time off work.'

'I know – but I don't like not to keep my word . . .'

'You're a very honourable person, Griff, and I love you for it,' she said.

NINETEEN

They always looked forward to the Christmas mail. There were birthday cards for Megan, of course, cards with warm greetings from family and friends, the ones from back home depicting snow scenes, not unlike here!

Mattie particularly enjoyed catching up with the once-a-year correspondents. This included Grace, with news of her family and recent changes in circumstances.

Dear Mattie and Griff,

Tommy graduated with honours from high school this summer. He applied, and was accepted by the Canadian Air Force. His ambition is to be a pilot. His father would have been so proud. The base is not too far from home, but he has not had a long leave yet.

Dear Mrs Mack has retired and I have at last regained my status as Housekeeper! I have staff under me now, and a good stipend.

These events have given me courage to sort out my marital arrangements. Edwin has moved into Tommy's room, and Lydia is sharing with me.

She is nine years old now but I have refused to allow her to work towards her keep, as Tommy had to do. Lydia and her father get on well; he found it easier to be a father when she was no longer a baby.

You asked in your letter if I had seen Mungo lately. The answer is no. He wrote to Tommy to congratulate him on his success . . .

Mattie sighed as she read the last paragraph of Grace's letter. Such a pity, she thought, that Grace and Mungo had met at the wrong time. Their attraction for each other had been immediate and strong, but they resisted temptation to take things further. Yet, life had obviously taken a positive turn and Grace and her family were doing well.

'Good for Tommy,' Griff said, when he heard about his ambitions.

The mail arrived at breakfast time. Mattie put the birthday cards and a couple of parcels addressed to Megan to one side. She must wait a few days! There was a letter from Sybil. Mattie handed it to Griff. 'You open that one!'

Griff glanced at the content, showed surprise, then read aloud:

Dear Mattie and Griff,

I apologise for not being in touch lately, but as you will see from the following, I have been very preoccupied!

Since Rufus passed away I have been caring for my parents, both suffering from increasing bad health, with help from my faithful Hilda, without whom I could not have coped. I had to get a manager in to deal with the farm – I have no talent in that respect.

I lost my father six weeks ago, and my mother only three weeks and two days later. As you may know, my parents were in their early forties when I was born, I am their only child, they were both over eighty, so it has not been such a shock as it was when Rufus died at just over the age of fifty.

I have already decided what to do. Money is no longer a worry. The farm will be sold, lock, stock and barrel. I have nothing to keep me here. I think of you as my family. If it can be arranged, I would like to join you in North Dakota, but only if that is what you want, too. There is the usual problem, in that I will need sponsors. Can I ask for your assistance in this respect?

As farm life has proved not to be the one for me, I would be looking to live in a nearby town, and would hope to be involved in a project dear to my heart, but also to see you often and I would be very willing to help in times of need.

I shall see that Hilda is set up for the rest of her life. She wishes to remain in England.

Please think this over carefully, and let me know what you decide. It would probably take several months to come about.

It would mean so much to me to be with you and to meet your lovely daughter.

May I wish you all a joyful Christmas, and Megan, a happy birthday.

With fondest love from Sybil.

'Well, what do you think?' Griff asked Mattie.

'I think we should do all we can this end to make it possible. I know she says to think it over, but that's my immediate reaction, and yours, I'm sure.'

'Thank you,' he said quietly. 'Sybil, I always felt, was on my side when Rufus was being difficult. Minot would be the place for her. Shall I write and say yes?'

'Tell her it will mean a lot to us, to have her around,' Mattie said. She felt a familiar pang: if only Evie would come here too, wouldn't that be wonderful?

There were no deliveries to make on Christmas Day, though the cows still had to be milked. No Bert to help out this year, as he had to work over the Christmas period, but would have two days off later to spend with his family. Gretchen and Kjetl had offered to help in the morning and evening. 'We have our main celebration on Christmas Eve,' Gretchen said.

She didn't ask about Bert, and Mattie felt a little sad that her romantic notions regarding Gretchen and Bert had not come to anything. Maybe it was because Bert was not one for writing letters. But she also guessed that the Norwegians liked the thought of marrying one of their own. It strengthened the ties between them, working together for the common good. They were generous too with support for their neighbours.

The living-room floor was awash with Christmas and birthday wrappings as Megan tore her parcels open, sitting in her warm dressing-gown on the rug before the fire, on Christmas morning.

She was pleased with all her presents, even the white box containing a pair of new school shoes with stout soles and high, laced fronts. The shoes were put to one side, the box would shortly become a doll's house at her mother's suggestion. Transparent, coloured wrapping from toffees eaten before breakfast, and silver paper which had contained chocolate coins would make stained-glass windows and tiny cutlery. There was a little cardboard cut-out clown with paper-fastener joints and strings to manipulate to make him dance; Megan would colour the clown with her crayons later. She had a pile of books which would keep her happily absorbed all winter.

'You are a very lucky girl,' Mattie observed.

'I know,' Megan said happily.

The workers were almost blown through the door by the wind, in a flurry of snow. They had cold, red hands which they held out gratefully to the glowing fire.

'My teeth are still chattering,' Gretchen said ruefully.

Mattie had laid on a second breakfast for them, and when they had warmed up they moved to the table where Griff carved thick slices of crumbed pink gammon, not the usual curls of ham that his wife and daughter preferred. Megan insisted that the boiled eggs should sit in the precious egg-cups decorated with brightly coloured cockerels which were the set her parents had brought from England.

'The cockerels didn't lay the eggs!' she told them solemnly.

'I somehow didn't think they did,' Kjetl said, equally straight-faced.

Mattie was not feeling too well; she had a thumping headache and a sore throat. She had dosed herself with hot lemon and honey and swallowed two aspirin first thing. She didn't want to say anything and spoil their enjoyment of Christmas Day. They had attended church on Christmas Eve, and it was then that she had experienced the shivery aches and pains which usually meant she was developing a cold.

Griff glanced at her with concern, but knew she would be cross if he commented.

'Well,' Gretchen said, looking at Kjetl, 'time for us to go home, I think.'

'Snowing quite hard now,' Griff observed, peering out of the window. 'Still, the worst hit is North Forks, I hear on the wireless.'

'Snow – oh good!' Megan wasn't interested in a place she'd not heard of before. 'Don't forget your promise, Dad – to pull me on the new sledge to Old Hick, will you?'

'Not today. You and Mommy must keep warm indoors. Thank you for your kind help this morning, Gretchen and Kjetl. Wish your families a good Christmas.'

'You sure you can manage this afternoon by yourself?' Kjetl asked diffidently.

'Yes, don't worry, but I will be glad to see you tomorrow.'

'We can do the deliveries for you,' Kjetl offered.

'Oh, are you old enough to drive?' Griff asked.

'We have both been driving round the farm since we were ten years old,' Gretchen put in. 'But Kjetl is seventeen and he can officially drive now.'

'We'll see, it depends on the weather – we may have to pull the sled after all!'

'We can do that!' they chorused.

When they had gone, Griff said to Mattie: 'Those Norwegian kids – they really thrive on hard work, don't they?'

'Did you know that Kjetl's little brother catches gophers for bounty money?'

Before her dad could answer, Megan butted in, 'Oh Dad, please can *we* catch gophers when we go to Old Hick, and buy lots of sweets with the money?'

'The gophers have sharp teeth, they gnaw at trees and burrow down in the soil to eat the roots of crops, but *you* won't have good teeth, if you eat any more toffee!'

*

By late afternoon Mattie was aware of a pain behind her ribs. She was sweating too, not just from the heat of the fire. Griff returned from the afternoon milking looking forward to turkey sandwiches and Christmas cake, having worked off the effects of a splendid dinner that only he could have done justice to. He found Mattie lying on the sofa with a cold flannel pressed to her brow, and Megan playing quietly with her dancing clown. No repast.

He tried a feeble joke. 'Rather a repeat of five years ago, eh?'

Mattie struggled to sit up. 'How can you say that!' She wept. 'At least I knew what was going on, then – and there was something good about to happen – Megan!'

'Yes, me,' Megan said uncertainly. It wasn't like her mother to be ill.

'You're very hot,' Griff told Mattie. 'You do have a high temperature this time. You need to rest in bed. I'll fill the stone hot-water bottle first.'

'Can we play snap?' Megan wheedled, showing her father her new cards.

'Let me just make Mommy comfortable, first. Then we'll have cake and mince pies and then we'll play cards – is that a bargain?'

'I think so.' Megan wasn't really sure what a bargain was.

'You must be tired,' poor Mattie said, as Griff slipped her nightdress over her head. She allowed him to help her into bed, to pile pillows behind her. She stretched her feet, clad in thick bedsocks, on to the warmth of the stone bed-warmer.

'I'm all right,' Griff insisted. He'd filled the water jug on the bedside table. 'I'd better keep my promise to Megan. I'll look in on you again soon . . .'

'You're so kind – I love you,' she said faintly.

'And I love you,' he told her. She mustn't know that he was worried sick about her. If things became worse, how could he go for the doctor, leave her and Megan?

By 8 p.m. when Megan was in bed, Mattie was worse. Every breath she took made her gasp with the searing pain in her chest. She clung desperately to Griff.

They didn't hear the first knock on the door until it was loudly repeated. Griff disengaged himself gently and hurried to see who was calling.

Gretchen and her father stood there, muffled in heavy coats and scarves, stamping their feet to warm them.

'Gretchen tell me your wife look not well. She ask me to bring her back to help you out,' Mr Larsen said in his slow, accented English.

'Thank God you're here!' Griff pulled them inside.

The visitors took one look at Mattie and acted swiftly.

'I got my truck outside and snow chains if I need them. I go for the doctor,' Mr Larsen decided. 'Gretchen get steaming kettle in room to help her breathe.'

When they arrived Doc, warmed by a generous nip of spirits from a flask, climbed aboard the truck and they began the cautious drive back to the farm.

It was a night Griff would never forget: a nightmare, he would say, except that he was awake and terrified. Gretchen's father had gone home to alert his wife to the emergency, but said he would return at first light. At Griff's insistence, Gretchen shared Megan's bed, but she slept fitfully, having said, 'Call me, if you need me, Mr Parry.' Doc and Griff remained at Mattie's bedside all night.

'I believe she has pleurisy, inflammation of the lining of the lungs,' Doc said. 'It may turn into pneumonia. There will be a crisis point. We can only watch and wait.'

The ambulance made it through the snow to the farm soon after daybreak. When Mr Larsen arrived he was despatched to Doc's house to telephone the hospital.

Mattie was rolled into warm blankets and carried gently outside to the waiting vehicle. She was lifted into the back and fastened by restraints to a stretcher bed.

'You must go with your wife,' Mr Larsen told Griff. 'We, your friends, will take care of your business. Gretchen shall stay to care for the little one, and the house.'

Griff kissed his small daughter. He tried to keep calm, for her sake. 'We are taking Mommy to the hospital, to be made better. Be a good girl for Gretchen.'

Gretchen cuddled her in her strong arms. 'What would you like for breakfast?'

'Pancakes,' Megan said hopefully. 'With lemon and syrup. Like Mommy makes.'

It was six weeks before they were able to welcome a frail Mattie home. No one told her how very ill she had been, but fortunately she had only vague memories of fever-ridden nights, the gasping for every breath, and the pain which had taken over her body. She had no concept of time. Sometimes she had been aware that Griff was sitting at her bedside, holding her hand, and once, she knew he was crying, but she couldn't say anything to console him.

Megan had started school while Mattie was in hospital. She walked there with Gretchen, as she now did to church on Sunday afternoons. She drew pictures for her mother, and the teacher and the other children made a special fuss of her, so although of course she missed Mattie she was made to feel secure and as happy as possible, in the circumstances. And she got plenty of hugs from her dad, as always.

When she and Gretchen returned from the school one day Megan had no idea that a wonderful surprise awaited her.

'Mommy!" she cried, rushing over to Mattie on the settee, still in her night clothes, and covered by a quilt. Her mother was so pale and thin, and Megan could hardly make out what she was saying, but she was smiling and holding out her arms to her.

Griff, standing by, watched anxiously, but didn't interfere, as mother and daughter embraced and kissed. He knew it would be hard to tell Mattie that the doctors had decreed it would be a long process before she was fit enough to get back to a normal life. She would be unable to resume her hectic working life on the farm. The weakness in her lungs would prevent that, especially in cold weather.

The friends had rallied round magnificently, but, come spring, decisions must be made. Griff knew they would have to let all this go . . . find another dream.

TWENTY

JUNE 1931

Mattie took the pictures down from the living room walls, interleaving them with great care between the pages of a scrap book. She'd already pasted in the stories she'd written, which Griff's pictures so vividly illustrated. He'd painted the design on the cover: OUR FAMILY STORY, PRAIRIE TIMES, 1925–1931.

The little house where they had been so happy, worked hard, and enjoyed life, was almost cleared of their furniture and belongings. Only a small table and one chair remained for Mattie to complete this last task in comfort.

She heard the arrival of the truck, then the door opened and Griff came in, as she closed the book and silently wrapped it in a piece of cotton sheeting.

'Are you ready now?' he asked. 'It's time to pick up Megan from school.'

She nodded, too emotional to speak.

'Come on then. We'll bequeath them the table and chair – somewhere to rest between the unpacking . . .'

'I must take a last look at my garden,' she managed.

He held out his hand for the book. 'I'll put it on the front seat in the truck. I'll meet you out the back.'

The flowers were wilting in the heat of day. The wind stirred the parched grass. Mattie could make out the cows moving slowly in the field beyond and the horses under the trees, tails swishing, no doubt at the irritating flies. The yellow rosebush was in full bloom. As she stretched out to pluck one, petals drifted lazily to the ground.

'Who will care for my garden?' she said aloud. 'To me, this will always be home . . .'

Griff gently touched her shoulder. 'Let's go. Before the new owners arrive, eh?'

In the spring they had mentioned to the Larsens that they must sell the farm, the dairy cows and the business, because if they tried to carry on they would most certainly be in debt. The hospital fees had drained them.

'You do not need,' Mr Larsen said, 'to pay us for our assistance. We help when and where we can.'

'We couldn't have continued this far without you!' Griff affirmed. 'But there will be no end to our problem, with my wife unable to work with me, unless we sell up.'

'Wait another week or two. I will find you a buyer . . . even for a scrabble-farm.' This was a description for a place without piped water or mains electricity.

The Larsen family grapevine was soon buzzing, and an offer was made, by a brother-in-law who wished to return to the family fold. He and his wife had no children of their own, but as they were aware that Kjetl was a most capable young man, they asked him to join them. 'If he should marry a suitable girl, one willing to work alongside us, that will be for our common good. I understand it is a family house,' his uncle said.

Kjetl, now eighteen, proposed to Gretchen, and was accepted. The marriage was arranged for this coming Saturday, when they would move in with their relatives. The wedding clothes would be no problem – the young couple would wear national dress.

'Gretchen is so young to be married,' Mattie worried as they drove to the school.

'You were not much older,' Griff pointed out, with a smile.

'I didn't really know anything about *anything*, you know . . .'

'You soon learnt. We both did, eh? Here we are, and Megan waiting at the gate.'

Megan's school bag was bulging with gifts from her classmates. She would start at her new school on Monday, in the middle of a term, which was daunting.

'Goodbye, good luck,' the youngsters called out, waving energetically.

There were other farewells to make, although they hoped to see most of their friends from time to time. Doc came out from his surgery, stethoscope round his neck, to tell Mattie she was looking much better, but not to try to do too much, too soon.

'We will still sell Mattie's ice cream,' the storekeeper said, 'Gretchen insists we keep the name. It will be the same recipe.'

Harry swung hand-over-hand along the beams in the garage, at Megan's request.

'Thank you, Griff,' he said, rolling down his shirtsleeves over his muscular arms. 'I appreciate you getting the accounts up to date, when you've been so busy. Join me in the café for a cup of Gary's good coffee and a slice of his crumble cake.'

'Smile, please!' Gary, in his spotless white apron, beamed, as he clicked his camera. 'I'll send you a copy when I've developed the photograph, and I'll put an enlargement on the café wall, so that folk will be reminded of the Parry family!'

'That's good. We'd best get on,' Griff said. 'It's a fair way to Minot and our new life in the city.'

'It'll take time to get used to city life again.' Mattie clutched the sheet-wrapped package to her, in the truck. They would be exchanging that for a small car tomorrow. The truck had played a vital role in moving their goods. She thought, I'll keep the scrapbook in the little trunk, as I won't be able to look at it again until I stop my inward crying. I'll take out the clothes that I last wore in Plymouth, even if they're out of fashion now, and pack away my dungarees. They're more patch than original denim; I probably won't wear them again, but they were given me by Ollie, at the trading post . . .

Minot had grown rapidly from humble beginnings and was designated a city in 1897. North Dakota had become a state in November 1889. There was still a strong Norwegian presence in Minot, with a good mixture of other pioneering descendants, which included Danish, German, English and Icelandic families. The Lutheran church remained prominent. The city was well-served by the great railway companies, there was an air force base thirteen miles north of Minot, excellent schools and colleges of further education and gas stations to fuel the increasing number of motor cars. There were well-stocked shops, cinemas and theatres, hotels, dance halls and musical entertainment – a lively social scene.

Their new home was on a lot developed by an enterprising builder, filling in the gaps between self-build houses erected a decade before. It stood in a pleasant, quiet setting with wide boulevards along which small trees, planted at intervals, bordered the sidewalks. It was a short distance to the small local shops and a dime store, so there was a sense of living in a village community. The city bustle was a bus ride away.

Number 43, a white-painted house behind a caragana hedge, had a front porch, with room for a swing seat, cane table and chairs, which had influenced their decision to buy the place. Somewhere to sit and entertain friends and neighbours.

Mattie longed to plant the front garden with a stretch of grass and flower-beds, but they were advised to clean and build up the soil with a first crop of potatoes. At the back was a square yard, still choked with builders' debris, but a concrete path had been laid and there were two poles for the washing-line.

The property next door was empty, but would soon be occupied.

The area of land around the house was small compared with all the space they had become accustomed to, but Mattie approved of the layout of the house. The rooms both up and down were a good size and there were interesting views from the windows. There was a lot of glass to keep clean and shiny, as Griff ruefully noted.

There was a gas cooker in the cream-walled kitchen, a boiler, which provided hot water; copious cupboards; a clothes-copper with detachable mangle, stowed under the draining-board by the deep sink; a walk-in larder with a cold cabinet, and dark-green linoleum on the floor. Their table and chairs fitted into the bay window recess.

Upstairs there were three bedrooms, a large airing-cupboard and a compact bathroom. There was a separate WC which they soon dubbed the sentry box.

The living-room had a double aspect, with windows at either end. The fireplace had a tiled surround, there was a picture rail, and Mattie thought immediately that the wooden plank floor needed shaggy rugs to make it more homely.

'The furniture's not in the right place,' she told Griff.

'We can soon shift it around, but not tonight, eh? I don't start my new job at the gas station until next Monday, there's plenty of time.' He flicked a switch, and the room flooded with light. 'Oh, the joy of instant electricity, Mattie!'

'Turn it off! We haven't any curtains up, either!' she protested.

On the floor above they could hear thumps and the banging of doors. 'Who would think one small girl could make so much noise?' He smiled. Megan was exploring, and she'd turned on every light upstairs, not caring about no curtains!

Mattie and Griff stood in the fading light. He drew her gently to him and held her close. 'I'll work hard tomorrow,' he promised. 'Let's heat up that casserole you prepared this morning, in the oven and have our first family meal in the kitchen. The agent lit the boiler, as promised, so later you and Megan can have a nice, relaxing bath, while I make up the beds – how does that sound?'

'*Perfect.*' The lingering kiss she gave him was full of promise for later.

Megan was pleased to discover that there were three children in the house next door but one. There were two boys, aged ten and nine, and their sister Kay, the same age as herself. She would be in Kay's class at school. Kay's mother said that when Mattie was satisfied that Megan was settled in she might like her to walk to school with Kay and her brothers. Mattie was actually rather hurt when, after the first morning, Megan said tactlessly, 'You don't need to take me any more, Mommy – I'd rather go with the Barkers!'

However, Megan didn't mind telling her parents what went on at school each day.

'I was just dreaming a bit, 'cos I know all my letters, and Miss tapped me on the hand with her ruler and told me to pay attention . . . I didn't close my eyes in prayers and she called me out the front . . . she said I didn't hold my pencil correctly . . . she said I stuck chewing-gum under my desk, but it wasn't me – honest, Mommy!'

'Oh dear,' Mattie said to Griff, 'That Miss sounds a bit of a monster! Megan's only a little girl, after all.'

'You're not going there to confront her, Mattie. Megan has to toe the line.'

Megan, apparently absorbed in rearranging the doll's shoebox house, heard their whispering. 'I got a gold star on the chart for being the best reader,' she put in.

'There you are, it's not all bad news!' Griff said.

He was smarting somewhat from the attitude of his own new boss. Griff had jumped at the chance to become an automobile salesman and to double up as bookkeeper at a big gas station on a busy road. There was a modest salary for the bookkeeping, which was guaranteed, but the salesmen were on commission, and the employer had his favourites. Life would continue to be a struggle, with a loan to repay. As Griff's boss remarked ominously, 'No one is indispensable if he don't meet the targets.'

Mattie had plenty to occupy her once Griff had dug over the front garden. Maybe Doc, she thought, would not have approved of her planting potatoes, shuffling along the ground on her knees. First impressions counted, and they were awaiting the imminent arrival of Sybil! She had purchased the house next door, but would stay with Mattie and Griff for a couple of weeks until her new home was furnished to her satisfaction.

The cab drew up outside number 43. Mattie was watching out for it, and hurried to the gate. An impressive array of luggage was decanted onto the path. Sybil had arrived in style, and looked as fresh as a daisy, but then, she'd travelled first class, all the way.

The cabbie carried the trunks and boxes into the hall. Mattie guessed there was more to follow. Sybil thanked him graciously and asked Mattie to sort out a generous tip from her purse. 'It will take me a while to get used to the new currency,' she said.

The beaming cabbie presented her with a card. 'Give me a call, if you need a cab.'

'I most certainly will,' Sybil said graciously.

When he had departed they went into the sunlit kitchen to drink coffee and to eat brandy snaps which Mattie and Megan had made, with varying success, the evening before. 'Hilda's specials!' Mattie recalled. Some of theirs were a funny shape.

They studied each other over the rims of their coffee cups. Mattie thought that Sybil had changed little in appearance since they had last met. Her hair was now ash-blonde, in a longer, sleeker page-boy bob. Her skin was smooth, her make-up as bold as ever: scarlet lips, darkened, curled eyelashes and finely plucked eyebrows. Sybil wore navy linen slacks, bell-bottom style, a fitted white jacket, with twinkling brass buttons and a jaunty beret. Mattie guessed it was an on-board-ship outfit.

'How do you spend your days?' Sybil enquired. She was relieved that Mattie was not pale and frail, as she'd expected after her serious illness. Mattie was a mature young woman, not the girl she'd been when they parted. She approved of Mattie's hairstyle, and button-through green and white candy-striped dress.

'I am concentrating on the garden. I like to be outside while the weather's fine.'

'What are you growing?'

Mattie giggled. 'Potatoes! Don't look surprised; I grew plenty on the farm.'

'Yes, but . . . *potatoes* in the *front garden* – it'll look like a jungle!'

'Visitors will have to fight their way through, then, won't they?'

'Oh, Mattie – you haven't changed in spirit at all,' Sybil said. 'I'm glad we've got some time to talk on our own, before the others join us.'

'Megan can't wait to see you; we had to coax her to go to school this morning.'

'Oh, don't make me sound selfish! I hope I've improved in that respect. I just wanted to tell you my plans, now I'm here. Get your opinion! I wasn't too sure, you know, whether it was fair to you and Griff to move into the house next door. It wasn't my original intention, and I want to assure you I don't want to intrude in any way—'

'You're family, Sybil! I know what you're trying to say, and I appreciate it, but we have honestly been looking forward to you coming.'

'Thank you! Well, first I must buy a small car. Griff can help with that, eh?'

'He'd be glad to, but . . . you can't drive, as I recall.'

'No, but you can, I understand! Would you be my driver, Mattie? I don't think it would take up too much of your time, and you would be paid, of course! I take it, that nod means yes. You look quite bemused, lost for words! You see, I know exactly what I intend to do: I shall open a beauty and hair-styling salon in the city – sell my own products. What d'you think? I could run courses for students in the art of make-up, too.'

Mattie found her voice. 'I think it's a great idea – I'd love to be involved!'

'It seems to me that women have become so used to the drabness of the depression, that they need a lift to their spirits. I don't want to sell in an exclusive fashion as I did back in Plymouth – I want to brighten the lives of women in general!'

'What will you call your business?'

'The Fullilove Beauty Experience. I think Rufus would have approved.'

TWENTY-ONE

APRIL, 1932

'It's good fun,' Megan observed, spooning up her breakfast porridge, 'having Aunty Sybil next door. She's taking me to the movies on Saturday afternoon—'

'Movies!' Mattie exclaimed. 'Back home we called it going to the pictures – that's all it was, when we left for Canada – now we have *talkies* . . . Can you choose the film?'

'Well . . . Kay's coming too, and her brothers said the new Harold Lloyd movie is *amazing* – he does tricks like Harry in the garage . . .'

'Fortunately, Harry confined his acrobatics to the garage beams. Well, off you go to school – it's time for me to honk the horn to let Sybil know her chariot awaits.'

'I haven't had a chance to look at the funnies yet,' Megan complained. 'Dad's allowed to read the paper at breakfast, why can't I?'

'Evie and I weren't permitted to read at the table.'

'That was in the old, old days, Mom!'

'Your dad says you'll look like Popeye if you keep reading under the covers when you should be asleep at nights. Got your lunch box?'

'Hope you made me corned-beef sandwiches? 'Bye, Mommy.'

'Have a good day, darling. Learn lots!'

As she went down the front path Mattie thought ruefully: Sybil's right, it *is* a jungle of potato plants but North Dakota reds are simply the best! In Sybil's garden, next door, the flower-beds appear to be manicured round the edges, and that's right for *her*.

She settled into the driving seat of the smart black box-shaped car, a new model from Ford, so easy to start after old Tin Lizzie. She squeezed the horn. No sign of Sybil yet. She sighed. Why does Sybil assume that she can take Megan out, and spoil her with treats, without asking me if I mind, first? Griff is happy with this, saying Sybil is family. It was he who suggested she should eat with us in the evenings – she still hasn't learned to cook, and as for housework, I'd have been landed with that, no doubt, if I hadn't known that Kay's mother was looking for a little job. Megan seems bewitched by her glamorous aunt – not that she's really an aunt, unlike Evie, whom she resembles so much, but Megan decided to call her that.

Mattie sounded the horn again, trying not to feel jealous. She reminded herself that Sybil often told them how happy she was to be with them again.

Sybil apologised profusely for not being on time. 'I didn't manage breakfast, so could we stop at the bakery on the way and buy a bagel?' Mattie nodded, as they drove off. 'D'you approve of my new perfume?' Sybil added.

Mattie smiled. 'It's very . . . potent. Have you named it?'

'Not yet. Any ideas?'

'I think you should call it "Sybil" Mattie said, tongue in cheek.

'Perfect!' Sybil agreed. 'I could hardly say that myself, but coming from you . . .'

'That's all right then, eh?'

The Fullilove beauty salon was situated in a parade of rather old-fashioned stores which had evolved from humble beginnings, opposite a modern lofty office block. There were beauty shops in the vicinity of the city centre, but this was a new venture here.

This was not a wealthy, big-business area, but it had survived the lean years, and seemed a good place to start working life. Stenographers in dark dresses brightened by colourful scarves and cinched at the waist by shiny patent leather belts (for hour-glass figures were back) and sometimes detachable white collars and cuffs, hurried in through revolving doors and took the lift up to one of the firms named on the brass plates in the foyer. The junior clerks wore tan-coloured rayon stockings and clumpy shoes; their superiors sported sheer silk hose and ankle-strapped shoes with heels. The majority were young or middle-aged, a good many were the family breadwinners, for unemployment had risen to twenty-five per cent. They shopped during the lunch-hour break. As professional women they must keep up appearances, and the salon had prices they could afford.

The beauty salon had been adapted from a store with an apartment above. The beauty treatments and hairdressing were accommodated downstairs. Upstairs, there were products for sale, and helpful assistants, who would oblige by filling the customers' own containers with lotions and creams. Beyond the sales area there was a door to the balcony. This spring, Sybil had invested in café tables and chairs and set them out. Clients were welcome to eat their packed lunches overlooking the busy street and to have a cup of freshly made coffee 'on the house'.

Sybil watched from the doorway to wave Mattie off, then she turned and went inside. She wished she had been able to persuade Mattie to work part-time in the salon, but Griff had worried that it would be too much for her. She inhaled with pleasure the exotic scents. The whole place was decorated in pale pink with chrome fittings. There were comfortable cane chairs, with heart-shaped cushions, a treatment couch, mirrors everywhere, a manicure bar with stools to perch on, and manicurists behind the counter. The curtained cubicles were for those requesting privacy. At the rear of the long salon a door marked PRIVATE led to a suite of rooms where new products were tested by an expert in the field before going on sale. Earlier, Sybil had been disconcerted when warned by the consultant, Lloyd Morris, that some preparations must be modified because of a toxic content. She'd learned to accept his wise advice.

She was greeted by members of staff she passed by on the way to her small office. They were pretty, smiling girls who naturally used Sybil's potions themselves.

Dolores, who dealt with the appointments book, was sitting at her desk, telephone in hand. Sybil lifted her hand in silent greeting, then hung her jacket and hat on the stand in the corner. She went to her desk by the window, but before shutting her handbag in a drawer, she removed a brown-paper bag. The bagel was still warm. She took a bite. Dolores would make her a drink when she had finished her call.

They drank their coffee together. Dolores had a doughnut in lieu of breakfast. She was enviably slim despite her consumption of such items, with a dark, natural beauty, large, expressive eyes and perfect white teeth, unlike many girls of her age who'd grown up in a poor area. Dolores was ambitious, already achieving at age twenty-two.

'No treatments booked until eleven,' Dolores observed. 'Axel is hoping you will have time to watch him using the new permanent wave machine – he has a client coming at 9.30 a.m.'

'Curls are in vogue again – the short, straight styles don't flatter all faces, do they? So I hope we soon recoup the outlay,' Sybil said. 'I may have a permanent myself . . . ' She remembered how she'd transformed her appearance, and upset her parents, when at sixteen she'd bleached her mousey locks, and begun experimenting with make-up.

The croquignole method of permanent waving had been developed for the liberated woman, freeing her from the time-consuming ritual of caring for long hair, when crimping meant applying sizzling-hot tongs, or curling with rags which were uncomfortable to sleep on. These curls were short-lived, especially when it rained.

Axel's client looked definitely nervous, despite the hair-stylist's soothing chatter as he wound strands of hair tightly on steel rods upwards to her scalp. There was a strong smell of chemicals, and she closed her eyes, which were smarting and watering. Fearsome dangling clamps were attached to the rods, the machine vibrated, and the resulting steam, with a strangulated yelp from the client, caused the audience to retreat.

'Phew!' Sybil told Dolores. 'I need more coffee. I hope she won't sue us!'

'Best dollar I ever spent,' said the satisfied client, some hours later. Her scalp still tingled, but the deep waves in her hair were indeed impressive.

Sybil was relieved that the client still possessed a full head of hair. However, she decided to forgo the experience herself. She was rather glad that the clever, aloof Mr Morris had not been at work today. He might well have disapproved, she thought.

Mattie was feeling at rather a loose end back at home. She'd found a letter from Evie waiting on the mat.

Been having fun! Mother said I must get out and about more, so I took her advice! Went to stay with Christabel and Walter for a few days during Easter break from school. Walter had to work, but C had two days' holiday owing, and was able to accompany me to the Crystal Palace – a wonderful experience! – I had my picture taken leaning against a dinosaur! I certainly wouldn't have got that near if it had been real!! The girls at school will have a giggle when I show the photo to them!

We went to see The Desert Song. The third time for C. Lovely! I don't know if she has told you yet, but I can't keep secrets from you. It wasn't intended, she says, but she and Walter are expecting a baby in September, after all this time! If it is a girl, they have decided on the name Dolly after her dear mum . . .

I'm jealous again, Mattie realised. Christabel and I were best friends, but she hasn't told me her news . . . what's the saying: Out of sight, out of mind? I need to be doing something – but what? – to keep me busy and happy.' This house is easy to clean, Megan is at school, and I miss, oh so much, working alongside Griff, as we did on the farm.

The thought of her beloved home on the prairie made her wipe her eyes on her apron. She went upstairs, opened the honeymoon trunk, as Griff had dubbed it, and took out the scrapbook of memories.

Much later she popped down to the dime store. She bought half a dozen cheap notebooks, a box of quality writing paper, a fountain pen and a bottle of black ink. She'd write her ideas in pencil in the notebooks, edit them, and then copy them out neatly on the good paper. First-person articles often appeared in the local newspapers. She enjoyed reading human interest stories herself. 'So,' she said aloud, 'I can but have a go ...' She had a title for what she hoped would be a series: PRAIRIE SONG. The inspiration had come from *The Desert Song*, the film mentioned in Evie's letter.

On Saturday both Griff and Sybil had a rare afternoon off. Sybil, as promised, took Megan and her friend to the local cinema. 'We'll catch the bus there, the girls will enjoy that,' Sybil said. 'Afterwards, Mrs Barker has invited Megan and me to join them for tea. We should be home around seven.'

Mattie cleared the lunch table and glanced at Griff, reading the paper. It seems ages since we've been on our own like this, she thought. What can we find to talk about?

I don't know why, but I want to keep my writing secret for the moment.

'D'you want me to help with the washing up?' he enquired, without looking up.

'Only plates and cups and saucers – you relax. You've had a busy week,' she replied, as she rinsed the crocks clean.

He took her by surprise, bending over the sink, as he had often done in the early days of their marriage, arms tight around her waist. He kissed the nape of her neck.

'That tickles.' She giggled. She shook the water from her hands and turned in his embrace. 'Give me a proper kiss.'

'I've got a better idea,' he said softly. 'Dry your hands, shed your pinny, and follow me upstairs. Take your own advice, relax, be Mattie instead of Mom for a few hours.'

She realised, with a pang of remorse, that it had been weeks since they last made love with abandon. Following her illness and slow recovery Griff had been patient, and understanding in that respect, as the doctors had advised. Then had come the big move to the city and she had felt drained and disappointed. Now it was another spring, and time to change, for she realised that Griff had suffered too.

She unbuttoned her frock, slipped it over her head, and lay back on the bed. 'Well, don't stand there looking mesmerised,' she said, 'come here!' And he did.

Some time later, she asked him: 'Are you happy now?'

'I am. How about you, darling?'

'I'm like a new woman,' she said solemnly.

'You feel like one . . . you obviously made up your mind not to fade away, eh?'

'I've a secret to share with you . . .'

'I'm listening,' he said, smoothing her hair out of her eyes. 'Not . . . ?'

'Not another baby, no. Unless we've crossed that bridge today . . . I want to *write*, Griff – about our experiences since we decided to emigrate, ten years ago. All the ups and downs, all the good friends we met along the way – what d'you think?'

'It's the best idea you've had in a long while,' he said, 'I love you so much, Mattie.'

Harold Lloyd had the audience gasping when, caught in a hoist, he was hauled up the side of a skyscraper in his latest film, Paramount's *Feet First*. Megan dropped her packet of popcorn and, later, crunched it underfoot before they emerged, blinking, into the afternoon sunshine in the street.

There was time to visit the drugstore for an ice cream before catching the bus home. After the mishap with the popcorn, Sybil thought it wise to save this treat for 'when you can see what you're doing'.

Others from the cinema had the same idea, so they joined a growing queue. There came a polite tap on her shoulder, and Sybil turned to see her colleague – she wouldn't have dreamed of calling him her employee – Lloyd Morris, smiling at her. He was accompanied by a boy of about Megan's age.

'Did you enjoy the film?' he enquired. 'This is my grandson, Max. He is visiting me this weekend. This is Mrs Fullilove, Max.'

'Good afternoon, Mrs Fullilove,' Max said, and it was obvious, unwillingly.

'It's nice to meet you, Max. This is my stepson's daughter, Megan, and her friend Kay. Oh, excuse me – I must pay for their ice creams.'

'I will see you on Monday, goodbye,' Lloyd said, as they moved away.

'That boy poked his tongue out at me,' Megan sounded indignant.

'Did you do the same?' Sybil asked.

'Oh, Aunty Sybil, of course I did!'

'My mom's a writer,' Megan told her friends proudly at school. 'You can read her story in the paper. They came and took her picture, and printed that, too. She's going to write lots more, and my dad's going to do some pen-and-ink pictures, he says. Tell your moms to buy the paper every Friday.'

'We only get it wrapped round meat from the butcher,' Kay told her. Then, 'That was meant to be a joke, Meg.' She added, to mollify her, 'My mom says I can go to the Saturday morning kids' club at the cinema, with my brothers – d'you want to come?'

'Depends what's on.' Megan was still huffy.

'*Our Gang* – kids who get up to all sorts of mischief.'

'Like us?'

'Like us, if we got half a chance!'

Mattie bought a gramophone with her earnings, and some big band records. The woodblock floor in the living room came into its own now; they rolled up the shaggy rugs, and on Saturday evenings, when Sybil was invited out for dinner by her friend Lloyd, and Megan was in bed, she and Griff danced cheek-to-cheek. She thought: No one would know we're an old married couple.

Megan, listening to the music, in bed, with her eyes closed in case Mom or Dad checked whether she was asleep, knew, of course, but although she wouldn't tell anyone their secret, even Kay, because they were too old, surely, she liked the thought of them being all silly and romantic.

To her surprise Sybil discovered that, despite her being over forty, romance was back in her life, too. Lloyd was proving an ardent suitor. He'd been a widower for several years, and he couldn't believe his luck at meeting a woman like Sybil when he was in his late fifties. No point in hanging about when you were older, they both believed that. They announced their engagement in September, and later that month there was more excitement when the family heard that Christabel and Walter had their daughter, Dolly.

TWENTY-TWO

1939

It was yet another hot, dry summer and dust storms were creating havoc on the prairies. It was enervating in the city, too, so the Parry family were nostalgic for the wide open spaces, forgetting the drawbacks.

Mattie was delighted when the newspaper editor suggested she should pen something along the lines of *A Return to the Prairie*. It was the summer vacation and Megan, who would not be fourteen until Christmas, had so far not been lucky with finding a holiday job. Kay and her brothers were picking peaches on a relative's farm, but Mattie thought Megan was too young to join them, unaccompanied by an adult.

'What is there to do?' Megan lamented loudly each morning. She loved high school, the course work and the sport. She and Kay were hoping to become cheerleaders for the football and basketball teams. Megan practised her moves in front of the long mirror in her parents' bedroom.

'She's obsessed with it!' Griff said wryly, when once they were wakened from slumber to see her twirling Mattie's feather duster.

Megan cheered up when Mattie suggested they might drive out to their old home and see Gretchen. It was hard to imagine her the mother of four children under seven.

When Sybil and Lloyd married six years ago he'd given up his apartment and moved in to her house. Lloyd was now her business partner as well as her husband, and the beauty salon was thriving. They made a good team. Sybil, now she was no longer in need of a chauffeur, generously donated her car to Mattie. Mattie was grateful for, as she said, 'Megan has a busy social life, and needs me to ferry her back and forth!' This was her chance to drive a longer distance, and to see old friends.

'I wish I could come with you,' Griff said, 'but it's not possible on a weekday. Try to be home before dark. The roads haven't improved out there – it'll be a rough ride.'

'Mom's a good driver, and knows the way,' Megan reminded her dad.

They left early and arrived mid-morning. Gretchen was plumper but so dear and familiar, with her long, braided blonde hair, though now she had little ones clinging shyly to her apron. She came to greet them with a welcoming cry of, 'Here you are, at last!'

Kjetl came out from the barn and gave them both a hug. He smells like Griff used to when we lived here, Mattie thought: of hay, sour milk from spills, manure on his boots. Griff now smells pleasantly of fresh laundered shirts and shaving cream; he polishes his shoes, but he was doing a real man's job then, and I know he misses that.

'Aunt has made a fresh pot of tea,' Gretchen said.

'Oh good,' Mattie said. 'We drink too much coffee nowadays!'

The house was much the same. Megan went up the ladder into the loft, now a bedroom for the three young sons, who wanted to show her their toys.

'Uncle and I are hoping to add two rooms on to the house; we need more space now our family has grown.' Kjetl said. He jiggled the fat little baby on his lap. 'Well, we got our girl at last, our Wenche.' He pronounced the name 'Vinka'.

Mattie sipped the hot tea, reflecting: it won't be the same house then. She said aloud, 'I like her name. It seems ages since Megan was that small.'

'We pasteurise the milk, it is the law, and we sterilise the bottles,' Uncle told them. 'Times have changed, Mrs Parry. Since we got real electricity, we have machinery and refrigeration – no more ice to cut and store.' He noted her expression. 'Ah, we still deliver by horse and wagon. Mama can crack a whip, but not drive a motor.'

'Come and see your garden,' Gretchen said quickly. 'I try to keep it the same.'

The garden seemed smaller, less flourishing than Mattie remembered. She told herself: Gretchen is not responsible for this torrid weather, the dust that coats petals and leaves. The air is still, but the sky above is grey, not blue, despite the heat.

'See,' Gretchen pointed out the yellow rose, now tall and spindly. 'We call it Mattie's rose.' It's nice, Mattie thought, she calls me by my Christian name now.

As they walked back to the house for lunch, fresh fish from the lake cooked by Aunt Lotte, Mattie thought: I shouldn't have come back. I suppose I knew that really, and that's why I always made excuses not to do so before . . . It's not my home any more, and I would rather remember it as it was. But I'm glad my friends are happy here.

Just before they went inside, Gretchen asked, 'Do you ever hear from Bert?'

'He's not one for writing letters, I guess you know that. But Anna gives me news of the family. Bert is doing very well in his job.'

'Has he married?'

Mattie said quietly, for her friend's ears alone, 'No. I don't think he could find a girl to match up to you, Gretchen.'

'He took too long to say it.'

'You were both so young . . . you are happy with your lot, aren't you?'

'We are well-suited, Kjetl and me, everyone says so!'

'He adores you, anyone can see that.'

'Dear Mattie, I love and respect him. But I don't forget that summer, you see.'

It was later than they intended before Mattie and Megan began the journey home. By the time they had driven through the little town and were travelling along in the open, it was suddenly dark, as a dust storm gathered momentum. They were still on the stony road, with all its hazards, including the cattle grids. Mattie stopped the car. 'Keep the door closed, don't open the window whatever you do, and leave the headlights on,' she cautioned Megan.

She stepped out to get their bearings. She could just distinguish a light glimmering to her left. Was there a track to a farm, where they might wait out the storm? She missed her footing and plunged down into a deep ditch, where she collided with a fence pole, to which she tried to cling as she scrambled up. Thank God, she thought, we didn't go over the edge in the car, it would have rolled sideways, and we'd have been trapped, and it could be hours before we were found . . .

There was an excruciating pain in her right shoulder, which had taken the brunt of the fall, as she crawled, clawed her way up hard-baked mud, towards the car beam.

'Mom, where are you?' Megan yelled, hammering on the closed window, as Mattie pulled herself up by the door handle with her sound arm. Megan screamed when she saw her, covered in dust and debris from the ditch. She was a tall, strong girl for her age, and she managed, somehow, to pull Mattie inside, where she slumped in the passenger seat. By then, like her mother, she was choking from the dust.

'Mom – are you . . . hurt badly?' Megan took off her jacket and put it round her mother's slumped body. 'What are we going to do?'

'I've put . . . my shoulder out, I think . . . We'll have to sit the storm out here.'

Even as she spoke, the car shook alarmingly. They were both too scared to say anything, but Megan clung grimly to her mother's good hand. Thick dust dimmed the head-lights. They were all too aware that the car could be bowled over and they would end up in the ditch, anyway.

Mattie moaned, then was silent again. Megan felt her mother's face: her eyes were closed. Mattie was uncon-scious.

Megan felt desperate. She knew how to drive, having observed her mother at the wheel often enough, but despite her pleas Mom had never allowed her even to move the car up the drive into the garage between their house and Sybil's.

'It's against the law, you know that, Megan. It doesn't concern us what other kids do,' she'd said firmly.

The engine was running, but she couldn't see the road ahead. She would have to drive blind. The car went in fits and starts at first, then she gained confidence. She had to get help for Mom's sake. Keep to the middle of the road, she told herself grimly.

It seemed like hours later when they lurched down the rough drive towards the light that Mattie had spotted earlier.

Mattie was conscious again, in a haze of pain, but aware of what was happening. She muttered a simple prayer: 'Dear God, save us please . . .'

Then she was lifted gently from the car and carried into the farmhouse.

Mattie spent three days in hospital. Her collarbone was fractured and her shoulder dislocated, but these would heal in due course in the comfort of her own home. The article she was writing for the paper would be late, but she certainly had more material, she thought. Young Megan was the heroine of the hour, of course, the story of her resourcefulness was headlined: DETERMINED DAUGHTER DRIVES THRU DUST STORM. Far from getting into trouble, she was presented with a certificate of bravery by the mayor, no less, and three dollars, which she spent on a wristwatch. Alas, it never went, because she overwound it when she took it home.

Evie, back in England, eventually learned of these exciting events, but the family there was undergoing great changes, partly caused by the threat of another war.

They had been looking forward so much to seeing Mattie and Griff again, and meeting Megan for the first time, for the Parrys had been due to visit home after seventeen years in Canada and the States. This visit would have to be postponed.

Evie was worried about Sophia's decline in health; her mother was becoming vague and forgetful since Will had passed away earlier in the year. She knew how much Mattie regretted not seeing her father again. It was decided that Sophia needed full-time care herself now that the Jacksons had left; the old lady was in a nursing home near her son in Norfolk, her daughter had recently retired and bought a cottage near her brother's house. Sophia was now living with Fanny and Ronnie in their home.

Out of the blue, Evie received a letter from the Amy Able College, informing her, that in the event of war, the Amy Able had agreed to accommodate youngsters evacuated to a safer area with their schools. More staff would be needed: some of these students were in the throes of preparing for matriculation. Would Evie be prepared to join them for the duration? It would certainly be classed as war work.

I need a fresh challenge, she thought. But what about the Plough? Everything seemed to fall into place. The Plough was requisitioned by the authorities; it would become a wartime hostel for refugees. In due course, as Evie had learned, when her father's will was read, the property would be inherited eventually by herself. Her brother had insisted on this because, he said, he and Fanny would have saved enough to buy a house of their own after he retired on a good pension. The only proviso was that the Plough would pass down to Robbie, his eldest son.

In September, two days before the official announcement, Evie was back in Lincolnshire, and reunited with her old friend, Rhoda, home from the mission field.

They were even accommodated in their old dormitory, which made them smile and reminisce about their college days as Amy Able students.

This was no longer a sleepy backwater. The fertile fields were still there, the wide open spaces, the vast skies overhead, the watery places; but now there were runways on the flat land and young men being trained to fly aeroplanes in combat and defence.

'I was sure you would marry, not be a spinster like me,' Rhoda observed. Evie looked youthful and pretty with her curly hair and laughing face, but they were both thirty-one. 'I always had the feeling I'd end up back here!'

'D'you know, so did I!' Evie admitted. 'What about Noreen?'

'Noreen? Oh, we wrote for a bit, then I heard she had married and gone to China.'

'China, eh? So I don't suppose she'll turn up here.'

It was a surprise to Evie and Rhoda when she did, accompanying her class of fourteen-to-sixteen-year-olds evacuated from a grammar school in London. Noreen, much slimmer than they recalled and now confident in her caring role, had returned to England two years previously when her husband had tragically died young. She had no children of her own. 'Which is all to the good, I believe, because I can concentrate on my girls, who need me even more now they are parted from their families,' she said.

'She's a good egg,' Rhoda observed to Evie. They applauded her attitude.

The three of them were together again, and still there was the morning rush for the hot water in the bathroom, and back to the diet of good food, but not too much of it.

Even the hierarchy was the same. Dr Anne Withers had postponed her retirement and was still at the helm. Miss Vanstone was now college bursar, and the little 'Sergeant Major', Miss Dodds, the games mistress, still blew her whistle and screamed, out in the playing field.

'The only difference is,' Evie said, defiantly applying Tangee Natural lipstick, which was too orange to look anything like natural, 'I don't have to torture my mop of hair into a tight elastic band nowadays!'

'Once an Amy Able girl always an Amy Able girl. Where's your breastplate?' joked Rhoda.

'I've got so skinny I discarded mine long ago!' Noreen said smugly.

War in Europe: the papers were full of it, and Mattie was concerned about her family back in England. They had recently enjoyed a surprise call from Tommy, Grace's son, now twenty-seven, and a flying instructor in the Canadian Air Force. He had literally made a flying visit to the American air base at Minot, but he'd not told them more than that.

'I couldn't go back to Moose Jaw without looking you up,' he said. 'I've got two days free, so I would like to spend them with you, if that's OK?'

Megan, of course, wanted to know all about life in Canada, as she'd been born in North Dakota. 'Is Mom's friend Ollie still at the trading post?'

He shook his head. 'I didn't know her, Megan, I'm afraid. Mum saw Mungo, my old teacher, for the first time since I left school, though. I'm sure she wrote to tell you, Mattie, that my stepfather had died? I'm afraid he took to the bottle after the horses were sold, and he lost his job. He stayed on there, because of Mum and Lydia.'

'What is Lydia doing?' Mattie asked. 'She must be getting on for eighteen now.'

'She says she'll join the forces like me, if war breaks out.'

'Why will Canada be involved, and not America?' Megan queried. 'We should all fight evil.'

'I believe the war will spread world-wide,' Tommy said. 'Now, cheer up, Megan, and how about I take you all out for a meal? Oh, I nearly forgot . . . Mum sent this letter for you, Mattie.'

Mattie went upstairs to get changed for the evening out, and opened the letter in the privacy of her bedroom.

Mungo and I are hoping to be together soon. I have to wait a decent interval, as Edwin hasn't been gone six months yet, but we have waited so long for this day. I know you will be happy for me . . .

'Dear Grace, oh, I am . . .' Mattie said aloud. She wiped the tears from her eyes. What wonderful unexpected news! Griff had just returned from work and she heard him talking to Tommy downstairs. It was lovely to see Tommy again, too, she thought. Though now it was likely to be a long time before the next reunion.

TWENTY-THREE

AUGUST 1941

Megan had work lined up all this summer vacation from school. She was a salesgirl in one of the big stores in the same precinct as Sybil's beauty shop. She earned twenty-five cents an hour. It didn't seem much, but Sybil told her that Dolores, her assistant, had an older sister working in Woolworths; her husband had died leaving no pension and she had several children to bring up. Somehow, they survived on her wages of thirty-seven dollars a month.

Bigelow's Store seemed, so her mother often said, a much larger version of the dear old trading post, for it sold everything a customer could possibly want. The clothes were old-fashioned, but so durable you couldn't wear them out, as Megan knew from experience. '*Farmers* buy their overalls here,' she reminded Mattie.

'When we were on the farm, we bought from their catalogue,' Mattie said.

'I can remember you cut the books up and hung the paper on a nail in the john!'

Still, even temporary employees were allowed a discount on purchases. Megan snapped up the first of a new line of dungarees, nattily striped in blue and white. Dad joked and said she looked like a hillbilly. Both Mom and Sybil reminisced endlessly about the wonderful Empire Emporium back in Plymouth. No sumptuous silk garments in Bigelow's, Mom sighed, but they had a good drapery department.

Megan and Kay spent most of their earnings on their social life. They went to the movies at least twice a week, to dances on Saturday nights, where girls often partnered other girls. They experimented with makeup and hairstyles at each other's homes.

The girls' bedrooms were all in similar states of chaos. Most of their mothers sighed and closed the doors firmly on the mess. They'd grow out of it, they said hopefully. Walls were decorated with pictures of film stars, sent by the studios as a response to fan letters. Mattie privately thought all the actresses looked much the same, pouting lips and peroxided hair, but she wouldn't spoil Megan's illusion that all the dashing signatures had been personally inscribed. It was the era of secret diaries, writing to pen-friends and singing along soulfully to records. There was much whispering about boys, especially the heart-throbs who excelled at sport, but these Adonises seemed to prefer the sweaty company of other adolescent males. 'Safety in numbers,' Griff said.

Megan was envied by her friends; she actually had an admirer. This was Max, Sybil's step-grandson. They'd had a mutual dislike of each other as children, and she found this new devotion irritating. Fortunately, he was only around in the vacations.

She had a photograph of Tommy, in his uniform, smiling at her from her bedside table. 'Will you write to me?' he'd asked, the only time they met, before he went back to Canada. 'I enjoy news from friends.' It was rather off-putting that Mom read her letters before she sent them off, adding a short message from herself and Griff. Maybe Mattie was recalling the young Evie's innocent attraction to an older man and wanted the letters to remain light-hearted. It had become rather a one-way thing, actually, for Tommy was too busy to write often, but said he sure appreciated Megan's efforts.

Britain was soldiering on, as Griff put it. He and Mattie were frustrated that they were powerless to do anything to help family back home. News of the bombing of London and other major cities was alarming. They were relieved to hear that Christabel, and little Dolly had been evacuated to Hampshire, although old Aunt Mary refused to budge from Mitcham. Walter had taken the Civil Service examinations after Christabel left work, in order to secure a better job. He, too was evacuated, with his department, but to the West country, so he and Christabel were living far apart.

Relations became tense between Britain and the States. However, there had been a boost earlier in 1941 when America presented the Royal Navy with fifty destroyers, which unfortunately proved to be not equipped for modern warfare. In return, Britain gave America long leases on bases in the West Indies. This was the start of the Lease-Lend policy.

There was exciting news of Robbie, now known as Rob, Mattie's eldest nephew. He'd joined the Royal Air Force, and was even now in Canada being trained to fly the Miles Majesta monoplane. There he'd met up with their friend Tommy!

Suddenly, it seemed, summer was over, and Megan returned to high school, as a senior student. She and her friend Kay were at last cheerleaders for the school sports and were proud to wear their attractive uniforms, gold satin blouses with full bishop sleeves and maroon pinafore skirts. The other girls envied her naturally curly hair, for shoulder-length curls were in vogue. Megan secretly wished she had inherited her mom's silky golden hair – didn't they say gentlemen prefer blondes?

*

Evie and her friends soon discovered that life at the Amy Able was not as hidebound as it had been a decade ago. In their student days the local pub had been out of bounds.

Now, when classes were over for the day, and homework marked up to date, there were house mistresses who looked after the younger pupils, and Evie, Rhoda and Noreen were free to go out to meet the local community.

'D'you know,' Evie confided, 'Mattie and I were never allowed even to peep into the bar at the Plough! Of course, we weren't old enough to drink, but Dad allowed us a drop of Stone's ginger wine at Christmas time. Mother was a teetotaller, apart from saying Christmas pudding and cake needed a generous helping of brandy!'

'Lemonade, then?' Rhoda enquired with a straight face, having decided it was her turn to buy the drinks.

'We . . . ell, port and lemon would be nice. Dr Withers welcomed us with a glass of that, after all. She said it was a drink favoured by the lower orders, but not too strong for young ladies!'

Even such a mild mixture saw them giggling over a second glass, and observing the regulars leaning on the bar.

'Not one under sixty,' Rhoda whispered.

'That old boy with the bulging haversack – poacher I shouldn't wonder – winked at me – bloomin' cheek,' Evie whispered back.

A couple of farm workers, yet to go home and get changed, were playing a noisy game of darts and downing pints of beer.

'Foul-smelling pipe tobacco.' Noreen fanned the air with her hand. 'We're the only females here . . .'

'Except for the landlord's wife,' Evie said. 'She's got a bust like a buttress.'

'Seen her muscles when she pulls a pint? She doesn't count,' Rhoda decided.

The outer doors were pushed open, and there was a sudden hush, as everyone looked to see who had arrived.

'It's the Brylcreem boys,' the poacher told the assembly.

'Not one of 'em over twenty,' Evie sighed.

The confident young men in air-force blue soon propped up the bar. They talked among themselves and their laughter was infectious. The poacher moved to the edge of the group. He patted his haversack and Evie and her friends caught the words: ' . . . should you be int'rested – half a crown . . .'

'Ah, if it can be eaten, they will be,' a man's voice observed. Evie looked up, startled, at the airman with the sergeant's stripes, who had entered after the others.

He smiled. 'May I join you ladies at your table? I'm just here to keep an eye on the lads, and to ferry them back to base in due course. I'm Dave Harrington.'

'Evie Rowley,' she returned. 'My friends and colleagues, Miss Rhoda Jefferies and Mrs Noreen Jones.'

'Glad to meet you! Colleagues sounds rather grand – d'you work locally?'

'We teach – or lecture, if that sounds grander! – at the ladies' college.'

'I was a teacher – rather than a lecturer! – in civvy life, myself. May I buy you ladies another drink?'

He's nice, about our age, too, Evie thought. No doubt married. But not the type to deny it. He's not handsome, but he has a cheerful grin and twinkling brown eyes.

Evie was right: before they'd had a sip from the fresh glasses the photographs of his family were passed around them.

'My wife, Vi. Pity the snaps are not in colour, she has the most striking auburn hair! Our son, named after me, Davy, he's two and a half, and the baby in the shawl – she's toddling now! – is Lucy, a miniature of her mother!'

'Are they here in Lincolnshire?' Evie asked.

Dave shook his head. 'No. When I was drafted here Vi took the children to her parents' place in Surrey. They're out in the country away from the danger areas.'

'Were you flying in the Battle of Britain?' Noreen wondered.

'I was still training then. I was in a reserved occupation, but I volunteered for call up. I'm a sergeant-pilot, but some of this intake will definitely be high-flyers, if you'll excuse the pun. They thrive on action. Is your husband in the forces?'

Noreen said evenly, 'I was widowed just before the war.'

'I'm sorry,' he said.

'We had four good years together. No family, in case you were about to ask. You see, we were in China then, and we always thought . . . we'd have children when we came home at the end of his working assignment there.

I'm really fortunate to have been reunited with my college friends, so life is good again.'

'Well, I'm glad about that,' Dave said sincerely.

Rhoda glanced at her watch. 'Drink up, you two, or we'll find the Amy Able blacked out inside as well as out . . .'

'So long as you're not locked out! Are you walking home?' Dave asked.

'Not likely, we've got our bikes outside and dimmed lights – it's not far. It was nice to meet you, Dave. Thanks for the drinks,' Evie told him.

'I hope we meet again.'

'I have a feeling we will,' she said. While he was talking to her friends, she had been aware of his sidelong glances at herself. She wasn't vain in the least, but he wasn't the first man to find her attractive. And she had to admit to herself that despite their brief acquaintance she felt drawn to this nice man.

The nights were drawing in, and now they often woke in the early hours to hear the roar of the big bombers leaving the base. They didn't talk about their fears. In the morning life was normal – or as normal as it could be, in wartime.

America was catapulted into the war on 7 December 1941, when Pearl Harbour, a natural harbour in Hawaii, where a great number of American ships were docked, was targeted by Japan, both at sea and in the air, with planes piloted by suicide bombers. The onslaught commenced just after dawn. It was a catastrophe on a massive scale.

It was followed by a Japanese attack on the Royal Navy in Southeast Asia. Two great ships and crews were lost, the *Prince of Wales* and the *Repulse*.

Great Britain and the United States were now united in their resolve to overcome the enemy forces.

'Thank God for that,' Mattie said simply, for naturally, she and Griff had divided loyalties. They were now Americans, but still British at heart.

'I hope you will forgive a word of advice in your ear,' Rhoda said, observing Evie making ready to go out one Sunday afternoon. 'You must know nothing can come of this friendship. I would hate to see you get hurt.'

Evie replaced the hand mirror on her locker top. She turned her flushed face and looked at Rhoda. 'You know me better than that. It's just a visit to the pictures, and tea in the ABC. He tells me the latest news about his family and I'll make him laugh at some of the pranks the girls get up to here. We won't mention this bloody war – and don't look so shocked at my language! – or the fact that there's always the chance he might not be around for another date. He has never once made any . . . overtures of any sort, or compromised my maidenly virtue.'

'Would you have minded too much, if he had?' Rhoda challenged her.

'I'm not going to answer that!' Evie picked up her bag, and brushed past Rhoda without her usual cheerful rejoinder of 'See you later, then!'

Dave was waiting outside the Amy Able gates, in his four-wheel drive. It was a windy, chilly January day, and the landscape seemed as grey and leaden as the skies.

'Hop in!' he invited. As they drove off Evie wondered if Rhoda was watching from the upstairs window. Their exchange had unsettled her.

'Everything all right?' he enquired.

'Not really. It seems that some might, well, be thinking we are more than just friends,' she said, in a rush.

'What rot!' he said robustly, but he kept his eyes on the road ahead. 'Your friendship means a lot to me, I admit, but—'

'You would never dream of cheating on your wife,' she concluded.

The conversation ceased there, as they'd arrived at the cinema, and after parking the car, joined a long queue outside, stamping and shuffling their feet in the cold. Evie turned up the fur collar on her plaid coat, which she'd bought before clothing was rationed. It had seemed extravagant at the time, but in this bleak weather she was certainly appreciative of its good quality.

Ninotchka, starring Greta Garbo, was a couple of years old, but still a box-office draw in small country towns. Fans were particularly eager to see this film, because for the first time, as proclaimed on the billboard outside the cinema, GARBO LAUGHS! The Pathé newsreel brought the audience back down to earth, with grim reminders of the Japanese advances in Singapore.

They drove past the teashop, but before Evie could say anything, they drew up outside the George Hotel.

'I thought we should have a special meal together on my last evening,' Dave said in a matter-of-fact way. 'I've booked a room – and before you jump to the wrong conclusion, it is a private sitting-room. Dinner will be served to us there.'

She made no attempt to get out of the motor. 'I have to be back at the Amy Able before 9.30. I don't understand. Are you . . . leaving here?'

'I shouldn't really say anything about this at all. Some of us are being deployed elsewhere. I couldn't just vanish without saying. I'll have you back at college on time.'

There was a modest fire warming the small room, which had ugly dark wallpaper, a couple of hard-backed armchairs, and a table laid for two. Dave pulled the curtains across the window. The blackout shutters were already in place.

The landlord's wife brought in the first course. 'Rissoles', she said apologetically. 'I can recommend the gravy though, made with good stock. Our home-grown vegetables, we store them in the cellar. Your beer, sir. Port and lemon for the lady. Would you care to listen to the wireless?'

Dave looked at Evie. 'No thank you. I must say this looks very nice . . .'

The rissoles were piping hot and indeed tasty. The apple tart which followed was tart, as sugar was used sparingly. The Bird's custard powder was mixed with dried milk.

When the table was cleared of dishes, they sat opposite each other in the armchairs. 'Let's talk, say all the things we should have learned about each other, but haven't. You first, Evie.'

'All I can say is, I know what's the most important thing in your life – your family.'

'Nothing about how you really feel about me – how you suspect I feel about you?'

'No. No!'

He stretched out his hand towards her, but she kept her hands resolutely folded in her lap. 'Please, Evie . . .'

'You would regret it for ever if you betrayed your wife.'

'I see your resolve is stronger than mine. I really didn't bring you here to make love to you, you know. I miss Vi terribly. She's not here. You are. I think it's highly probable I won't see either of you again,' he said flatly.

'I think we should leave now.' Evie rose. He stood up, in turn. 'I'll fetch our coats,' he said.

They parted outside the main gates of the Amy Able. She didn't resist when he pulled her to him and kissed her. 'Goodbye,' he murmured.

'Goodbye. Good luck,' she managed in return.

Rhoda and Noreen didn't question her about her delayed arrival back. But that night, as they settled down in their narrow beds, she told them: 'Nothing happened. Nothing at all . . .'

TWENTY-FOUR

CHRISTMAS 1943

Megan's last shift on the general ward in the hospital, where she had been working since she'd graduated last summer, was on Christmas Day, her eighteenth birthday. She was paid thirty cents an hour for basic domestic duties, and Mattie insisted that she should save her earnings for the future.

'Perhaps you will decide on a career in nursing,' Mattie said hopefully.

'I don't think I'm cut out for that, Mom. Oh, I'm real glad to be helping out the way I do now, though I hate being on bedpan duty – and the patients say I make 'em smile.'

'Haven't you any idea what you might do, after this?'

'Wait and see, eh?' Megan knew, of course, what she intended to do. She just wasn't sure that her mom and dad would agree with her choice.

The nurses sang favourite carols and the few patients who had not been able to get home or had no family to care for them, sat up in bed, or in chairs with a blanket over their knees, to open the presents the hospital staff had delivered. The cleaners hovered in the background, to watch. They would collect up the torn wrapping paper and generally tidy the ward before going off duty. It was late afternoon.

Megan was thinking about Tommy. He was a long way from his own home in Canada. Tommy was somewhere in England, attached to the RAF. She'd posted him a photograph of herself, with the message, *Love always, from Megan*. The photographer's art had made her look like a film star, she mused. Surely he would see how grown-up she was now.

With a start, she realised that her name was being called. Sister Julienne was holding out a parcel. 'Miss Megan Myfanwy Parry – please step forward!'

As Megan did so, voices were raised in song once more, some old and quavery and out of tune, a pleasing baritone from one of the doctors, but all knew the words: HAPPY BIRTHDAY TO YOU – HAPPY BIRTHDAY TO YOU – HAPPY BIRTHDAY DEAR MEGAN, HAPPY BIRTHDAY TO YOU!

*

There was more warbling back home, where the family had kindly postponed opening their own presents and sitting down to their Christmas dinner until Megan's return.

They'd been joined as usual by Sybil and Lloyd and, for a few hours, Max, who was fortunate to have leave from the army before going overseas to the battle zone. He was six months older than Megan and had joined up immediately he left school.

'Sorry, I didn't manage to get out and buy you one present, let alone, two,' Max apologised. 'But I do have a little something for you, don't worry.'

'Well, I didn't know you were coming today, so I've nothing for you, either!'

Griff fastened his and Mattie's gift, a gold chain and heart-shaped pendant round her neck. 'Oh, you still smell of carbolic – but this is with our love,' he said.

'Mom, Dad – it's beautiful! Thank you so much.' Megan's eyes brimmed with tears. 'I'll have a quick squirt of Sybil and Lloyd's scent, eh?'

'Do you mind,' Sybil smiled. 'It's Chanel No 5 and so no squirting, just dabbing!'

'You can open the pendant,' Mattie told Megan. 'Put a tiny photo inside, or a lock of hair. Not your father's, he can't spare any, these days.'

'Cruel woman, your mom,' Griff said fondly.

Megan postponed her announcement until after they'd eaten. She thought, Dad will understand, he's more placid than Mom. He's always smiling since he left that dreary job at the garage, just after America went to war. He loves his work in the planning department at the aircraft factory, he's doing something worthwhile again . . .

Max gave Megan his present when he thought no one was looking. A small box, which he slipped into her hand as they sat side by side at the table. 'Don't open it now – it's not much, but I hope you'll wear it and think of me,' he whispered.

She said in her forthright way, 'I'm sorry I didn't have time for shopping this Christmas. I thought you'd be too busy too, so—'

'You needn't make excuses. Just say you'll knit me some socks.'

'What makes you imagine I can knit?' she challenged, but she didn't feel irritated, as she usually did, at his persistence. He was a goodlooking fellow, tall and athletic, but, despite the uniform, he still seemed immature compared with Tommy.

Griff and Lloyd were sharing the carving duties, one with the turkey, the other with the ham. Not quite the spread of pre-war days but, as Mattie observed: 'We're so fortunate. Evie is still eating college fare, and Ronnie's Fanny is feeding the five thousand she says, on short commons . . .'

The pudding arrived, and generous portions were served, with custard and cream. Then they raised their glasses to salute Christmas and Megan on her special birthday. 'To Megan, may you have a good year to follow!'

It was time to tell them. Megan looked round at the smiling faces. 'Well, it's beginning well. I'm following Max's good example and joining up before conscription. I've decided I want to train to be an army driver. In fact, I've already had an interview. I was asked what my strengths were and all I could think of was, I drove my mom to safety through a dust storm!'

There was a stunned silence. Then Griff cleared his throat, stood up and said huskily: 'We've always been proud of you, Megan, but especially today. Raise your glasses all of you, to a wonderful girl. Megan.'

'Megan!' they echoed.

'You're crying, Mom,' Megan said, concerned.

Mattie dabbed at her wet face with her table napkin. 'I'll miss you – but, oh, Megan, I know I would have done the same, at your age!'

'Of course you would,' Griff agreed, adding: 'Didn't cousin Bert once say you were a girl and a half, Megan? You certainly get that spirit from your mom!'

Sybil tapped her glass with a spoon to gain their attention. 'I've some news to impart, too. Lloyd and I have decided to close down the beauty parlour side of the business, for the duration. It doesn't seem appropriate at this time. However, we'll keep the hairdressing salon going, as we have more mature staff there, who are past call-up. Lloyd is concentrating on his laboratory work, and me – I am offering my services to the military hospital to help those service personnel who suffer burns or other disfigurement in the fighting. My skills at concealing scars and blemishes could aid rehabilitation, I'm told.'

'Sybil, that's a great idea!' Mattie assured her. She thought, there must be something *I* could do, too, to help the war effort. Selling war bonds perhaps? Or maybe working in Bigelow's part-time – they're suffering from a shortage of staff now. Will we have a family gathering like this next Christmas, I wonder?

'When are you leaving?' Max asked Megan.

Attention focused once more on Megan.

'Next week,' she said, 'Mom and Dad, I hope that's not too much of a shock!'

Griff squeezed Mattie's hand, answered for them both. 'Having made up your mind, the best thing to do is to get on with it! We're behind you, all the way!'

After the guests had departed, Megan helped her parents with the clearing up, then went off to bed. She settled under the covers, comfortable in old pyjamas, fingering the locket round her neck. She'd write to Tommy and ask if he had any spare Polyfotos, she mused. She didn't need to say what for. She suddenly recalled the little box which Max had given her. She'd put it on her bedside table. She reached out, and opened it. His high school fraternity pin! With a rueful smile, she pinned it to her jacket. It was obvious what he meant by this gift. She'd thank him, of course, and wear the pin for friendship's sake.

The fierce hug he'd given her earlier when he was about to leave, the way he'd kissed her full on the lips for the first time and murmured, 'Think of me – sometimes – Megan, *please . . .*' had made her realise the extent of his feelings for her. Now, as she checked that the pin was fastened securely, she sighed. 'I don't suppose,' she said aloud, 'that *Tommy* thought of *me*, today . . .'

April 1944. Somewhere in England

Megan had come through her basic army training with flying colours. She had been flown over with other young women drivers to a secret location deep in the country-side. They were aware that they were here to chauffeur their superiors to important meetings, that something very exciting was about to happen, which could lead to a break-through in the hostilities, but they didn't talk about it, even among themselves, or allude to it in letters home.

She was becoming accustomed now to driving down narrow, leafy lanes, the lack of signposts, disguised or removed when there had been a very real threat of invasion after Dunkirk, even to the rain and ensuing damp conditions of an English spring. Banks of delicate, lovely wild flowers made Megan catch her breath. Land girls driving tractors; women riding bicycles with baskets on the front, and toddlers strapped in little seats behind, raised a hand in greeting as the staff car passed them.

Two of the most senior officers were to attend a weekend conference in London. Megan was chosen to drive them there. The officers would be staying at a big hotel, where security was already in place: Megan would put up at a smaller establishment, and was told to enjoy her short break, but to stay within the hotel at all times in case she was needed.

She told herself there was no reason why she shouldn't contact Tommy and ask him over on the Saturday evening; he was stationed in Surrey and grounded for a spell. It was a pity she wouldn't be able to see anything much of London, she thought, on her first visit. She knew that her mother was disappointed too, that she hadn't yet been able to get in touch with her Aunt Evie in Lincolnshire, or the relatives in Suffolk.

Driving through bomb-ravaged London was a sombre experience. Some of the buildings were mere shells. Having come from the lush countryside, she realised just what London and the other big cities had suffered two years previously.

The great hotel, however, was seemingly untouched. Megan was not invited inside but drove away immediately her passengers had alighted. Her more modest destination was some miles away.

Her arrival was expected. She was escorted to a pleasant room on the first floor, where a tray of refreshments was delivered shortly afterwards. 'Dinner at seven, madam, in the dining room.' The young woman who'd accompanied her opened a door. 'Your private bathroom. There's enough hot water if you wish to take a bath.'

'Thank you,' Megan said. 'I'd sure appreciate that.'

She took off her cap and threw it on the bed. It would be good, she thought, to hang up her uniform, to change into something pretty and feminine before Tommy arrived. That was if he did, of course. He hadn't confirmed that he would.

It was four o'clock. Time for tea. She settled herself at the small table in the sitting area. A silver tea service was a pleasant change from the tin mugs she'd become accustomed to. She'd hoped for a gooey cake or two, but there was a single scone on a plate, already split and spread thinly with butter.

Refreshed, she rested on top of the coverlet on the bed and closed her eyes for a brief nap. She awoke with a start, to discover that it was past six. I'll have to hurry, she thought ruefully – but I'm not going to miss out on my bath, or washing my hair!

Fortunately, she'd brought bath salts, soap and shampoo, because these luxury items were no longer provided. However, there was a big white towel, embroidered in one corner with the name of the hotel, and a smaller towel for drying her hair, which she'd wash in the bath, to save time and water.

The pale pink chiffon dress, with cap sleeves and cross-over bodice sparkling with silver sequins was the one she'd worn for the studio portrait she'd sent to Tommy. She'd had no chance to wear it since. It was lined in silk, so she'd no need of a petticoat, only minimal underwear. She smoothed her nylon stockings carefully over her legs, then slipped her feet into borrowed silver dancing shoes, with heels. Her hair was still damp but she swept it up off her neck with a pair of glittery combs. No worries about setting a style – her hair was curly, and that was it, she thought.

Megan looked at her face in the dressing-table mirror. Just a dab of powder to disguise the shine bestowed by steaming water, coral-coloured lipstick and touches of the expensive perfume given her by Sybil last Christmas.

She took a deep breath. Just on seven. Would he be already at the table, waiting for her to appear? I can't hurry in these heels, she reminded herself.

The dining-room was almost deserted: no Tommy. A couple of women in sensible tweeds sat at a corner table. Megan immediately felt conspicuous. In wartime, she realised, it was not necessary to dress for dinner.

She was guided to her table by a middle-aged man, with sleek pomaded hair and a pencil-thin moustache. 'Good evening, madam. My name is Louis. Do you wish to order now, or wait for your guest to arrive?'

'I'll wait, thank you,' she said. She was aware that the women were regarding her from their table. Did she look that much out of place?

'Would you like a drink while you study the menu?' Louis prompted.

Megan felt flustered. She'd never ordered a drink for herself.

'A little wine, perhaps?' Louis persisted.

'A small glass of sherry,' she decided. Sybil was the most sophisticated person she knew, and that was usually her choice.

She picked up the menu nonchalantly. Most of the items were crossed through. The selection of food on the base was more appetising, mostly flown over from the States. They enjoyed fresh-baked white bread, and deep-fried doughnuts.

'Chef's choice of the day . . . stewed rabbit and savoury dumplings,' she read aloud in disbelief, wrinkling her nose. 'I wonder why they didn't translate that into French!'

'Doesn't sound too bad to me,' remarked a cheerful voice.

Megan looked up, couldn't suppress a gasp. 'Tommy – you got here!'

'Sure did. I've even booked a room overnight. Glad to see me?' He slid into a chair opposite, placed his cap on the table, and sat smiling at her, still in his uniform.

'Oh, I am!'

Louis appeared, removed the headgear smartly to a curved coat-stand. 'Good evening, sir. Would you care for a drink? Are you ready to order?'

'Whisky, please. Say, can't you rustle up something more special than rabbit?'

Louis stiffened. 'Are you not aware, sir, of the strict rationing over here?'

'You think I come from the States? Well, I'm from Canada, of British parents, and I've been over here almost from the start of the war . . . It's just that this is by way of being a reunion, and I guess I hoped to impress a beautiful girl.'

'In that case, sir, I apologise, I'll see what I can do. Leave it to me,' Louis said.

The wait was worth it. Toad in the hole, one fat, herby sausage each, in batter made no doubt with dried egg and milk, served with thick brown well-seasoned gravy, mashed potato and glazed carrots. Some of the batter was reserved for crispy pancakes, served, to their delight, with maple syrup.

Louis beamed at their obvious enjoyment of the meal, but it was time for vacating the dining-room to allow the staff to clear up and lay the tables again for breakfast. It was past nine o'clock.

'Would you like coffee in the foyer – or perhaps in your rooms?' Louis asked.

He didn't even blink when Tommy said immediately, 'In your room, I think, Megan? Booking at the last minute, the only room available to me was on the top floor, next to the staff WC.'

'Not quite, sir, it's closer to the broom cupboard. You'll find it adequate, I'm sure. Do you want your bag taken upstairs?'

'No, I'll keep it with me, thank you. Lead the way, Megan!'

They drank their coffee, sitting side by side on a *chaise-longue*. Megan removed her shoes and wriggled her toes. She gave a contented sigh. 'This is nice. D'you have to go up to your attic? There's a spare blanket, you could sleep on the couch, couldn't you? I don't want the evening to end yet.'

'Nor do I,' he said softly.

She didn't look at him when she said, 'Or, as you've noticed, there is a perfectly comfortable double bed . . .'

His arms encircled her, he turned her gently towards him. 'Are you ready for this?' he queried, his breath fanning her cheek.

'Not quite . . . I don't want to crush my best frock . . .'

'That's easily solved,' he whispered. 'You don't have to do this, Megan, you know. I didn't realise you were all grown up, I admit. But please remember I'm older, and yes, more experienced than you. I don't want to take advantage of you—'

'I'm in love with you Tommy. I can't help myself. I intend to marry you one day!'

'Oh, Megan, how can I resist you? I think I'm falling for you, too . . .'

*

The talking, the meticulous planning was over – the D-day landings began in June, 1944. Europe would be liberated at last. Amid the euphoria, there was the cruel reality of great loss of life for the Allied forces. Tommy was among those who would never return. Also, the war in the Far East was not over yet.

In August, Megan was flown home to North Dakota on compassionate grounds. Her war was over, too, because she was four months pregnant.

TWENTY-FIVE

'No more weeping, Mattie darling,' Griff said gently to her that homecoming day. 'No recriminations – promise?'

Mattie's lips trembled. 'I'll try . . . promise. It's just that—'

'You're her mother – it's natural you should feel the way you do. Disappointed – let down – we both feel she's too young. If . . . things hadn't turned out the way they have, well, we would have been shocked and angry that Tommy was so irresponsible, as Megan is so young.'

'She's not grown-up enough to be a mother! Nor was I, at that age. We were married almost four years before she put in an appearance! Another thing, I don't feel ready to be a grandmother – at just forty-two! I *could* still have a baby myself . . .'

Griff hugged her tight. His voice was muffled as he rested his face against her hair. 'This one will do . . . Megan has suffered enough, losing Tommy. We must support and love her, and her baby. Is her room ready?'

'You know it is. Oh, Griff, how will I know what to say to her?'

'You will. She's still our Megan.'

They had both taken the afternoon off work. Mattie had decided on a simple supper, Chicken Maryland. Not too heavy a meal, but nourishing for an expectant mother, she thought. This was a favourite family dish: chicken portions, coated in breadcrumbs, fried to a golden brown; sweetcorn picked from Mattie's front vegetable garden and made into fritters, served with sliced, cooked bananas. Megan had written that bananas had been unobtainable in England during most of the war. For dessert, Mattie baked individual blueberry tarts, and whipped up a jug of cream.

She wondered whether Megan had an aversion to certain foods, as she had had when she was expecting her daughter; she hoped that Megan might be past the morning sickness stage. She mustn't treat her as an invalid – she hadn't allowed that herself, she recalled wryly.

After Griff had gone to collect Megan from the station Mattie sat watching the clock, trying to relax, as Griff had suggested. She heard the car arrive, but she waited for the tap on the door, which would mean that it was Megan, for Griff had his key.

She opened the door slowly. Griff was backing the car into the garage. Megan stood there, pale-faced and unsmiling. Mattie held out her arms. 'Welcome home, darling!' She drew her daughter inside the house, pulling the door to; Griff would be tactful, she guessed, and allow them a few minutes together.

Megan followed her into the kitchen and Mattie set the kettle to boil for tea. Megan wore the striped baggy dungarees she'd bought at Bigelows in 1941, which accommodated her baby bump. She didn't look much like the cheerful girl in uniform in the full-length photograph she'd sent her parents before she left for her duties in England. This young woman was obviously desperately unhappy.

They were aware that Griff had come in, but he went straight upstairs with Megan's baggage.

Megan spoke at last. 'Poor Dad, I couldn't say anything to him except hello . . .'

'I'm sure he understood. Mug or cup, dear?'

'A cup and saucer – I missed your china tea set. I missed you, Mom. I missed Dad! I wanted you to be proud of me.'

'We are,' Mattie assured her. 'Drink your tea. I have a letter here for you from Grace. I had to tell her about the baby, of course.'

'Did she – understand?'

'She said it was helping her to cope with her grief. It's brought us even closer.'

'Tommy didn't know. I wasn't sure, you see, at that time. After he'd – gone – I had a letter. He said he loved me, that we'd be married as soon as we could – how wonderful it was that we'd come together – destiny, he said . . .'

'You didn't tell *us* for some time, did you? I was worrying myself sick about those awful flying bombs, knowing you drove into London quite often. Please God, I said, let Megan come safely home to us.'

'And here I am,' Megan said simply.

'Any tea left in the pot?' Griff asked, joining them.

Later, in her room, resting on the bed, Megan unfolded Grace's letter.

Dear Megan,

You will soon be home, so I am enclosing this letter with your mother's. I am still trying to come to terms with my loss, but I am grateful for the years I had my son – he was brave and resolute like his father, who also died young, doing his duty.

He wrote to me, you know, after you met in London last April. He could hardly believe his luck, he said he knew you and he were meant for each other, and he was going to ask you to marry him. I was so happy then – your parents befriended me on the boat over here, and we have been pals ever since – this would be a further strong bond between us, I thought.

Now, Mattie tells me that you are carrying Tommy's baby! Please allow us to be part of your life, for dear Tommy's sake.

Take care of yourself, and God bless, with love from Grace, Mungo and Lydia.

The sobbing began then. She turned her face to the pillow, trying to stifle the sound.

A hand gently caressed her hunched shoulders. Her father sat down on the side of the bed. He used the soothing voice he had used when she was upset as a child, or had shouted at Mom when she was a teenager, railing against not being allowed to do some activity her parents didn't approve of. He was the family peacemaker.

'What's up?' he asked, as if he didn't know.

'Oh, Dad, I've let you down, you and Mom, and now I'm going to be a burden, because I haven't any money, though the army says it will help, and how can I get a job, in my condition?'

'Look, you don't need to worry about that now. All that matters is that we are here for you, and always will be. If you want to pour your heart out, now is the time. I'm listening. Mom will call us when supper's on the table.'

Megan sat up, and reached for his hand. 'We were only together for a weekend, Tommy and me. Don't blame him – please ` . . .'

'It takes two,' Griff said softly. 'You may find it hard to believe, but your mom and I almost succumbed to all that, before we were married. Of course, times were very different then, but, it was frustrating. Barriers are broken down in wartime. A last chance to be together, who knows what will happen next? Is *that* how you felt?'

'Yes. I don't feel guilty!' She fingered the pendant round her neck, remembering. 'He said: "Let me see whose picture you have next to your heart," then he opened it, and looked inside. I said, I had to cut you down . . .' She gave a little hiccupping giggle.

Griff cleared his throat. 'Good to see you smiling. Want to share the joke?'

'Well, now, you've confessed about you and Mom – I omitted to say that when we were in bed, that the pendant was all I was wearing!'

'Mom's calling! Ready to come downstairs?'

Mattie refrained from asking what they had been talking about. She said only, as she dished up the meal: 'Oh Megan, after you left home I was sorting out the washing and I found a fraternity pin on your pyjama jacket! I put it back in that little box on your bedside table. Didn't you miss it?'

'I thought I'd lost it – I expect you realised that Max gave it to me that Christmas? I never heard from him – I guess he found a nice girl!'

'I doubt it, in the jungle in Burma. Eat up, before it gets cold.'

Megan wasn't prepared to stay at home putting her feet up for five months. She had too much nervous energy for that. She asked Mattie to approach Bigelow's and ask whether they could do with another member of part-time staff. 'They can hide me in a back room, and disguise me in one of those old-fashioned farming smocks,' she said.

Bigelow's was also adapting to a fast-changing world. There were two other expectant mothers, GI brides both of them, who were allowed to perch on stools behind the counter, and they welcomed their former student helper back.

'I can work until I go pop!' Megan told her mother.

'I'm sure Mr Bigelow Junior didn't put it quite like that!' Mattie mock reproved. She was aware that Megan was determined to make everyone believe that she was all right. She wasn't, of course, but it was good she was keeping busy until the baby was born.

Mattie accompanied Megan to a prenatal appointment at the hospital in late November, six weeks before the birth was due. The doctors warned that her blood pressure was soaring, and there were the first ominous signs of toxaemia. They said that she must give up her job immediately and have bed rest in hospital for 'a week or two'. Megan was not convinced. 'Supposing they make me stay there until my due date?' she fretted.

Megan wasn't allowed to go home, but was shortly lying on a bed, in a cubicle off the main maternity ward, dressed in a well-laundered hospital gown, which she complained was indecent because it was open at the back, while Mattie went home to pack a bag hastily for her. Meanwhile, Megan was given a sedative, tucked up and told to have a good sleep.

Sleep was just what she did, for the following two weeks. She was woken to take tablets, to be helped to a commode, washed like a baby herself as she lay on the bed. Visitors came and departed at different times of the day. Sometimes she was aware of their presence, sometimes she slumbered on. A delicious fragrance caused her to open her eyes one day, to see Sybil leaning over her to bestow a gentle kiss on her damp forehead. It was the perfume she had worn herself, the day Tommy came back so briefly into her life. Sybil brought flowers and also a special bunch of red roses. 'These are from Max. He asked me to bring them, as he couldn't come himself. He sends his love and best wishes,' she said, not sure whether Megan could hear her.

Mattie busied herself at home, preparing for the baby, something Megan had put off, saying there was plenty of time. The old trunk yielded up a few items she'd forgotten, like two tiny flour-sack night-gowns, trimmed with lace at neck and cuffs. She washed them by hand, and pressed them carefully, as she had for the little Megan.

A specialist was called in to give an opinion. He thought that the baby should be delivered a month early by caesarean section. Mattie and Griff were asked to give permission as her next of kin. They were told gravely that time was of the essence. Both the mother and her baby's life were in danger.

Megan awoke at last to see a nurse with a thermometer in her hand and a big smile on her face.

'I'm ... still here?' she managed. Her mouth was very dry, and although she wanted to, she couldn't manage to struggle up in the bed. Her hands strayed to her abdomen.

It was flat, but padded with dressings. She winced as pain gripped her, then receded.

'You're still here,' the nurse agreed. She opened the cubicle door, called out: 'She's come round – you can see her for five minutes, but no more, this time. She is due for some pain relief.'

'Mommy, Dad.' Megan lay there, with a drip attached to her arm. 'What's happened?'

Mattie couldn't speak for a moment. Griff took Megan's limp hand in his warm clasp. 'You have a baby daughter, Megan . . .'

'Where is she?' Megan asked.

'She's in the nursery with other premature babies, but she's fine. Not a bad weight. The doctors are checking her over. You'll see her very soon.'

'I thought it would be a boy,' Megan said, like her mother before her.

'But you don't mind?' Mattie found her voice.

'No . . . so long as she's all right . . . Mom, I can't remember . . . the baby being born.'

'That's because they had to put you out, operate,' Griff said.

'You'll have to stay here while you recover,' Mattie had to tell her.

The nurse came back. 'Time's up. Oh, have you a name for your baby, Megan?'

'I thought . . . I'd call her after her two grandmas, but I'm not sure which – Grace Matilda, or Matilda Grace.'

Her tactful father said, 'There's only one Mattie, eh? Your Mom. Grace is good.'

Megan and Grace came home just before Megan's nineteenth birthday, and Christmas. At Megan's suggestion Mattie and Griff had redecorated her bedroom. Down had come the childish posters, the film star photographs, but the picture of Tommy remained. They papered the walls with pink paper with a tiny silver star pattern, and Griff made a mobile of hand-painted butterflies to hang over the crib.

Mattie gave up her job. She was needed at home, she said. She could tell that Megan was not really ready to be a mother. 'I can do the practical bits,' she told Griff. 'She'll grow up fast. All she needs to do for now is give Grace plenty of love.'

TWENTY-SIX

APRIL 1945

Mattie had not written much since her prairie articles for the newspaper; in wartime there was not much call for nostalgia, with more immediate action to report. She missed the quiet enjoyment of sitting down with pencil and paper and expressing her thoughts. Among the gifts for the baby was a book to record her progress, with space for photographs and anecdotes.

'You might as well have this, Mom,' Megan said casually, passing it over. 'I know I wouldn't keep it up to date – I never did with diaries, eh?'

'She's depressed,' Mattie thought with a pang of fear, as she remembered what had happened to Ena, young Robbie's mother.

This was confirmed when she went into Megan's room one morning, carrying Gracie, as Griff had soon dubbed her, freshly bathed and fed, to lay her down for her nap. Megan had gone back to bed – not downstairs to tackle the baby's washing, as her mother believed.

'What's up?' she asked, when Gracie was in the crib. She suddenly realised: it must be exactly a year since Megan and Tommy had been together, in London . . .

'Oh, Mom, I didn't get much sleep last night. She wouldn't stop crying . . .'

'She just needed a cuddle, maybe, and a drink.'

'I know. It would have been so much easier, she would have been more contented, if I'd been able to nurse her myself, wouldn't it?'

'Darling, you couldn't help that. You were so poorly after she was born, it seemed best to start her on the formula milk.'

'Mom – I keep thinking what I could have done with my life, if—'

'Well, you would have married Tommy, I guess, and *then* had a baby.'

'Perhaps not. I thought it was real love – but we didn't have time to find out whether it would last, did we? Mom, when I was in the bath earlier, I looked at my scar. It's still livid. They told me at the hospital it would be unwise for me to have another child. I don't suppose any man would want me, knowing that. I guess I'm stuck with my lot for a good few years yet, and I don't have a career to fulfil me, like Aunt Evie.'

Mattie surprised herself. 'You could do something about that. You could apply to go to college in the fall. I'd look after Gracie, with help from your dad . . .'

Megan sat up. 'Mom, d'you mean that? Isn't it too much to ask of you both?'

'Of course it isn't,' Mattie said firmly, hoping that Griff would agree. 'Why not write to Evie, and ask her advice?'

'I will, *today*!' Megan threw back the covers, swung her legs out of bed. She'd donned a clean pair of pyjamas after her bath, and on impulse, she'd fastened Max's pin to the lapel. Mattie noticed but, wisely, didn't comment.

Evie, in England, was considering her own future. The evacuees were returning to London and the suburbs, to schools preparing for the influx. The war in Europe was not officially at an end, but there was renewed determination among the population that things would be better in the future. Rationing was still strict, and it was just as well that folk were unaware that this would carry on for years after the war was over.

The year of 1944 would never be forgotten because of D-Day, but also for the white paper in Parliament, outlining the proposed National Health Service, and R.A ('Rab') Butler's Education Bill, which promised good secondary education for all children.

Their friend Noreen resumed her teaching post in London, but Evie and Rhoda were still undecided. In due course, the Amy Able would be once more a teachers' training college, but the original staff, including Dr Withers, were taking well-deserved retirement, which had been deferred due to the war. A new head was to be appointed; both Rhoda and Evie received letters asking them if they were interested in applying for this position.

Rhoda's father was now vicar of a country church. The mission field was unsafe still in many parts of the ravaged world. Evie decided she wanted to continue teaching, rather than be in administration, so she urged Rhoda to put her own name forward.

'Only if you agree to stay. I'd need your back-up if I get the job,' Rhoda insisted.

Both appointments were confirmed a few days before Evie received Megan's letter, enclosing a brief note from Mattie: *Please don't feel you should discourage her, for my sake – you did your bit all those years ago with young Robbie – now it is my turn!*

Megan studied Evie's response, then she passed the letter to her mother, at the breakfast table. Griff was just leaving for work. 'Tell me later, after you've talked it over,' he said. Gracie jigged in her high chair, knowing she was about to have a kiss. She loved her grandpa, that was obvious, and the feeling was mutual. 'Look after my girl,' he added, and Mattie and Megan knew he meant his little grand-daughter. Gracie was not a bonny baby, as Megan had been – she didn't take after her mother in looks; she was small and skinny, with wispy brown hair and dark eyes with a fleeting squint. However, there were definitely signs of Megan's spirit when she refused to swallow a spoonful of spinach purée. Her red face and tightly closed mouth showed her determination.

Dear Megan,

My advice is, if your parents are happy to look after your baby while you gain further qualifications, send off those applications now! Just what Mattie urged me to do, at your age! Like you, I had family responsibilities, but 'there is always a way'.

Why don't you apply for teacher training? Over here, because of the urgent need for experienced staff, the courses have been shortened to two years, instead of three. Is it the same in the States? I'd be thrilled if you decided to follow in my footsteps!

I have decided to stay on here at the Amy Able as a lecturer in English. So, I have had to make a decision regarding Plough Cottage, which will shortly be derequisitioned. I hope to retire there in twenty or so years' time, but in the meantime, I am offering it as a home for young Robbie, when he is demobbed and marries his fiancée. He will inherit the place eventually, as Mattie knows, but why shouldn't they have the pleasure of living there now?

Good luck, my dear – my best love to you and Gracie, Mattie and Griff.

From Evie.

'Right!' Megan cried. 'I'll be a teacher! Long vacations will make life easier for you and Dad. I'll enjoy playing mom to Gracie then!'

Mattie wasn't quite sure that 'playing mom' was the right expression, but, as she'd learned to do with Megan lately, she kept that thought to herself.

VE Day, 8th May

'We'll have an early, extra Thanksgiving celebration,' Mattie decided. 'A family affair, I think – the war is far from over in the Pacific—' she was about to add: *when the boys come home for good, that'll be the time to pull out all the stops,* when she thought of those who would never return, including Tommy. She glanced at Megan, but she was engrossed in a bulky letter which had arrived among others for her in the morning post.

Megan looked up, flushed with excitement. 'I didn't expect a reply so soon, but I've been invited to an interview! I'll need references – from school, the army and from a "professional person" it says. D'you think Lloyd would qualify, being a professor?'

'I imagine so. They'll be joining us for dinner, you could talk to him then. Not much point enquiring about others for a day or two, till all the excitement dies down, eh? You didn't say where the letter was from, Megan.'

'Well, not Minot State Teachers College, only a mile or two from home, as you hoped. It seems too many applied earlier than me. I'd have to live on campus, if I get a place at this one. It's still North Dakota, but *miles* away.'

She doesn't sound as she'd mind that at all, Mattie reflected wryly to herself. I hope it's not rattlesnake territory – no poisonous snakes in Minot, thank goodness! You could even enjoy the song of the meadow lark when they picnicked in the hills on a summer's day. She'd liked the idea of the local college, which had a mainly female intake. She said: 'Look, I need your help now. Your father's out front cleaning the car, as he's got a day off. Tell him to leave the bucket and sponge and get over to that farm where they promised us a turkey. First come, first served, remind him.'

'I'll go with him, shall I?' Megan was too eager.

'I'd rather you looked after Gracie for the day, if you want to avoid being too involved in the kitchen!' There, I've made my point, Mattie thought.

Unabashed, Megan returned: 'OK Mom! I might push her to town in the pram, to see all the flags flying!'

'I wonder if they've decorated Teddy Roosevelt's statue in Roosevelt Park?' Mattie mused. 'Plenty of high jinks in Trafalgar Square in London, I heard on the wireless. Street parties being organised – I can't imagine much going on at the Amy Able, can you, though? Just a few staff in residence, life will be pretty much the same as usual there . . .'

'Maybe not, with the Yanks not too far away!' Megan grinned.

Sybil hadn't dressed up for the occasion, which was unusual. She wore a simple white blouse and, to Mattie's surprise, serviceable blue jeans. Her hair, which she had grown, was now more white than blonde, and was combed back into a chignon; it actually made her look younger. She had retained her trim figure into her early sixties. She sat down gratefully on the proffered chair and sipped a celebratory glass of sparkling wine while talking to Mattie, who was taking a breather before serving dinner. Megan was actually putting the baby to bed upstairs.

'Lloyd will be over in a little while. He's been working far too hard, and the doctor says it's time he gave up. I'm still busy, of course, with my cosmetic courses, but I have some very capable assistants who could take over. It's time we both retired.'

'You're thinking of moving away from here?' Mattie asked.

'In the autumn: I still can't think of it as the fall, as you do! First, we plan to take a holiday during August: visit Lloyd's sister Ruth and family on Juan Island, a ferry ride from Puget Sound, Washington. She and her husband have a ranch there – together with comfortable quarters, all mod cons for visitors who enjoy helping with the chores. There's not the usual student lot, due to the war, so I wondered if you and Griff would join us there for a couple of weeks, and if he would like to be involved in the harvest?'

'Well, I know Griff will jump at the chance! But what about Megan and Gracie?'

'They can come too! It would do Megan good to work hard outdoors in the fresh air – while you and I relax in the sunshine and keep an eye on the baby.'

'Megan'd be fit to go on to college then. I'll persuade them, don't worry!'

'Lucky I didn't let you throw out my old farm boots, Mattie!' Griff teased her, as he finished carving the turkey, and the plates were passed round the table.

'Oh, those monstrosities! Wait till you see them, Sybil; I did dispose of the old knee britches he wore with 'em – they were so stiff, they could stand up without him in them! Those boots were the very devil to do up, a double row of flat hooks down the front, and long laces which crisscross one to another, and tuck behind the hooks.'

'They don't make them like that nowadays,' Griff said regretfully.

'Just as well!' But Mattie was smiling, too. 'Now, pass the vegetables round.'

Never mind that the pastry on the pumpkin pie was not as short as prewar, fats being rationed. They drank to a liberated Europe and to a speedy end to the war with Japan.

In Lincolnshire Evie and Rhoda attended a thanksgiving service in the local church, followed by a lively social gathering in the village pub. A band played music out on the green, and there were indeed American servicemen dancing with local girls.

Evie and her friend sat a little apart, enjoying the music and the fun, but lost in their own thoughts. Evie hoped that Dave, whom she hadn't heard from again, had come through safely and that he would soon be home with his family. She was content with her lot; it was not the life she had envisaged, but still a good one.

August 1945

Four months previously President Roosevelt had died, and Harry Truman, the Vice-President, took his place. On 23rd May, Winston Churchill resigned, but formed a caretaker government. There was a general election on 5th July. There had been general unrest in the country since the spring, and despite the promise of sweeping changes in health and education, the Labour Party was ready to take over. It took time to count all the votes, especially from those serving overseas in the armed forces.

When the Potsdam Conference resumed it was Clement Atlee who joined Truman and an increasingly dominant Stalin. Churchill was rejected, and dejected.

The family were on San Juan Island when the news came that the atom bombs had destroyed Hiroshima on the 6th of August and devastated Nagasaki on the ninth. The war was over, and the harvest was under way.

Megan was in her element. 'You can drive?' Ruth's husband, Jock, a Scotsman by birth, was delighted when she said 'yes'. After the wheat had been cut and piled into stooks Megan drove to the field in a truck and stopped by each stook in turn. Sometimes it was Griff who stuck his pitchfork into the stook and tossed it into the truck, where another man dealt with it. She drove through woodland to an outlying barn where it was unloaded, then back to the ranch to repeat the performance.

Gracie, in gingham rompers and a tiny baseball cap, crawled on a rug on a stretch of grass under a shady tree. Mattie, in shorts and T-shirt, and Sybil, in a dirndl skirt and sleeveless blouse, sat on canvas seats, taking it in turns to jump out and propel Gracie back on to the rug whenever she tried to venture further. She thought it was a good game. Lloyd sat engrossed in a book. Ruth joined them with a tray of lemonade and home-made shortbread.

'I've never been so lazy before in my whole life,' Mattie confessed, 'I like it!'

'Your Megan's a marvel,' Ruth commented, watching the truck in the distance.

'Yes she is,' Mattie agreed. Megan was enjoying being young and unattached again, she thought. She was sure now that they were doing the right thing, leaving her free to go to college with other girls of her age.

It was a golden holiday, golden grain, glorious sunshine and best of all, *peace*.

TWENTY-SEVEN

Gracie was eight years old and still living with her grand-parents in spring, 1953. Sometimes Mattie looked at her, wondering where all the years had gone to. Not that she or Griff could imagine parting with her now. When Megan qualified as a primary school teacher she had been offered a post near the border of North Dakota and Manitoba, in Canada. It was a small school, taking pupils up to seventh grade, and she said it reminded her of the one she had attended herself before the move to the city.

They'd agreed then that it would be easier for Megan to carry out her duties if Gracie were to join her mother when she was of school age herself, but so far this hadn't happened, because Gracie needed frequent visits to the ophthalmic clinic as her squint became more of a problem. It was Mattie who patiently applied eye drops, supervised special exercises to try to strengthen and straighten the weak eye, and persuaded Gracie to wear spectacles with one blacked-out lens. Eventually, an operation was deemed necessary. It was an anxious time, reassuring a fractious child, but fortunately it was a success. Mattie convinced herself that Megan would not have had the time to deal with all this.

They missed Sybil and Lloyd too, but they were happily settled in the Californian sunshine. Before they left, Sybil received a civic award, a medallion, for her services to humanity in wartime. Many who were helped to conceal their battle scars had regained confidence 'to face the world', as the citation put it. Her family were very proud of her.

Next door there now lived a widow who took in lodgers and was too busy to make small talk. Their other neighbours, Kay's family, were out at work all day. Mattie looked forward mostly to Gracie's return from school, and later, Griff's from work. Visiting family back home in England was further delayed while they brought up another child.

Megan had been with them every other Christmas, weather permitting, and during the school summer holidays she came for a couple of weeks. Last year Griff, Mattie and an excited Gracie had made the lengthy journey by car to stay with Megan. It was not so daunting a ride as it had been all those years ago: their vehicle was comfortable and reliable, there were now places to put up over night, and gas stations which not only had rest rooms and snacks, but could assist, if your transport broke down *en route*.

They kept a long-standing promise to go on to Moose Jaw to see Grace and Mungo, who was now retired. 'Grandma

Grace', Gracie called her other grandmother, but she kept to 'Mommy Mattie', which she'd decided on when she was two years old. She called Megan by her Christian name, and Mattie suspected that Megan thought of Gracie more as a younger sister rather than as her daughter. Grace confided to Mattie that she was disappointed that Gracie had her mother's surname, Parry, rather than Tommy's, but Mattie explained that as he hadn't known of her impending birth, Megan didn't feel she should use his name. Mattie added, 'Gracie, will, I promise be told about her father when she is old enough to understand.'

When Lydia, newly married and living near her parents, came to see her niece Mattie realised that it was Tommy's sister whom Gracie most resembled. Lydia was a tall, thin girl with straight, long brown hair kept off her face with an Alice band, and large, soulful dark eyes behind her glasses. Gracie had recently been prescribed new glasses to correct short sight. She seemed to have more in common with her aunt than her mother. They whispered and giggled together and Lydia spoiled her when they went shopping.

This rapport did not go unnoticed by Megan. I'm jealous, she realised, like Mom was when I was a child, and enthused about being taken out for treats by Sybil. Gracie thinks of Mom and Dad as her parents: they appear to think I'm not responsible enough to care for my own child, when I have *thirty* children in my class at school! She made up her mind to broach the subject when she was next home at Easter, in early April.

Mattie, too, was keeping something to herself regarding Lydia, not even confiding in Griff. Lydia had seized the chance to have a private word with her, when they volunteered to do the washing up together after lunch.

She said: 'If ever you find it too much, looking after Gracie, I would be glad to take her on. My husband has been married before and has a grown-up family – he doesn't want to deal with the baby stage again. Gracie is just the right age—'

'No,' Mattie exclaimed vehemently, if she leaves us, it will be to join *her mother*.'

Megan shared the schoolhouse with the senior teacher; they divided the chores, but Megan took on the small, neglected garden. Her social life, she thought ruefully, was practically non-existent in this rural outpost. She wrote to her mother for advice, and was told to clean the soil by planting a potato patch!

One Saturday morning she was digging and turning over clods of earth, wearing her now ancient dungarees with one of the straps pinned to the front because sewing was not her forte, when she was hailed by a familiar voice from beyond the garden gate. She straightened up, then let out an unladylike squeal: '*Max*! Where have you been all these years? Come in. I'll wash my hands and put the kettle on.'

'Let me hug you first,' he said, as he came up to her. He didn't kiss her but ruffled her curls, as he had as a youth when he wanted to rile her. 'We've got a lot to catch up on.' He followed her indoors.

Megan was glad her colleague was away for the weekend, as this meant she could entertain him. The acerbic Miss Rodda didn't approve of what she called, 'followers'. She'd been at the school since 1935, and had seen younger teachers come and go.

'Sit down,' she invited, in the tiny kitchen. She removed a pile of laundry waiting to be ironed from one hard bentwood chair. 'Now, you start first.'

'Did you know I went to med. school, after demob?'

She nodded.

'I qualified last year. I'm working as a temporary locum not far from here. I am taking up a great opportunity at the end of May, a post at one of the big London teaching hospitals. Grandfather helped to fix it up for me; he still has his contacts in England.

'Sybil sent me your address, and when I discovered how close we were I decided I must look you up before I go. I thought it was time for a reunion.

'I gather you haven't married. Nor have I. We've both been too busy, I guess.'

'I have an eight-year-old daughter, as I believe you know,' Megan said evenly.

'She's being brought up by your parents, I gather?'

Megan's eyes filled with tears. Her voice wobbled. 'Yes – they've been wonderful – but now – well, I want her back. I can cope with being a mother, now.'

She was sitting beside him at the kitchen table, and he put a comforting arm round her shoulders. He said quietly: 'Then you must tell them that, Megan.'

'Gracie, my little girl, she might not want to live with me.'

'You're her mother. It might take time, but you should try, I believe.'

'I must tell them face to face. I'll be home for Easter, next month.'

'I was thinking of paying them a visit myself – maybe you could do with some moral support.'

'I sure could,' she agreed. 'Oh Max, I really hoped to see you again . . .'

'This time I intend to keep in touch.'

He still has his blond good looks, she thought, looking into his blue eyes, but, he's a man now, not an infatuated boy, and me – I'm a woman who loved and lost someone a long time ago.

'I've still got your fraternity pin,' she whispered.

Max had the weekend off, too. 'Let me take you into town later for dinner,' he suggested.

She blushed. He'd obviously seen there wasn't much in the fridge when she'd foraged for something to make him a sandwich at lunchtime. 'The local diner will do,' she told him. 'They do a nice hot chilli con carne. I always cool my mouth with a whopping big ice cream after a plate of that!'

They didn't stop talking all day. Megan reminded him how they had spent much of their childhood making faces at one another. 'You were always so neat and tidy, with your hair slicked back, while I was always' – she indicated the large safety pin on her front ruefully – 'a mess, despite Mom's best efforts. You spent all your holidays with your grandfather, I guess he was old-fashioned. We never heard anything about your parents.'

'That's because my father, my grandparents' only son, left my mother when I was very young. They felt responsible for me, paid for my education. I was sent away to school when my mother remarried. She had another family, and my stepfather didn't care to have me around . . . Like your Gracie, I was very close to my grandparents. My grandmother died while I was still at school, and later grandfather married Sybil and so I sort of felt connected to your family, in a way. Not that you appreciated that, eh?'

'We did become friends later,' she said. 'D'you remember the rodeo which we went to, just before the war, when we were both still at school?'

He grinned. 'I saw you in a new light then – when you volunteered to spin a rope!'

'I made a bit of a fool of myself.'

'You were always ready to have a go. I envied that. Your family encouraged you. My grandfather was too protective. That's why I joined the army straight from school.'

Very late that same evening, back at the schoolhouse, he said regretfully, 'I'd better go.'

'Yes,' she agreed. 'Will you come back tomorrow?'

'You want me to come?' They were standing by the front door, and she nodded.

'I might even put on a dress!'

'This is how I always remembered you, in your dungarees!' He inclined his head towards her. 'Do I get a goodnight kiss?'

'Why not?' she said, as he drew her to him. 'Watch out for the safety pin,' she murmured.

They met as often as possible during the ensuing weeks. Just before Easter, before the trip home, he told her, as they went for an evening stroll in a nearby wood, 'Well, that's it. I took the locum's job for three months, and I've finished there now. There's something I want to ask you. Will you come with me to London? I—'

'Are you suggesting I marry you?'

'I'm not suggesting – I'm asking! As usual you didn't give me time to finish what I was saying! I don't suppose the school will be happy at the lack of notice, but I'll take the blame for that. And before you start finding reasons to say you can't – of course I want Gracie to come with us.'

'You haven't even met her yet! Max, there's something I should tell you – you may change your mind when you hear it. I was very ill when Gracie was born. I was advised not to have more children. That wouldn't be fair to you, not to have a child of your own!'

'I hope, in time, I could be a father figure to your daughter, Megan. My grandfather fulfilled that role very well, for me. Please say you'll think about my proposal, but I need an answer before we leave for Minot.'

'I'll give you my answer now, if you tell me what I most need to know.'

'I love you, Megan.'

'That's all right then and I love you, too! *Yes*!' she almost shouted.

'You'll frighten all the birds out of the trees!' he said.

'It's hard to take all this in,' Mattie said, when they broke the news to her and Griff after Gracie was in bed. Megan had written to ask if it was all right for her to bring a friend home with her for Easter, and they had assumed it was a girlfriend.

'D'you remember Max?' Megan said, when they arrived.

'Of course I do. Why didn't you say who it was?' Mattie asked. She thought: Megan will have to share with Gracie now, and Max can have Megan's room.

'Isn't this rushing things?' Griff put in mildly, now.

'I know, you're thinking of what happened in London, aren't you? It's not like that at all. Yes, we intend to be married as soon as we can arrange it, because Max had already planned to go to England – London again, I admit – and now we've got together again we are *not* going to be parted!' Megan insisted.

Max said quickly: 'Calm down, Megan! Look, all we need to say is that we are both sure of our feelings.'

'I've given my notice in at school,' Megan said defiantly. 'I'm not going back.'

'How long have we got, to make ready for the wedding, and when are you leaving?' With Mattie speechless for once, Griff had to smooth things over.

'Oh, Dad – I knew you'd come up trumps! We'll get a special licence. We're expected in London, in late May. Just in time for the coronation, Mom. Won't Gracie love that!'

'Gracie . . .' Mattie said faintly.

'Yes, Mom. I'll tell her our news tomorrow. She'll be coming with us, of course!'

Later, when Mattie and Megan went upstairs to bed, the men stayed downstairs for a nightcap and a chat.

Mattie paused outside Gracie's door. 'Are you sleeping in here? Or—'

'Oh, Mom darling – I'm not making the same mistake as last time. Max respects that. We haven't slept together

334

yet. I love him, Mom, oh, I *do* – please be happy for me!'
She hugged her mother close. 'I know how much you and
Dad will miss Gracie, but I have to try to make up to her
now, for not being a proper mom, myself . . .'

TWENTY-EIGHT

It wasn't the wedding Mattie had dreamed of when Megan was a teenager: a long white dress and veil, a church packed with wellwishers and rose petals drifting down as the cameras clicked.

'What did you wear on your wedding day?' Megan asked her mother.

'It was thirty years ago, you know! A pale pink linen two-piece, and artificial rosebuds in my hair . . . You could wear something more striking, with your black hair. How about sunshine yellow? I wore a yellow dress once,' she reminisced.

'I remember you telling me, it was when you had your portrait painted, wasn't it? I'm thinking of buying a full-skirted frock, with petticoats, nipped in at the waist and the new mid-calf length, I think, with flat ballet pumps to match . . . don't look so amazed! I like the idea of decorating my hair instead of a veil!'

'You'd want yellow rosebuds if you follow my suggestion, not pink, like me. Is Gracie to be a flower-girl?'

'We're going to ask her. Did you have attendants?'

'I did. They wore pretty cream frocks. My friend Christabel's mother, Dolly, made them. I hope you'll look Christabel up! Her husband is my cousin Walter, and her daughter is Dolly, after her mother.'

'All these people you want us to meet! We'll do our best. But, naturally, Aunt Evie is top of the list!'

It was a civil ceremony, but old friends, including Megan's school pal, Kay, came along, as well as a couple of nurses she had known from working at the hospital, and some of the Bigelow's staff. Others, like Sybil and Lloyd, too far away to attend, sent warm wishes and gifts. There were gifts too from Anna at Red River, the family in England and Grace and Mungo.

Grace wrote: 'May you find happiness a second time, like me with dear Mungo.'

Mattie was sure she would when Megan walked into the registry office on her father's arm. She looked so beautiful, Mattie caught her breath. A beam of sunlight through a window glinted on Gracie's new glasses, the blue frames complementing her taffeta dress. *She* was slowly blossoming, her grandmother thought happily.

Young Gracie was swept along by all the excitement, but the magnitude of what was about to happen, the parting from her beloved Mommy Mattie and Grandad Griff, moving to a strange country, suddenly overtook her later, when Mattie discovered her, crying her eyes out in her room, after they realised she'd crept away from the family party back at the house.

'Come here,' Mattie held out her arms to comfort her.

'Oh, Mommy, I don't want to leave you!'

'You like Max, don't you? You must call Megan Mom, now. She loves you so much and it'll be fun, you know, having a young mother who can do with you all the things I can't, because I get wheezy, and have to rest up at times . . .'

'But she told me she loved my dad, and would have married him.'

'That's true, and she'll never forget him, I know that, but – she has someone else she cares for now, who cares for her, *and* for you. Max is a good man and you're both lucky to have him. We'll write to each other, eh? You'll meet all my lovely family in England, and tell me how they are, won't you? I know you'll miss us, just as Grandad and I have missed the folk back home all these years, too.'

Mattie gently removed Gracie's glasses, lifted the hem of her skirt and, after huffing on them, polished the lenses on her new silk underslip. Gracie's big dark eyes blinked at her grandmother, but she managed a little smile.

Mattie said briskly: 'Now, wipe your eyes, and come and see Grandad and me dance to the old gramophone – that's if we can clear a space in the middle of the company! We'll be good for a laugh, even if we've forgotten the steps!'

Griff whispered in Mattie's ear as they whirled around in their version of the quickstep, 'You look really nice today, Mattie – still got your trim waist, so I can get my arms round you!' He demonstrated.

'I thought of wearing pink again, but I didn't want to clash with the bride. So ivory seemed a good compromise. It's heartening to see all the bright new fashions in the shops again, though it made it hard to choose. I'm glad you got a new suit.'

'Had to,' he admitted ruefully. 'You're such a good cook, Mattie, *my* waistline isn't what it was!'

Gracie was staying with her grandparents for two more days: Megan and Max had booked in at a hotel and from tomorrow would be making last-minute preparations for the flight.

By 10 p.m. the party was over. Gracie was insisting she wasn't tired, which her yawning belied. Mattie and Griff were ready to put their feet up too, to unwind before going to bed.

'It was a lovely day – thank you for all you did to make it possible,' Megan said, hugging them in turn.

Mattie straightened the lopsided band of rosebuds on her daughter's head. 'Now I won't have to worry about you any more – Max can look after you!'

'You can count on it,' he said sheepishly.

When they had gone Gracie was determined not to cry, because she guessed Mommy Mattie and Grandad Griff needed her to be cheerful. They must make the most of this time together, as Grandad quietly said.

*

Another hotel, Megan thought, but no austerity now that the war was behind them. She mustn't think of Tommy tonight . . .

Max slipped into bed beside her, turned off the bedside lamp. 'Are you wearing my fraternity pin on your pyjama jacket?' he joked, reaching out an exploring hand. Then he gave a soft exclamation: '*Oh*—'

'Pyjamas,' she murmured. 'They're in Mom's rag-bag. I meant to replace 'em with a frilly nightdress, but I forgot. You'll have to take me as I am.'

'I don't mind that at all,' he said. 'I'll follow your example, eh?'

'Just us again,' Mattie gripped Griff's arm as they watched the plane take off.

'Yes, another turning point,' he said. 'I'm happy as long as I've got you.'

'I just wish we were back on the farm; city life is becoming so – busy.'

'One day, Mattie, when I retire, we'll go back to the old country, I promise. We've had a good life, in Canada and now here, and I don't regret it, but I know that you—'

'Still dream of picking watercress with dear Evie,' she said simply.

Gracie kept her promise and wrote to them regularly.

I like our new apartment – they call it a flat here. We are on the third floor, and go up in an elevator – they call it a lift. (That is much easier to spell.) Max often works late at the hospital, but Mom and me have, guess what, a television set to watch. Mom makes us popcorn and we pretend we are at the movies. The picture is rather small, but we sit close, because the room is not very big. If the picture isn't right Mom bangs the top of the set, then it gets better. We got the television so we could see the coronation. It went on all day, so we were quite glad when the Queen got crowned. Mom said it was a moment in history.

We are going to Plough Cottage next weekend. Aunty Evie will be there, too. My cousin Robbie who is old to be a cousin, lives there with his family. Mom says we will pick watercress and think of you.

Write soon, I love you, Gracie xx

P.S. At my new school they are impressed I can write and spell so well – they say I am preco – etc. only I can't spell that! I was going to look it up, but Mom says I am getting out of going to bed.

'She *is* precocious,' Griff said fondly to Mattie. 'Not our shy Gracie any more, she's becoming just like her mom and you!'

'I shall ignore that,' Mattie said. 'I'm going to start a new scrapbook: *Letters from a granddaughter in England*. I might even make a copy of the letters I send to Gracie, because I don't suppose she'll keep my replies. I'll stick in photographs, just as I did with my prairie book.'

'Good idea,' he approved. 'Though she might be embarrassed when she rereads her letters when she's grown up!'

'Mommy Mattie was right, Aunty Evie – you and Mom are like two peas in a pod!' Gracie told her, soon after they arrived at Plough Cottage.

'My hair wouldn't be as dark as Megan's, I'm afraid, if I didn't give it a helping hand now and then!' Evie smiled. Like her sister, she'd kept her trim shape.

'You dye it, you mean? Mommy Mattie had her hair *styled*, before Mom and Max got married – at Aunty Sybil's old shop, only it isn't hers now, 'cos she sold it when they went to live in California.'

'I don't suppose Mattie is grey like me, she seems to have kept her hair colour.'

'She says you're still her best friend, as well as her sister.'

'You've made my day, Gracie, telling me that.'

'I've heard so much about Plough Cottage,' Megan said. 'I think I know every corner of it.'

'Of course, I haven't lived here myself since just before the war. Fifteen years – it hardly seems possible to me. Dear Robbie and Vi have kept it all in splendid order – it was never wallpapered in my day, just whitewashed! When I retire, I've suggested that we divide the house between us. I'd like to be this side, which was once the pub, where the rooms are kept ready for my visits – we could call it 1 and 2 Plough Cottages maybe – but that's quite a way in the future!'

'Mum and Dad will be over this afternoon,' Vi said, pouring welcome cups of tea.

'Ronnie is Robbie's father – and Mattie's and my elder brother,' Evie told Gracie.

'I guess I'll work out eventually who you all are,' Gracie said, amid laughter. She added: 'When can we go and pick watercress? I promised Mommy Mattie I would.'

'It's a lovely day – what do you say we all go and pick together?'

'Whatever's this?' Griff asked, when they found a small flat object in Gracie's next letter.

Mattie knew. 'She's pressed a sprig of watercress – just as you do flowers! Careful, it's very fragile. That'll certainly go in the scrapbook.'

TWENTY-NINE

In November 1960 Griff had the opportunity to retire within three months. Their longed-for trip to England could be possible in the spring. Mattie was advised by her doctor to wait for better weather, not to arrive to cold and damp conditions in the UK.

Megan, Max and Gracie had been back to the States once, two years previously, when they managed only a fleeting visit to Mattie and Griff because they were responding to sad news from Sybil, in California. 'Please come, your grandfather is dying, and asking for you . . .' Within six weeks of losing Lloyd, Sybil had a fatal stroke. Griff, as executor of their estate, had to deal with everything. It was a stressful time. A modest legacy had come their way then, but Max and Megan were the main beneficiaries.

'Please allow us to book your flights,' Megan wrote. 'Stay as long as you like!'

Mattie replied, 'As soon as your father finishes at work . . .'

Gracie hadn't corresponded with them for several months, and Mattie realised, she's growing up fast, almost sixteen: I'm not Mommy Mattie any more, but 'Gran'. I must seem incredibly old to Gracie! At her age I'd left school and was a working girl.

Megan wasn't going to upset her parents by telling tales. Gracie was becoming rude and rebellious, intent on doing all the things her mother and stepfather would rather she didn't. She was a bright girl, but she'd skipped school on several occasions recently. Megan had been summoned by the headmistress and told her daughter would be suspended if this continued.

When Megan and Max managed to sit down with Gracie to try to sort out matters, Gracie sat there sullenly, then said: 'Does *he* have to be here? He's not my father. It's nothing to do with him!'

When Megan opened her mouth to make an angry reply Max put out a restraining hand. 'I've always thought of you as my daughter, Gracie,' he said evenly. 'We've had a good relationship, haven't we?'

Gracie turned her head away. 'I don't like school, Mom. I don't want to sit silly old exams. Don't you know I can leave home when I'm sixteen? If you don't stop going on at me, I will!' Then she flounced out of the room.

She was closeted in the bathroom for the next couple of hours. In the morning she appeared with a 'don't you dare say anything' expression. She was wearing her school uniform, but she had dyed her hair jet black.

'All right, I'll go to school. I'll do those stupid O levels, then I'll get a job – and I'll choose what I want to do myself!'

When she'd flounced out, Megan sat down again at the kitchen table and cried floods of tears.

'I must go,' Max said awkwardly. 'Teenage hormones – she'll get over it—'

'Hormones? I know I was a bit of a monster at that age, but not as bad as that!'

'Different times.'

'What are the school going to say about her hair?'

'Nothing, if they're sensible. She'll get fed up with it, if no one appears to notice.'

Max buttoned up his overcoat to go to work. 'Why don't you write to Evie and ask her advice – she's had plenty of experience with adolescent girls, after all.'

'I will! Max – you don't regret taking Gracie on, do you?' Megan's voice was muffled by the thickness of his coat as she clung to him, 'I *need* a hug this morning!'

He obliged. 'I've never thought of it like that. You, me, Gracie, we're a family. She's *our* daughter. There, feel better now?'

'Oh darling Max, I do!'

Evie's response was by return of post. She wrote:

What a coincidence! I was about to write to you as Rhoda and I are booked to attend a three-day seminar in London the week after next. Amy Able is now under the umbrella of the local education authority! A good thing in many ways, but it seems we need to become more up to date in some respects.

Noreen has invited us to stay with her, but I had already decided to visit you one evening as it seemed too good an opportunity to miss. I can't promise to solve your problem, but I'll certainly have a try! Will ring, love Evie.

There was the weekend to get through first, Megan thought ruefully. After her outburst, Gracie maintained an aloof silence when her parents were around. She didn't rise from her bed on Saturday until lunch-time, when she spoke three words to her mother. 'I'm going out.'

'Come away from the window, she'll think you're spying on her,' Max told Megan.

'She got into an open-top car – in this weather! Some lout sitting at the wheel, he didn't open the door for her. Probably hasn't got a licence – he's got dyed hair too!'

'How can you tell?' Max asked mildly. 'I gather you didn't recognise him?'

'No. He drove off too fast. Didn't you hear that noise from the exhaust?'

'Mmm. Relax, Megan. They won't get far in all the Saturday traffic. Just be thankful she's not perched on the pillion of a powerful motorbike, eh?'

'Oh, you! You're just like Dad with Mom – that soothing voice . . .'

'Is that so bad?' he asked.

'No-o. What d'you mean by "relax"?' she demanded.

'I'm open to suggestions,' he said, with a smile.

She plumped down on his lap, wound her arms round his neck. 'A kiss?'

'That's a promising start,' he murmured. 'We're unlikely to be interrupted . . .'

'This is deliciously decadent,' Megan giggled, snuggling up to him in bed. 'What a way to spend Saturday afternoon at home!'

'It beats watching horse-racing on TV,' Max agreed. 'It's rather inhibiting, you know, with a glowering teenager playing loud music on a record player in the next room. We've made up our minds to live permanently over here, so we ought to think of moving out of London, buying a house while we can afford it. You miss having a garden, I know . . .'

'We can't do anything until Gracie leaves school,' said Megan.

'Which now looks likely to be soon, eh? You could go back to teaching; that's if you want to, of course.'

'I do – but I didn't like to say! Oh, I've enjoyed my voluntary work at the hospital, because I could fit that in round Gracie, but I know every book in that library trolley by now, and as an old patient told me ungratefully the other day, "You can't make a decent cup of tea, gal!" '

'That's true – but you make an excellent pot of coffee!'

He was distracting her now, lightly caressing her throat and bare shoulders with his fingertips. 'You haven't worn your gold chain and pendant since our wedding day.'

'It didn't seem right. I – couldn't bring myself to remove Tommy's photograph. I thought I'd give it to Gracie on her eighteenth birthday.'

'You still think of him? You don't regret . . .'

'Regret marrying you? Max, it was the best decision of my life!'

'And mine,' he said. 'Well, how about coffee, and cake? I'm getting hungry.'

'You'll have to wait! I fancy a bit more relaxing first. Then we'll have toasted crumpets in bed. Cake makes too many crumbs!'

At just after eight in the evening, the phone shrilled. Max rolled over in bed, reached for the instrument, on his side of the bed. 'Not the hospital,' he hoped.

Gracie's agitated voice almost deafened him. 'We're in Richmond – we had a meal at a roadhouse – the car had a flat tyre, and there isn't a spare – we had to leave it on the roadside, and walk a couple of miles here . . . We – we haven't got enough money to pay for the meal, but the manageress took us in to her office and said "ring your father and tell him to come and get you . . ." You will come, won't you? Digby will give you directions . . .'

'*Digby*,' Max said sotto voce to Megan, who had overheard all. 'The lout has a name!' He said into the mouthpiece: 'I'll have to get dressed first, I may be some while. Why don't you offer to wash up to cover what you owe? Put Digby on.'

'Why have you gone to bed this early?' Gracie demanded.

'Tell her we're old and need our sleep,' Megan put in.

'Mom? Is that you?'

'Who else would be in bed with your dad? Where's Digby? I'll write down the details while Max gets ready.'

Megan filled a flask with coffee, slipped a bar of chocolate in the bag. 'Your good deed should hopefully guarantee restored communications! Drive safely. At least you're not going into a dust storm.'

Gracie and Digby were sitting in the reception area of the roadhouse when Max arrived some two hours later. Max noted that Digby was hardly dressed for the cold weather, in a hand-knitted tank top in lurid stripes over a summer shirt and patched jeans. Gracie at least wore over her jeans and T-shirt what she called a sloppy joe sweater, with sleeves so long, she'd pulled them down over her cold hands. Digby was occupied in gnawing his nails, but managed a grunt: 'Thanks mate.' He didn't appear to be one of the sixth-formers at Gracie's school, whom Gracie referred to disparagingly as 'swots'.

The manageress had declined their offer of washing up and presented the bill to Max. 'They offered me five shillings in coppers between them, but I said, "I expect your dad will pay – they usually do." '

It was too dark and too late to inspect the car. 'Your father can see to that,' Max said briefly. 'Where do you live?'

'Stepney. It's my uncle's car.'

'Are you insured to drive it?'

'Yes. I drive him around, he's disqualified. He's in a band, so am I.'

'How did you meet my daughter?'

'She and her mates came to one of our gigs. I play drums.'

'Aren't you usually making . . . music . . . on a Saturday night?'

'I was supposed to be meeting up with the lads later. Too late now . . .'

'What a pity,' Max said acidly.

From the back seat Gracie exploded: 'Oh, leave it, Dad! *Please!*'

Dad, he thought, she called me Dad. Megan will be pleased.

The rest of the journey passed in silence.

*

Evie came to see them on Tuesday evening. Max was working late, and Megan was busy in the kitchen, making Gracie's favourite meat-loaf supper. This involved browned steak mince, seasoned well, spread with half a bottle of tomato ketchup (which she still called catsup) topped with mashed potato, sprinkled with cheese, and baked in the oven. She intended to stay out of the way while Evie and Gracie talked.

'I like your hair,' Evie said, meaning it. 'It suits you.'

Gracie was pleased. The dye was not a permanent one, but she'd hastened the recovery process by having her hair cut fashionably short, with a gamine fringe. Her friends said she looked like Audrey Hepburn, when she'd had her hair shorn in *Roman Holiday*, that was when she didn't wear her glasses but looked out on a misty world with those huge, dark eyes.

Gracie came straight to the point – she was her mother's daughter after all. 'I suppose you know I want to leave school after my exams, and not stay on for the sixth form in the hope of going on to university?'

'Yes. I'm not here to make you change your mind. But I'd like to see you train properly for whatever job you have in mind. Any ideas?'

'I want to be an actress. I love reading aloud, performing in school plays. But I don't know how to go about it. My school doesn't teach drama as such.'

'There are stage schools. You might get a scholarship to one in exceptional circumstances, but your parents would probably have to pay for your tuition. Even then, they will only take pupils who have real talent, and determination. You could back up what could be a precarious living with extra training as a drama teacher. Would you like me to find out some facts about possible schools or colleges while I'm in London?'

'Oh, I would! Thank you, Aunty Evie.'

'I was helped to fulfil my ambitions by a friend,' Evie said quietly, 'My mother thought I should stay at home to care for the family. I hope I am there for them when needed, but I wanted to make my own way in life.'

'Didn't you want to get married?'

'Maybe I thought about it, once or twice, but you know, it's possible to be happy and single! It has quite a lot to recommend it, in my experience. I'm very fond of my nephews and nieces, which, of course, includes you! I still miss my wonderful sister Mattie. She's founded quite a dynasty – a *female* one!'

Megan was banging a spoon on a mixing bowl. 'Supper's ready, you two!'

THIRTY

SPRING, 1961

The United States had a brash new young President, John F. Kennedy, known as Jack, warmly endorsed by the outgoing incumbent of the White House, General Dwight D. Eisenhower. The Cuban crisis was about to erupt. The Americans were heavily involved in the space race with Russia. Khrushchev was negotiating a peace treaty with East Germany, American troops were fighting in Vietnam, and US Polaris submarines were based in Scotland.

Great Britain, too, had seen political changes over the last few years, but Harold Macmillan was now apparently steady at the helm. National Service was no more. There was unrest in the Colonies: the UK was making overtures to the EEC and inflation was escalating.

We have a new home! (*Megan wrote to her parents*.) A spacious ground-floor flat in an Edwardian terrace in a quiet situation. No front garden (for potatoes!)

but a courtyard at the back. A real sun-trap and not overlooked. I am buying lots of pots to grow all my favourite flowers.

We decided to stay in London because of Max's work. He is in line for a consultancy, we hope! Also, when Gracie leaves school this summer she will enrol at the polytechnic for theatre studies, just a short bus-ride away!

Please come to see us soon, as promised!

Your loving daughter,

Megan.

Mattie was nursing an unexpected bout of hayfever when the airmail arrived. Griff brought it up to her on her breakfast tray, which he balanced carefully on her knees.

Wiping her streaming eyes and blowing her sore nose, she said huskily: 'You open it, and read it to me, there's a dear. I really shouldn't be so lazy, lying in bed expecting you to wait on me, you know.'

'A retired husband's privilege,' he returned. 'It's coming up to our thirty-ninth wedding anniversary. Next year it'll be our Ruby wedding!' He felt for his reading glasses in a pocket, sat on the edge of the bed, while she cracked the top of the soft-boiled egg. When Megan and then Gracie were small girls, she'd cut thin strips of bread and butter for dipping in the yolk. Griff had done the same for her. There was a pink rosebud in a second egg-cup.

She looked at him lovingly as he bent his head to decipher Megan's large, looped handwriting. The bald patch on the crown of his head was visible, which it wasn't when he stood up, because he was taller than she was. She was suddenly aware that he was faltering in his speech – the flimsy blue paper was wavering in his hands. As if in slow motion, he slumped forward, across her lower legs.

Mattie endeavoured to shift up in the bed, to free her trapped limbs, while the tray went crashing to the floor. She stepped over the debris and attempted to lift him to a sitting position, but was unable to do so. Trembling, she picked up the bedside phone, dialled the emergency code.

Then she knelt beside him and cradled his inert body in her arms. She heard a voice say loudly, not recognizing it was her own: 'Wake up, darling, I'm here . . .'

There was the sound of splintering wood downstairs in the entrance hall, as the front door was forced open, and then footsteps pounded up the stairs.

They tried everything they could to resuscitate Griff, but it was too late, he was pronounced dead at the scene.

'He is sixty years old,' she said simply, when they asked his age.

'A massive coronary – a long-standing heart condition,' was the medical verdict.

Mattie just couldn't take that in. Griff had never complained: he'd cared for her and boosted her spirits during her own spells of poor health. How could she carry on without him? She could only take it day by day.

So it was that Mattie's family came to North Dakota, instead of the way it should have been, Mattie and Griff flying home to England to be with them.

Mattie, of whom Griff once said, 'You always seem to feel better when you've had a good cry,' had been resolutely dry-eyed since the family arrived. She comforted Megan and Gracie and tried to reassure them by telling them that Griff couldn't have suffered, because the end had mercifully been so quick. Max was kind and thoughtful in his quiet way, and took over the funeral arrangements. They could only stay a few days.

'Mom, leave everything, and come back with us,' Megan entreated.

Mattie shook her head. 'I can't just walk away from here after thirty years.'

'You've nothing to keep you here now.' Megan instantly regretted saying that.

'I imagine I will come home for good at some time in the future, but I'm not ready to let all this go, all that your father worked so hard for. I need to come to terms with what has happened. I'm not yet over the shock.' Mattie thought: maybe I never will be. I've lost the love of my life. I can't . . . *abandon* him . . .

Easter had been at the beginning of April this year. The last excursion, as they called it, which they had enjoyed together, was the hundred-mile drive to the Peace Garden, on the border between North Dakota and Manitoba. This beautiful sanctuary symbolised the long friendship between the United States and Canada. It was also symbolic to Mattie and Griff of the link they themselves had with both countries and where they had embarked on their great adventure.

In the Peace Garden the wild prairie rose, the State flower, designated as such in 1907, bloomed alongside more exotic varieties. It was soft pink in colour with a golden centre, and reminded Mattie of the briar roses in the hedgerows she'd loved, in her childhood in Suffolk. Griff had instantly recalled the pink costume she wore on their wedding day. 'Your colour, Mattie.' He sketched her sitting in the garden, with roses in the background.

Now, she said, 'No hothouse flowers for Griff, please: just the prairie rose.'

Griff hadn't been a regular churchgoer, nor had she, since the days when she'd gone on most Sundays to the Lutheran church, while they lived at the farm. His mother, she knew, had been a chapel-goer in Wales, where she had met and married Griff's father.

'We'll take him back to the prairie, to be laid to rest in the cemetery there,' she decided. 'It was the first place he thought of as "home" – after an unsettled childhood.'

'I'll drive you over,' Max offered. 'See if it can be arranged . . .'

'We'll all go, if Mom doesn't mind,' Megan suggested. 'I've not been back there since we got caught in the dust storm. Gracie should see where I was born.'

'We never went again either. I felt sad, you see, after that last visit, because I was reminded how much I loved – and still missed – the old place,' Mattie told them. She paused. 'I need to go there now, for Griff's sake.'

The little township had expanded even further, people looked prosperous, there were more shops, but the garage was still in place, even though it had been modernised by a new owner. The provision store was now a regular drug-store, but there was still a sign: MATTIE'S ICE CREAM SOLD HERE.

'Same recipe, I hope,' Megan said, as she and Gracie went to buy a cornet each. They were able to tell Mattie that the ice cream was still made in the same way from the same dairy products, by 'Your friend Gretchen.'

They stopped off at Gary's café, and there he was, grey-haired now, but smiling to see old friends, then concerned when he learned why they had returned.

'Please don't think it's an intrusion,' he said, reaching for his camera, under the counter. 'I must have a picture to prove I saw you again . . .'

Gretchen, still blonde and braided but more buxom, was at the church to greet them, and to introduce them to the new pastor, still considered by his flock to be a relative newcomer after ten years.

'Later,' she said, 'you must come back to the old place and eat with us before you journey home. My uncle and aunt have both passed away since we last met, and now we farm with the help of our three big sons. Wenche was married a year ago.'

Gracie took her grandmother's arm as they went together to look at the dairy, and the cows lined up for the afternoon milking.

'Let them go on their own,' Max told Megan gently, as she made to follow.

Gracie said, as they walked slowly back to the farmhouse: 'Oh, Mommy Mattie – how could you bear to leave all this?'

The tears rained down Mattie's pale cheeks then. She stood stockstill, and Gracie clutched her in a fierce embrace. They cried together, united in their sadness.

Mattie said at last: 'This was a dream fulfilled, when we came here. It was a great deal harder to survive than we ever imagined it would be, but Griff and I were proud of what we achieved. Those days are past. We made a good life for ourselves in the city, too, and we had Megan, and then, you. Grandad Griff and I were looking forward to a happy retirement, starting with a visit to England. We never intended to leave it so long – I regret I never saw my parents again, although we always kept in touch . . .'

'Aunty Evie wants you to come, very much.'

'Tell dear Evie, I will – but not just yet.'

'I still miss you a lot. Mom and I – well, we clash sometimes. She doesn't understand me, like you do.'

'She does, but she was headstrong when she was your age, and she's afraid—'

'I'll make a big mistake, like she did?' Gracie challenged.

'I never think of it like that! Nor must you, Gracie. Look, if you'd rather talk to the older generation, like me, go to Evie – she'll soon put you right!'

It was a simple service, following the long, slow journey by the cortège. A lovely day, though with the need to hold on to hats and to smooth down skirts in the strong breeze. Family were joined in the church pews by those who had known the Parrys years ago, and came to pay their respects. The harmonium swelled, there was heartfelt singing, prayers, and then they followed Griff to his final resting place.

Mattie, Megan, Max and Gracie went back to the farm for refreshments before driving home.

As she had said, twenty odd years ago about Bert, Gretchen observed quietly to Mattie, 'I don't ever forget you, you see . . .' She paused. 'I will take care of him.'

'I know you will . . . Gretchen, can't you call me Mattie after all this time?'

Gretchen smiled. 'To me, you'll always be "the Missus". Did Bert ever marry?'

'No – but he's done well: chief engineer on the railway. Anna, his grandmother, is still alive. Bert takes care of her nowadays. I'm sure he has his memories too.'

She said goodbye to her family at the front gate. 'Don't come to the airport,' Megan insisted. 'We love you Mom!' The taxi was waiting.

'I know you do.' Mattie said. She actually wanted to be alone now, to cope in her own way with her loss. She hugged Megan, then Max, and last of all, Gracie. 'Try hard in your exams; follow your dreams,' she whispered. She thought: Griff never achieved what he might have with his gift for drawing. I let my writing lapse, but we did follow our dream.

She looked at the weeds in the garden. It needed digging over. There were seed potatoes to plant. Griff had done all the heavy work for years now, but if she took it at a steady pace, she thought, she could do it herself. She wouldn't be able to sort through things indoors yet, that could wait. She needed to be physically tired to be able to sleep at night. Maybe she could grow enough vegetables to sell at the gate – the thought actually made her smile – and she could experiment with her ice-cream making. She'd have to buy a book on it, for nowadays there were all sorts of rules and regulations, but this was yet another beginning, and this time she had to go it alone.

THIRTY-ONE

1971

The house echoed in its emptiness as it had the day Mattie, Griff and Megan had arrived to live there – was it really getting on for forty years ago? It was ten years since Griff had died. Mattie hadn't intended to stay there so long. When Evie retired from the Amy Able in 1968 and returned to Plough Cottage, she'd written to her sister: 'Now you have no excuse not to come – oh, the two of us together again – how wonderful!'

Mattie had seen Megan and Max several times during these years, including last fall, when Megan said bluntly, 'Don't you want to sell up after all?'

Gracie, of course, was long since grown up. There had been more adolescent *angst*, and she hadn't lived at home since she was eighteen, when she had her first walk-on part in a touring play. Megan hadn't confirmed it, but reading between the lines in the occasional postcard Gracie sent her grandmother, Mattie suspected that Gracie was living with her boyfriend, an actor named Lachlan. Megan sent Mattie a snap of the two of them at a party: Mattie hardly recognised the sultry, pouting young woman with long, straight hair, in a skimpy dress, with a brimming glass in one hand and a cigarette in the other. Lachlan, on whose lap she perched, had long locks, too, an earring, and a shirt open to the waist. How was it, she thought dismayed, that she could discern a similarity to the young Griff? Perhaps because Lachlan too had a dark Celtic air.

The world was changing at an accelerating rate. There had been the terrible assassinations in America which stunned the population. On the other side of the Atlantic there were the dark troubles in Northern Ireland. Decimalisation of Britain's coinage had taken place, the Common Market was in sight. The trade unions were in an uproar, strikes were frequent, unemployment rising.

Mattie realised that she would have to prepare herself for a few shocks when she returned to England. But surely, she thought, Plough Cottage will be as it was?

Her luggage was piled ready for collection in the hall. The little trunk was there, with all the treasures she'd collected together over the years. She'd looked in there once more, then closed the lid and fastened the straps to keep it secure. The furniture had gone to auction. Her good neighbours would let her know how that went, in due course. She glanced at her watch. There came a knock on the door. The new owners were on time. She was glad the house was going to friends: Megan's schoolfriend Kay's son and his wife.

She opened the door, welcomed them in. They were going to measure up for curtains and decide where their furniture could go. They were in their twenties, with no family as yet, the girl was in blue jeans and a sweatshirt which matched her husband's.

'I can't wait to plant all my favourite flowers in the front garden.' Katy smiled.

Mattie smiled back, thinking, she'll be surprised when she digs up the odd potato!

'I left the kitchen curtains up, I thought you might like those,' she said.

She saw the girl bite her lip. 'Thank you.'

Mattie added quickly, 'Of course, you may want a different colour. You can always start a rag-bag with mine!' She sensed they were waiting for her to go, so that they could explore the house on their own, and make plans. 'Well, your grandfather will be waiting to take me to the hotel. Then he has kindly offered to take me to the airport tomorrow morning. Good luck! I hope you'll be as happy as we were here.'

I don't suppose they'll stay forty years, as I have, she said to herself. And I wonder if Mattie's Ice-Cream Kiosk will open up again this summer in the park by the pool? Will they find someone to run it who enjoys watching the kids at play, as much as I did? That kept me going on the days I missed Griff most.

The flight was all that Megan and Max had assured her it would be. It was amazing to think that this time the journey in reverse would take hours, not days. She sat back in her comfortable seat and actually dozed, for she had been too excited to sleep much last night.

Her daughter and son-in-law were waiting to greet her when she came towards them, trundling her baggage. The necessary formalities completed, they drove home.

'Will Evie be there?' Mattie wondered hopefully.

Megan was in the back with her mother, holding tight on to her hand as she had as a child. 'Mom, she said she'd see you in a couple of days, when we take you to the cottage. She said it ought to be just family today. You'll have all the time in the world to catch up, after all.'

'Gracie?'

'Gracie and Lachy are appearing in a show in Drury Lane! They don't rise very early, but they'll make an exception for you, and join us for lunch.'

'No wedding bells yet?'

'Not even a tinkle! She's only twenty-six. I guess you're hoping for a great-grandchild, eh? There's nothing maternal about our Gracie, I'm afraid!'

'I knew someone else like that! And here you are, enjoying supply teaching nowadays, eh?'

'Gracie may do the same one day – if the starring parts continue to elude her.'

Later, as she changed out of the smart pants suit into a shirtwaist frock, and tidied her hair, she looked round the guest room, wondering who had chosen the geometrically patterned bright wallpaper and the jazzy curtains. She glanced through the window, saw that it overlooked the courtyard, and smiled to see a tiny, splashing fountain and pots both large and small, with unusual plants. Not a potato in sight!

Gracie had long ago discarded her glasses. 'Contact lenses,' she confided. 'At least I can see where I'm going now, and am in no danger of falling off the stage!'

Mattie thought immediately that Gracie was far too thin, but she knew better than to comment on that. Actually, Gracie had a good appetite, and obviously enjoyed the smoked salmon, tiny buttered potatoes and green salad, with crusty bread. She declined the lemon meringue tart, saying she preferred a cigarette with her coffee.

Lachy said very little, allowing Gracie to do all the talking. Mattie was relieved to see that his shirt, with its tapering collar, was buttoned to the neck and that he even sported a bootlace tie. He'd grown a lot of facial hair since that photo was taken.

Some time later, in the comfortable sitting room, Mattie rested her head back in her armchair, and before she knew it, she was asleep. The journey had taken its toll.

'We must go, Mom.' Gracie dropped a light kiss on her grandmother's forehead. 'Tell Mommy Mattie we'll see her again soon. If she feels up to it, before she goes to Aunty Evie's, why don't you bring her to the theatre? I could wangle some seats.'

They were driving through the countryside, and Mattie kept exclaiming, 'Oh, it's just as I remembered it!' She'd only passed through London on a bus on her way to catch the train to Plymouth when she was eighteen years old, but it had changed in many ways since the wartime bombing and later rebuilding.

The door to Plough Cottage stood open. Megan and Max let Mattie go forward on her own, to greet her sister. The two women embraced, and then there was laughter and tears, and the welcoming words from Evie, 'Here you are at last, then!'

After the others had left for London, and Robbie and Vi, who had joined them for a while, retired to their side of the old house, Mattie went from room to room with her sister, exclaiming with pleasure as she recognised the old and familiar things.

'I had the kitchen made more up to date,' Evie said apologetically.

'You haven't got a washing-machine,' Mattie noted.

'No, just a Baby Burco boiler. Gets the sheets as white as Mother did!'

'Well, please let me contribute a few things – like a washing-machine and a spin dryer. We don't want to be all day doing chores – I've been looking forward to revisiting all our favourite local places.'

'The stream, and the watercress bed, I imagine?'

'That most of all,' Mattie said softly. 'Now I'm here, and will be *for ever*.'

1985

Gracie telephoned and asked if she might visit them one weekend in May.

'Is Lachy coming?' Evie asked.

'No. We are both not working at present, and there's not much prospect of me doing so, but he has an audition for a radio play.' Gracie sounded rather off-hand.

'Oh dear.' Evie turned to Mattie as she put down the phone. 'I wonder if they are thinking of splitting up . . .'

'Megan hinted that something was up.' Mattie was reclining on the sofa. She'd been laid low with a chest infection which stubbornly resisted medication.

'Are you up to a visitor, old dear?'

'Not so much of the old; you make me feel over eighty!'

'Well, you may not look it, but you are, and I am going to take care of you, whether you like it or not!'

'Of course I want to see Gracie. She's forty now . . . doesn't seem possible.'

'Forty she may be, but she's taking her time to grow up, eh?'

'I thought she'd be married by now,' Mattie said. 'Probably too late for a family.'

But when they saw Gracie they realised instantly that it wasn't too late, at all.

Gracie was wearing a fine almost transparent Indian dress in an unusual shade of green, fitted under her breasts and flowing loose over a definite bump. 'Yes, I'm pregnant,' she said defiantly. 'Just as much a shock to me as it obviously is to you both.' She moved a footstool next to the sofa and sat on it, looking up at her grandmother. She was actually wearing her glasses today, which somehow made her look vulnerable.

Evie hesitated, then said, 'I'll make the tea. You two – *talk*.'

Mattie fingered the soft material of Gracie's long sleeve. 'I remember we had a lovely range of Indian silks and cottons in the emporium at Plymouth. Christabel and I, we had dresses made from remnants bought for a few shillings, when we went on a bank holiday outing . . .'

'The only outing I have in view is to the maternity hospital,' Gracie said.

'What does Lachy think about this? Isn't he going to ask you to marry him now?'

'He's been on at me for years about that! He's a vicar's son, didn't you know?'

'No . . . I didn't know.' Mattie was aware she was wheezing; she must keep calm.

'Well, when I get used to the idea, I might,' Gracie sounded less defiant. 'I-I thought you'd be upset and say how could I, and all that . . .'

'I didn't say that to your mother, though I was worried stiff because she was so young, and I won't say it to you, either. In my view, and your dear Grandad's, a baby is always a blessing! Does Megan know?'

'Yes, and she said I must tell you myself – that's why I'm here.'

'I'm glad. I really am.'

Evie wheeled in their latest acquisition, a tea trolley. 'Is everything all right?' she asked anxiously.

'Everything is very all right,' Mattie said. 'Except I need a spoonful of linctus in case I cough all over those lovely cakes!'

Gracie and Lachy had a quiet wedding in September: the baby was due in November. They were staying with Megan and Max in London as Lachy had a regular spot in a series on radio.

It was obvious that Mattie's health was declining, but she was determined to see the baby soon after it was born.

'You mustn't think of travelling here. Mom and Dad have promised to drive us to Suffolk, as soon as I am up to it! Ask Aunty Evie if the crib is still in the loft,' Gracie said over the phone as she settled in at the hospital for the birth.

Evie, who was on the receiving end of panic calls from Megan, wisely kept the news of Gracie's difficult confinement from her sister. It was a great relief to her when she was able to tell Mattie, 'It's a girl! Six pounds something – I didn't quite hear all Megan was saying, she was so excited!'

'Is all well? I was rather hoping it would be a boy, because Gracie said she'd call the baby after Griff . . .'

'I think you'll be pleased when you know the baby's name, Gracie wants to tell you herself, and yes, all's well, it seems, thank goodness.'

A week later Gracie placed a small bundle in her grandmother's arms. 'She's Matilda, after you, Mommy Mattie – are you pleased?'

'Oh, I am, but you might prefer to shorten it to Tilly, this time.'

'Would you like that?'

'Yes.' Mattie, propped up by pillows on the sofa, cuddled the baby close. 'She's got dark hair, so far, maybe she'll have curls like your mom and Evie.'

'I don't know about that, but she's got a lot to live up to,' Gracie said softly.

EPILOGUE

Tom had gone abroad after their graduation, as he had always planned. He wanted Tilly to accompany him on his travels, for them to paint together in exotic locations, 'before they disappear for ever,' he said.

Tilly had another idea. 'It's Aunt Evie's hundredth birthday just before Christmas. She's getting very frail – she has a full-time carer now. But her mind is as sharp as ever, and she still writes to me regularly, as you know. She took over keeping in touch with the family from Mattie. She's the last one of that generation left. She wants me to be at her party.'

'You could come home for the celebration,' Tom thought. 'Think about it.'

'I already have. There's something I want to do in the meantime.'

'What?'

'She sent me that slip of paper in her last letter – the address where the painting of Mattie, or rather the unknown girl was sent to, can you believe, over ninety years ago? I want to follow the trail – find the picture – take a photograph of it, if it still exists, and give it to Evie on her birthday.'

He gave her a fierce hug. 'I'll miss you.'

'And I'll miss you. But we both have to do our own thing,' Tilly said. 'Like the artist, wish me good luck.'

'I do. Keep in touch . . .'

'Always,' she promised.

It was a time for writing letters. First to the address in Somerset given by Mr B., but although Tilly promptly received a pleasant reply, the present occupant had only lived there for four years. She knew nothing of the artist, or the picture. However, she recalled that the previous owner had mentioned that the family for whom the house had been built had lived there until the 1970s, when the property was sold for the first time.

The letter concluded: *I enclose an address for my predecessor. We exchange Christmas cards, so I know this lady still lives there. Perhaps she can help?*

Tilly had decided that she should correspond in her own handwriting, not dash off something which might appear too official on the computer. She had forgotten, she thought ruefully, how long it took to put pen to paper and write a letter a stranger would want to read. The older generation preferred a fountain pen to ballpoint.

There was a frustrating two weeks before she had a response to her enquiry.

I found your letter most interesting! I was told by a surviving member of the original family at Moat House when I moved there with my husband and young children, that her grandfather had been an esteemed surgeon at one of the big London teaching hospitals. Sadly, his wife died young, and he brought up a large family with the help of his unmarried sister and quite an army of servants (I had to manage with one splendid local daily help!) because, naturally, he was not often at home.

I do not remember seeing the picture you mention when we were shown over the house for the first time, but the granddaughter, who lived there then had most things packed away, the furniture under dustsheets and so on. She had lost interest in the place. I'm afraid this lady is no longer with us.

I wonder if you have thought of writing to the Academy to find out if they have any record of the artist's descendants?

Well, Tilly now knew just a little about the place, and to whom the picture had gone. Another letter to write! But first, she must research the artists of the time and try to find the mysterious Mr B!

At her parents' home in Surrey one of the walls in the sitting-room had been fitted with shelves for books. There was a whole row of weighty encyclopaedias encased in grainy leather with copious illustrations. These had been published at the end of the nineteenth century. There were several artists with a surname which began with 'B' but only one who seemed a possibility: the son of German immigrants, a tailor and a seamstress who took up residence in the east end of London in the 1870s. There was a short piece on the artist and his work, but no photograph of him or facsimile of any of his pictures. He was said to be a painter of rural scenes, mainly watercolours, but it was noted that latterly the artist had executed some portraits in oils, one of which had been accepted by the Royal Academy.

So, Tilly said to herself, it might be worth writing there to see what they know of this particular artist and where he was after the outbreak of the First World War.

She received a formal acknowledgement of her letter within a week or two, with a note saying that her communication had been passed on to someone who might be able to help her with her quest. They must leave it to this person to get in touch and not reveal any further details, they said.

Oh, another wait, (she wrote to Tom) and it's already November! Maybe I am on a wild goose chase, after all . . . I'm glad I decided to make this a surprise for Aunt Evie, because if I don't manage to find the picture then she won't be disappointed. How I wish you were here!

A month went by. Tilly was ready to give up. Then a letter in unfamiliar writing arrived. She opened it with shaking hands. Was this a polite rebuff? As she began to read, delight spread across her face.

Dear Tilly (if I may call you that),

You have found me out! I am a cousin, several times removed of the artist. I never knew him personally because he died during the Great War. Broken-hearted, my grandmother said, because he was forced to leave his home. I am the custodian of his unsold paintings, which I am afraid are stacked in the attic of my modest home some distance from you, in fact in Cardiff!

If you should wish to talk to me further, you are welcome to visit me. Please telephone before you come.

Yours sincerely,

Daphne Shelby.

Tilly's mother lent her the money for the train fare, with a sigh. 'Let's hope that you will feel able to settle down in the new year, and find a job . . . time to grow up, Tilly.'

'Just what your Grandma Mattie's mother said to her, according to Aunt Evie,' Tilly told her ruefully.

Daphne Shelby, a woman about her mother's age, took Tilly up the winding stairs to the attic in her tall, terraced town house.

'You'll have to sort through all these, I'm afraid. Not quite my taste; I like contemporary art. What branch of art are you in?'

'I studied fine art. Cézanne is a favourite of mine.'

'An Impressionist, eh? He must have influenced my relative, if this particular painting is anything to go by. It's unusual because the face is left blank – I thought at first that it had faded, because it has leaned for years against the windowsill. I don't suppose . . .' She lifted a small canvas, turned it round to show Tilly.

Tilly said faintly, 'It *must* be! The portrait of the unknown girl in the yellow dress, the one my great-grandmother sat for.'

'I wonder who returned it to my cousin's estate?'

'Maybe the person it was painted for didn't want it, because it was unfinished. I don't suppose we'll ever know now, but I made up a story about why he commissioned the picture, to explain it to myself,' Tilly said. 'I thought the portrait was to represent a young girl who had died. The artist was given her photograph in order to complete it, but he apparently sent that back too to the client for safe keeping. May I take a photograph of the picture, Daphne, please?'

'Better still, you must take the picture and give it to your wonderful aunt. I'm sure the artist would have wanted that. Let's go downstairs and dust it off, eh?'

*

379

Tilly's family gathered for the party. Tom was there, too. He couldn't stay away, he said.

There was a long silence while Tilly carefully unwrapped the painting for Evie.

Then Evie touched it very gently, as Tilly held it so that she could see it.

'Thank you, Tilly. So many memories ... I never thought I'd see this again. Dear Mattie's crowning glory, her hair, and that lovely, yellow dress. Just one thing will make it perfect.'

'What's that, Aunt Evie?'

'Will *you* paint her face for me? There's that photograph of the two of us, on the hall table, with our basket of watercress – would that help?'

'I can see her face in my mind's eye already, I'd love to do it,' Tilly said, as Tom slipped his arm round her waist and squeezed it.

'Let's go down to the stream and pick watercress,' he whispered. They hadn't been alone together since he returned from abroad.

'But it's not the right time of year for that,' she protested.

'You go,' Evie said wisely. 'The others will have tea ready when you come back.'

ACKNOWLEDGEMENTS

The Meadow Girls is dedicated to the five 'Mackley Girls' who grew up variously in Moose Jaw, Saskatchewan, Canada and Minot, North Dakota, USA.

Also, to the memory of two lovely English sisters, Lottie, who was painted as a child wearing a yellow dress, and her sister Clare, missionary and teacher.

I would like to thank my Canadian/American cousins, Jean (Mackley) and Del Plaisance for their warm encouragement, vivid recall of past times, and help with my research, (which included splendid photographs by their nephew Gary Hagen).

Also 'over here', Sara, Glenys, Joyce, G.C. and, as always, John.

Welcome to the world of *Sheila Newberry*!

Keep reading for more from Sheila Newberry, to discover a recipe that features in this novel and to find out more about Sheila's upcoming books . . .

We'd also like to introduce you to MEMORY LANE, our special community for the very best of saga writing from authors you know and love and new ones we simply can't wait for you to meet. Read on and join our club!

www.MemoryLane.club

Meet Sheila Newberry

I've been writing since I was three years old, and even told myself stories in my cot. So it came as a shock when I was whacked round the head by my volatile kindergarten teacher for daydreaming about stories when I was supposed to be chanting the phonetic alphabet. My mother received a letter from my teacher saying, 'Sheila will not speak. Why?' Mum told her that it was because I was scared stiff in class. I was immediately moved up two classes. Here I was given the task of encouraging the slow readers. This was something I was good at but still felt that I didn't fit in. Later, I learned that another teacher had saved all my compositions saying they inspired many children in later years.

I had scarlet fever in the spring of 1939, and when I returned to our home near Croydon, I saw changes which puzzled me – sandbags, shelters in back gardens, camouflaged by moss and daisies, and windows reinforced with criss-crossed tape. Children had iron rations in Oxo tins – we ate the contents during rehearsals for air-raids – and gas masks were given out. I especially recall the stifling rubber. We spent the summer holiday, as usual, in Suffolk and I remember being puzzled when my father left us there, as the Admiralty staff was moving to Bath. 'War' was not mentioned but we were now officially evacuees, living with relatives in a small cottage in a sleepy village.

On and off, we returned to London at the wrong times. We were bombed out in 1940 and dodging doodlebugs in 1943. I thought of Suffolk as my home. I was still writing – on flyleaves of books cut out by friends – and every Friday I told stories about Black-eyed Bill the Pirate to the whole school in the village hut. I wrote my first pantomime at nine years old, and was awarded the part of Puss in Boots. I wore a costume made from black-out curtains. We were back in our patched-up London home to celebrate VE night and dancing in the street. Lights blazed – it was very exciting.

I had a moment of glory when I won an essay competition that 3000 schoolchildren had entered. The subject was waste paper, which we all collected avidly! At my new school, I was encouraged by my teachers to concentrate on English Literature and Language, History and Art, and I did well in my final exams. I wanted to be a writer, but was told there was a shortage of paper! True. I wrote stories all the time and read many books. I was useless at games like netball as I was so short-sighted – I didn't see the ball until it hit me. I still loved acting, and my favourite Shakespearian parts were Shylock and Lady Macbeth.

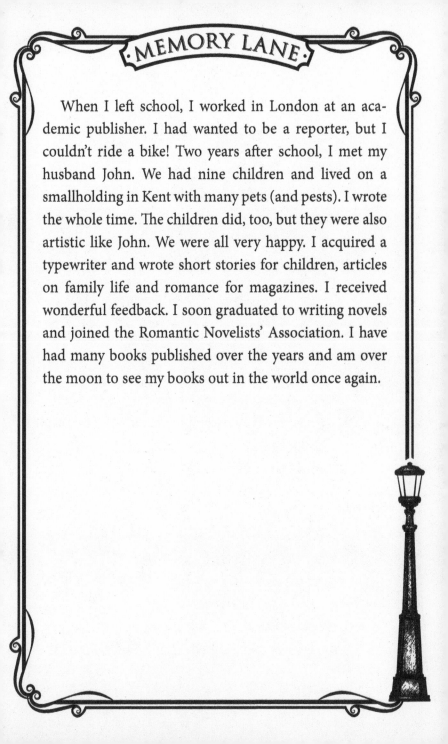

· MEMORY LANE ·

When I left school, I worked in London at an academic publisher. I had wanted to be a reporter, but I couldn't ride a bike! Two years after school, I met my husband John. We had nine children and lived on a smallholding in Kent with many pets (and pests). I wrote the whole time. The children did, too, but they were also artistic like John. We were all very happy. I acquired a typewriter and wrote short stories for children, articles on family life and romance for magazines. I received wonderful feedback. I soon graduated to writing novels and joined the Romantic Novelists' Association. I have had many books published over the years and am over the moon to see my books out in the world once again.

A Recipe for Cheese and Potato Pie

During her time at Amy Able College, Evie and her fellow students enjoyed a warming supper of cheese and potato pie. Now you can try it too . . .

'They sat at long refectory tables to eat their simple but satisfying supper after saying grace: cheese and potato pie, nicely browned on top, with a fresh green salad. Baskets were piled high with warm rolls, butter was apportioned on a plate: there were jugs of water.'

For the pie
750g of potatoes
100ml of crème fraiche
A pinch of grated nutmeg
Ready-made puff pastry – 2 × 375g
250g of camembert cheese
One egg – beaten
Plain Flour – for dusting

For the salad
One shallot – finely chopped
Half a shredded lettuce
A handful of spinach
Half a cucumber – chopped
Olive oil – to drizzle
The juice of half a lemon
Salt – a pinch

Method

1. Heat the oven to 200°c. Wash the potatoes, then place them in a deep pan of water and bring to the boil. Cook for a further two minutes. Once cooked, remove the water and mix the potatoes with the crème fraiche. Season by sprinkling with nutmeg and then set aside.

2. Dust your work surface with flour and roll out the puff pastry and cut a circle of around 28cm wide. Then place on a baking tray.

3. Place a third of the potatoes in the middle of the pastry and sit the cheese on top. Then place the remaining potatoes around the cheese, leaving a 1cm border at the edge of the pastry.

4. Roll the second puff pastry sheet out and cut into a circle around 30cm wide and brush the edges with egg. Drape the circle over the cheese and potato mixture, crimping as you go around. A tight seal is important to avoid leaking.

5. Brush the egg over the lid and gently score the pastry. Bake for thirty minutes until golden brown and puffed up. When removed from the oven, brush the pastry with a little more egg and leave to cool for five minutes.

6. Place the salad in a bowl with the dressing and enjoy!

Don't miss Sheila Newberry's next book.
Coming November 2020 . . .

THE MOTHER AND BABY HOME

Sunny grew up in the mother and baby home on
Grove Lane, London.

The daughter of a wartime nurse from Trinidad and
a Polish pilot, Sunny was abandoned by her mother
shortly after her birth and taken in by Nan,
the warm and gentle proprietress.

Never having known her parents, Sunny has always felt
like she doesn't quite fit in, but at sixteen-years-old, she
is ready to find her place in the world. Heading
out to start her first job, she finally feels she has
some idea of who she wants to be.

As 1950s post-war London is changing at a rapid
pace, so is Sunny.

And when someone from her past returns, Sunny
has some tough decisions to make. Decisions
that could affect the rest of her life . . .

**Sign up to Memory Lane to find out more and do follow
us on Facebook and join in the conversation
🆕 MemoryLaneClub**